Exploring Microsoft® SharePoint® 2013: New Features & Functions

Penelope Coventry

Published with the authorization of Microsoft Corporation by:
O'Reilly Media, Inc.
1005 Gravenstein Highway North
Sebastopol, California 95472

ISBN: 978-0-7356-7552-0

2 3 4 5 6 7 8 9 10 LSI 8 7 6 5 4 3

Printed and bound in the United States of America.

Microsoft Press books are available through booksellers and distributors worldwide. If you need support related to this book, email Microsoft Press Book Support at mspinput@microsoft.com. Please tell us what you think of this book at *http://www.microsoft.com/learning/booksurvey*.

Acquisitions and Developmental Editor: Kenyon Brown

Production Editor: Rachel Steely

Editorial Production: Dianne Russell, Octal Publishing, Inc.

Technical Reviewer: Neil Hodgkinson, Microsoft

Copyeditor: Bob Russell, Octal Publishing, Inc.

Indexer: Ron Strauss

Cover Design: Twist Creative

Cover Composition: Zyg Group, LLC

Illustrator: Rebecca Demarest

[2013-03-12]

Contents at a glance

Contents

What do you think of this book? We want to hear from you!

Microsoft is interested in hearing your feedback so we can continually improve our
books and learning resources for you. To participate in a brief online survey, please visit:

microsoft.com/learning/booksurvey

Chapter 2   Introducing the new search architecture   63

What do you think of this book? We want to hear from you!

Microsoft is interested in hearing your feedback so we can continually improve our
books and learning resources for you. To participate in a brief online survey, please visit:

microsoft.com/learning/booksurvey

I dedicate this book to my husband Peter—
where my heart lives.

Introduction

Welcome to *Exploring Microsoft SharePoint 2013*. The purpose of this book is to point out both the new and improved capabilities of SharePoint 2013. As with previous versions of SharePoint, SharePoint 2013 contains many features with which you will be familiar; some features might not have changed at all; others will have changed, but at a high level will provide similar functionality that will not be new to you; and then there will be components that you will need time to fully understand before you can decide how they can benefit you and your organization.

With this version of SharePoint, Microsoft focuses on what a user can do, and therefore the focus of the improvements with SharePoint 2013 places users at the center of the SharePoint installation. In the coming months, as you learn more about SharePoint 2013, no longer will Microsoft talk about what SharePoint can do by using the six-segment SharePoint 2010 circle that consisted of the Sites, Communities, Content, Search, Insights, and Composites. You will hear that SharePoint 2013 provides a new way to work together and is the new collaboration platform. It will talk about how users can Share, Organize, Discover, Build, and Manage ideas and content in a SharePoint environment. Following is a description of each of these concepts:

- **Share**   You can share when talking about your content and information, spreading it socially, spreading it online, spreading it easily across multiple places and devices where you might need to interconnect, whether it is on-premises, mobile, on a tablet in a cloud, or at a client site.

- **Organize**   This is how you structure and categorize the information, whether it is a project, team, or information held in documents using SharePoint Office 2013 applications, such as Microsoft Outlook, Microsoft Project, and syncing your content in SharePoint to your desktop with Microsoft SkyDrive Pro.

- **Discover**   This concept includes connecting people across your organization, the discovery of insights and answers through the use of Business Intelligence, and finding what you're looking for by using enterprise search. In this version of SharePoint, Microsoft has invested a great deal of effort into the integration of enterprise search.

- **Build**   SharePoint 2013 has undergone major changes to the application model for how to build applications that are hosted on systems that are maintained by organizations on-premises, or when the systems are maintained outside of the control of an organization, in the cloud; how to publish these applications internally through a corporate catalog; and publishing them outside an organization as well as sharing them across on-premises farms and cloud-based farms through a public store. The new application mode also makes it possible for applications to be shared within office applications by using the new Windows 8 interface-based computers, laptops, ultrabooks, tablets, and Windows Phone. These are now introduced to the Microsoft Office 2013 applications.

- **Manage** SharePoint 2013 provides better support for managing SharePoint as a platform. It can be run in the cloud with Microsoft Office 365. It contains new archiving, eDiscovery, and case management capabilities that include SharePoint 2013, Microsoft Exchange Server 2013, and Microsoft Lync 2013.

 More Info You can find more details about Office 365 at *office365.microsoft.com*.

Microsoft's aim is still for SharePoint to be a self-service product; that is, providing users with the ability to complete their tasks using no-code solutions by using the browser and Microsoft Office applications.

SharePoint 2013 consists of two products: SharePoint Foundation 2013 and SharePoint Server 2013. The exposure of two sets of functionality still exists in SharePoint Server, but is implemented using standard and enterprise client access licenses with a new licensing model. There is no longer a separate Microsoft FAST Search Server for SharePoint. You will find much of the functionality that was included in that product now incorporated as part of SharePoint 2013. Another change is that Microsoft Office Web Apps is a separate product and should be installed on servers on which SharePoint is not installed. Also, if your organization is a heavy user of SharePoint to automate business processes, there are changes with which you can distribute the workflow business logic onto servers where SharePoint is not installed.

As usual, the user interface has changed, but only slightly, as detailed in the following list (see also Figure I-1):

- The ribbon is still there but not automatically visible when the Browse tab is active.

- Some of the components have moved. For example, the Site Actions tab has been replaced by a Settings icon that is now in the upper-right corner of the page.

- Some components are no longer displayed. For example, the navigation up icon and the portal connection link are still placed on the master page, but the default CSS rules prevent them from being shown.

Hopefully, you will consider that these changes are minor, and as you pilot your upgrade to SharePoint 2013, the user feedback will confirm that it will not be necessary to formally retrain your users when you do upgrade.

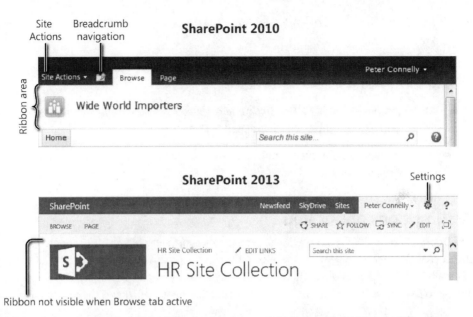

Figure I-1 Comparing the SharePoint 2010 user interface to the new SharePoint 2013 user interface.

Who this book is for

Although this book offers an overview of the new features of SharePoint 2013 from the perspective of an IT professional, it also introduces features that are important to the end user and business user. This should foster a solid understanding of why your organization might want to install or upgrade to SharePoint 2013 and help in the conversations you might have with these users.

This book does not provide step-by-step instructions on how to install or complete tasks by using SharePoint 2013 or provide an in-depth coverage or analysis of the new functions. Those details you can find in the following Microsoft Press books:

- *Microsoft SharePoint 2013 Plain & Simple* by Johnathan Lightfoot, Michelle Lopez, and Scott Metker, which is aimed at end users who are new to SharePoint.

- *Microsoft SharePoint 2013 Step by Step* by Olga Londer and Penelope Coventry, which is aimed at new and intermediate end users.

- *Microsoft SharePoint 2013 Inside Out* by Darvish Shadravan, Penelope Coventry, Tom Resing, and Christine Wheeler, which is aimed at intermediate and advanced power end users (who are also referred to as *citizen* or *consumer developers*). This book is also aimed at project managers, business analysts, and small business technicians.

- *Microsoft SharePoint 2013 Administrator's Companion* by Brain Alderman, which is aimed at IT Professionals.

- *Microsoft SharePoint 2013 App Development* by Scot Hillier, Ted Pattison, and Mirjam van Olst, which is aimed at professional developers.

- *Microsoft SharePoint 2013: Designing and Architecting Solutions* by Shannon Bray, Miguel Wood, and Patrick Curran, which is aimed at IT Architects.

Regardless of your role, I hope this book helps you to discover the features in SharePoint 2013 that are most beneficial for you.

Assumptions about you

This book is designed for readers who have experience installing Microsoft products. In a book of this size, it cannot cover every feature; therefore, it is assumed that you have some familiarity with Share-Point already. The focus is on the new functionality incorporated in SharePoint 2013 and is likely to appeal to readers who have knowledge of installing SharePoint 2010 and the functionality it provides.

Organization of this book

This book provides a high-level preview of the various new or changed features you might want to use in SharePoint 2013. This book is structured so that you as an IT professional understand the architectural changes before detailing features that the business might need you to install.

Chapter 1, "Architectural enhancements," discusses the critical infrastructure and service application improvements, including support for mobile devices, SharePoint development and changes, and Identity Management.

Chapter 2, "Introducing the new search architecture," deals with the new search user interfaces. Relevancy, search architecture, and topology are introduced.

Chapter 3, "Enterprise Content Management," covers records management and compliance, web content management, including the new Web Designer, and developer enhancements.

Chapter 4, "Social computing," discusses the user interface improvements to My Site, microblogging, activity feeds, Community Sites, and the User Profile Service Application process.

Chapter 5, "Building composite solutions," explores the improvements in Business Connectivity Services (BCS), Access Services Application, Workflow, and changes to Microsoft SharePoint Designer 2013.

Chapter 6, "Business Intelligence," examines the enhancements in Microsoft Excel 2013 SharePoint integration, including PowerPivot and Power View, Excel Services, Performance Point Services, and Visio Services.

Acknowledgments

It is never easy to write a book, especially one that covers such a vast subject area. Although I have been working with SharePoint for more than a decade—and with SharePoint 2013 for more than a year—it is still true to say that this book, as every other technical book, contains a snapshot of what the author knows at this particular moment. I'm happy to have the opportunity to share the knowledge I have gained so far with you. And, I'm also happy to pass along my thanks and appreciation to everyone in the SharePoint community who helped to bring this all about.

First, I'd like to include special thanks to Kenyon Brown, Microsoft Press Senior Editor, who offered me the opportunity to write this book and yet again kept me on track, and to Steve Smith of Combined Knowledge and Brian Alderman of MicroTechPoint for their assistance. Also, I would particularly like to thank Neil Hodgkinson (Technical Reviewer), for his invaluable insights and guidance. Knowing that he was reviewing the content was a great comfort and his contributions have made this a better book.

Huge thanks go out to the following people for contributing to the production of this project: Rachel Steely (O'Reilly Media Production Editor), Bob Russell of Octal Publishing, Inc. (Copyeditor), and all of the other people at O'Reilly Media who helped with the production of this book.

Last but certainly not least, my biggest thank you goes to my husband Peter Coventry for his continued support while I wrote this book. For his love, support, and understanding, I am forever grateful.

Support & feedback

The following sections provide information on errata, book support, feedback, and contact information.

Errata

We've made every effort to ensure the accuracy of this book and its companion content. Any errors that have been reported since this book was published are listed on our Microsoft Press site at oreilly.com:

> *http://go.microsoft.com/FWLink/?Linkid=279114*

If you find an error that is not already listed, you can report it to us through the same page.

If you need additional support, email Microsoft Press Book Support at *mspinput@microsoft.com*.

Please note that product support for Microsoft software is not offered through the addresses above.

We Want to Hear from You

At Microsoft Press, your satisfaction is our top priority, and your feedback our most valuable asset. Please tell us what you think of this book at:

http://www.microsoft.com/learning/booksurvey

The survey is short, and we read every one of your comments and ideas. Thanks in advance for your input!

Stay in Touch

Let's keep the conversation going! We're on Twitter: *http://twitter.com/MicrosoftPress*.

CHAPTER 1

Architectural enhancements

Microsoft SharePoint 2013 is built on similar architecture to that of SharePoint 2010; therefore, the architectural scenarios that you will use for SharePoint 2013 have not changed much. There are still web servers, application servers, and Microsoft SQL servers on which data is stored. Logically, a SharePoint farm consists of a number of web applications, and each web application can consist of one or more site collections. A site collection can have one or more sites and can be stored in one content database. A content database can contain more than one site collection. Sites are created from templates and contain lists and libraries.

As the following list indicates, the way you install and manage your SharePoint farm will also be familiar to you:

- Plan your topology, security accounts, and so on.

- Install the binaries on your SharePoint servers after you have installed any prerequisite software and hotfixes, such as Microsoft .NET Framework 4.5, Windows Identity Foundation and Extensions, Windows Server AppFabric, and Microsoft WCF Data Services.

- After SharePoint is installed, run the SharePoint Products Configuration Wizard to create a SharePoint 2013 farm, the configuration database, and the Central Administration website.

- Register your managed accounts, and create your service applications and web applications as needed. As with SharePoint 2010, you should only use the configuration wizard on the Central Administration website if you are building a development environment.

More Info You can find an overview of the deployment process at *technet.microsoft.com/ en-us/library/ee667264.aspx*.

Note As with SharePoint 2010, you can install and manage your SharePoint farm by using Windows PowerShell cmdlets; the only difference is that there are more of them in SharePoint 2013. The stsadm command-line tool is also still available but contains no enhancements over the version available in SharePoint 2010.

As with other SharePoint 2013 web applications, the Central Administration website sports a new look, as shown in Figure 1-1. When the Browse tab is active, neither the ribbon nor the navigation breadcrumbs are displayed. To navigate to the home page, at the top of the Quick Launch list, click either Central Administration or the icon just above it.

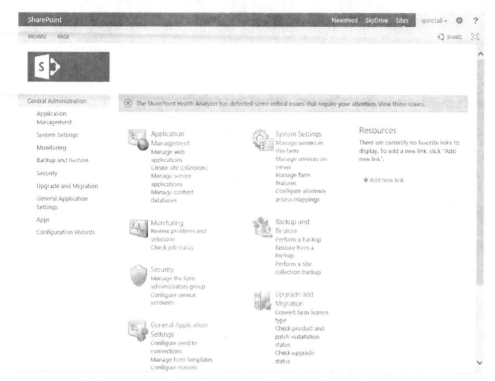

FIGURE 1-1 The SharePoint Central Administration website.

Many of the architectural enhancements you will see within Microsoft SharePoint 2013 were, for the most part, there in SharePoint 2010. The biggest single change for multi-tenancy support is search followed by Managed Metadata Service (MMS), which have made it possible for Microsoft to extend the hosting of SharePoint Online within its Office 365 service offering. These changes provide Microsoft with the opportunity to reach a vast new customer base and ensure that its customers receive the latest that it has to offer, quickly, while still keeping the users productive.

This chapter provides an overview of the architectural changes of SharePoint 2013. It details the infrastructure improvements and service applications that are new in SharePoint 2013, as well as those that are deprecated or changed, and what's new with web applications and site collections. This chapter also details the new application model and the introduction of the SharePoint App Catalog. The chapter finishes by discussing how to upgrade from SharePoint 2010 to SharePoint 2013.

Infrastructure improvements

Because the core infrastructure has not changed significantly, the infrastructure changes are progressive rather than revolutionary. There are, however, a number of platform-level improvements and capabilities of which you can take advantage, such as the following:

- Information storage in databases.

- Routing incoming user requests to specific or healthier web servers.

- Workflows with the introduction: a new, highly scalable workflow framework.

- User experience (UX) improvements.

These improvements are discussed in more detail in the next subsection.

 Note SharePoint 2013 must be installed on a server that is running the 64-bit edition of Windows Server 2008 R2 Service Pack 1 (SP1) or the 64-bit edition of Windows Server 2012. You can find information on the hardware and software requirements for SharePoint 2013 at *technet.microsoft.com/en-us/library/cc262485(v=office.15)*. When you first look at the memory requirements, these might seem larger than those you are used to for a SharePoint 2010 installation; however, they are in line with guidelines that most SharePoint experts would recommend for SharePoint 2010.

Database improvements

Two areas in which major improvements have taken place in SharePoint 2013 are the following:

- Taking advantage of Microsoft SQL Server functionality.

- Using shredded storage reduces the size of content databases when storing file versions and optimizes network traffic by reducing the need to transfer the entire document at one time.

SQL Server-related improvements

You can use SharePoint 2013 with either the 64-bit edition of Microsoft SQL Server 2008 R2 SP1 or Microsoft SQL Server 2012. SQL Server 2012 is Microsoft's latest cloud-ready information platform. It extends the functionality found in Microsoft SQL Server 2008 R2.

 Note To test the Business Intelligence capabilities available in the Microsoft Office 2013 and SharePoint 2013, SQL Server 2012 SP1 is required.

SharePoint 2013 database improvements include the following:

- All databases conform to Microsoft SQL Azure compliance criteria.

- Redundant and unused tables are removed as well as indices to track links.

- The design reduces Input/Output (IO) operations while browsing document libraries.

- Simplified database schema and optimized data access. In SharePoint 2010, when a list contains more columns than can fit in a row in the content database, multiple rows are used. Such a list is known as a wide list. The occurrence of these lists is reduced in SharePoint 2013, which uses features such as sparse columns that was first introduced with SQL Server 2008. You can gather more information on sparse columns at *msdn.microsoft.com/en-us/library/cc280604.aspx*.

- Improved large-list dependency.

 Note Business Intelligence capabilities are described in Chapter 6, "Business Intelligence."

Shredded storage

This enhancement reduces the amount of data that is saved within the SQL Server content databases and reduces the amount of network traffic between the SharePoint web servers and the SQL servers. This should also reduce the time needed to back up the content databases.

In SharePoint 2010, when a user wants to save multiple versions of a document, entire files are saved—one file for each version that you want to save. If a user downloaded a 200-KB Microsoft Word document from a SharePoint 2010 document library and then changed just one character in a sentence, the single change between the two files is not saved; instead, two 200-KB files are saved in the content database.

Bandwidth improvements are possible when Microsoft Office 2010 and SharePoint 2010 are used together to modify XML-based Office file formats, such as .docx, .xlsx, and .pptx files. When a user modifies one of these documents by using a Microsoft Office 2010 application, using the File Sync via SOAP over HTTP (MS-FSSHTTP) protocol locks portions of a file and downloads the file into the Office 2010 local file cache, the Office Document Cache (ODC). The ODC resides on the user's computer. The Office application opens the document from the ODC. When a user saves the document back to SharePoint, the Office application saves the document into the ODC and then uses the MS-FSSHTTP protocol to upload only the file differentials asynchronously in the background to the SharePoint server.

 Note You can access and manage the ODC settings and features through the Upload Center, which is automatically installed with Office 2010.

Because SharePoint 2010 is unable to send the modifications from the SharePoint server to the SQL server by using the MS-FSSHTTP protocol, SharePoint must incorporate those changes into the document on the SharePoint server. Then, the entire document is sent across the network to the SQL server, where it is saved into the content database.

SharePoint 2013 can now use MS-FSSHTTP not only when communicating with applications running on a user's computer, but also when communicating with SQL servers. Now, only the changes made while editing a file are stored in the content database. This is known as *shredded storage*, and it makes the following possible:

- A user can open a previously cached document, even if the SharePoint server is offline or not available.

- Network utilization is reduced, which improves both performance and costs.

- Users can start working with the document before it is completely downloaded.

- When a user saves a document to SharePoint, the document is uploaded to the server in the background; thus it seems as if the save happens immediately and control of the application is returned to the user nearly instantaneously, providing a great UX.

 Note For binary file types such as .doc, .ppt, and .xls, shredded storage is accomplished by using the Remote Differential Compression (RDC) feature, which was first introduced with Windows Server 2008. The RDC feature is not enabled by default. With earlier versions of Office, such as Office 2007, BranchCache could be used to reduce bandwidth utilization and download times for frequently accessed content, but as with MS-FSSHTTP with Office 2010, BranchCache does not reduce the amount of network bandwidth that is used when a file is saved to the content database. If both BranchCache and MS-FSSHTTP are available, MS-FSSHTTP will be used. For more information on SharePoint 2010, BranchCache and MS-FSSHTTP, go to *blogs.msdn.com/b/michaelp/archive/2010/06/12/does-sharepoint-2010-support-branchcache.aspx*.

When two users edit the same document simultaneously, SharePoint uses the same multimaster conflict used in co-authoring for the Office Web Applications. Thus, when two users change different sections in the document, the changes will be merged; if they change the same sections, the users will need to resolve the conflict.

Now, in SharePoint 2013, SharePoint does not need to merge the changes—only the changes go to the SQL server. Moreover, it is also not limited to Office-formatted files; it will work on any file type, such as PDFs. The SQL Server is able to manage the changes because the document is now not saved as one blob. Instead, it's saved as multiple blobs. In SharePoint 2013, there is no concept of duplication. The new version of a file is not a complete copy of a file. Therefore, in SharePoint 2013 you can expect the size of your content databases to go down.

Be aware, however, that when you upgrade from SharePoint 2010 to SharePoint 2013, your content databases do not automatically reduce in size. Shredded storage will only be used the next time the user needs to modify a file, after the upgrade has been implemented.

More Info To learn more about shredded storage, read Bill Baer's blog posts at *blogs.technet.com/b/wbaer/archive/2012/12/20/shredded-storage-and-the-evolution-of-sharepoint-s-storage-architecture.aspx and blogs.technet.com/b/wbaer/archive/2012/11/12/introduction-to-shredded-storage-in-sharepoint-2013.aspx.*

Request management

When most organizations implement a web-based solution, for resiliency and scalability they also implement it with a hardware or software load balancer, which routes incoming user requests at a network level to web servers. However, such a configuration might not meet the entire needs that an organization requires. This is where the SharePoint 2013 Request Management feature can be useful in large deployments because it routes incoming requests at the application level. With Request Management, SharePoint can refuse or redirect HTTP requests individually within the farm to dedicated or different servers in the farm for specific workloads. This means that you can configure the farm so that the availability and responsiveness of the web servers that are satisfying requests for web pages from the majority of your users are not compromised.

Note A SharePoint web server is a server that runs the SharePoint Foundation Web Application Service (SPFWA). On such servers, the Request Management service instance is installed but not started by default.

SharePoint can now recognize the origin of incoming requests; for example, from external search engines, from different types of browsers, or specific applications. SharePoint can then reduce the priority of certain requests and raise the priority of others, depending on different criteria. SharePoint can look at the packet headers, the requester's IP address, or subnet and decide to block that request, redirect it to another server, SharePoint farm, or web application.

Request management rules

Request management rules are applied per web application and are either throttling or routing rules. No rules are enabled by default. Throttling rules are always evaluated before routing rules, and if the incoming HTTP request matches the criteria, the request is refused.

Routing rules have a set of properties such as an expiration time. Routing rules are associated with execution groups 0, 1, 2, and so on. You can have as many execution rule groups as you need. Rules in execution group 0 are evaluated before rules in execution group 1, which are evaluated before rules in execution group 2, and so forth. Each routing rule is associated with a machine pool, which contains one or more SharePoint web servers. Each server within a machine pool—known as a routing target or routing machine—has a static weighting and a health weighting, as specified in the following:

- A static weight, as the name implies, is a constant that you can use to identify powerful or weak servers.

- A health weight is evaluated dynamically by Health Analysis and is a score from 0 to 10.

If an HTTP request matches all the criteria for a routing rule, that request is routed to the associated machine pool, where it is prioritized and load balanced between the target machines. When a rule contains more than one criterion, they are joined by using an AND.

It is common practice that the last execution group contains a catch-all rule (*) that is used to process incoming request that do not meet the criteria specified in earlier rules and route them to a specific machine pool. You should not have a * rule as the first rule, because the incoming HTTP request will never be processed against subsequent rules.

If you decide not to have a catch-all rule, when an incoming request does not match any rule, the request is routed to any server in the farm that is not in a machine pool, based on the health of the servers. This might be a reason to turn on Request Management with no rules, execution groups, or machine pools in your farm, because this will prompt SharePoint to route requests according to what it believes to be the healthiest server.

 Note When you route an HTTP input request to a machine pool, you need to ensure that the appropriate service that is needed to process the input request is active on at least one of the servers in the machine pool. Otherwise, the request will not be processed.

Request Management Criteria

The criteria for throttling and routing rules use the following HTTP request header properties:

- *CustomHeader*

- *Host*

- *HttpMethod*

- *IP*

- *SoapAction*

- *Url*

- *UrlReferrer*

- *UserAgent*, such as a Microsoft Office OneNote client application

The criteria operators, known as *MatchTypes*, are as follows:

- *EndsWith*

- *Equals*

- *Regex*

- *StartsWith*

Creating and managing Request Management

There is no administrative user interface for Request Management. The creation of rules, the setting of rule properties, execution groups, and machine pools are managed by using SharePoint Windows PowerShell cmdlets. To create your first routing rule, perform the following steps:

1. Get a reference to the necessary web application and save it in a variable:

   ```
   $webapp = Get-SPWebApplication http://intranet.adventure-works.com;
   ```

2. Get the reference to the Request Management settings object for the web application and save it is a variable:

   ```
   $rmsettings = Get-SPRequestManagementSettings $webapp;
   ```

3. Create a machine pool:

   ```
   $MachTargets = @("SP1");
   $machpool_1 = Add-SPRoutingMachinePool -RequestManagementSettings $rmsettings '
       -Name "Machine Pool 1" -MachineTargets $MachTargets;
   ```

4. Create one or more rule criteria to match all .docx files:

   ```
   $RMrulecriteria = New-SPRequestManagementRuleCriteria -Property Url '
       -MatchType Regex -Value ".*\.docx"
   ```

5. Create a routing rule and then associate it with execution group 0, a machine pool, and the criteria:

   ```
   $DocRule = Add-SPRoutingRule -RequestManagementSettings $rmsettings -Name "DocRule" '
       -ExecutionGroup 0 -MachinePool $Machpool_1 -Criteria $RMruleCriteria
   ```

To view the Request Management settings for the web application, type the following command (the output for the command is also shown):

```
Get-SPWebApplication http://intranet.adventure-works.com | Get-SPRequestManagementSettings
```

```
Name                    :
MinimumCacheRefreshTime : 00:00:15
RoutingEnabled          : True
RoutingScheme           : Default
RequestBufferLength     : 524288
```

```
MaxRequestBufferCount               : 1000
RequestTimeout                      : 00:01:40
RoutingHealthScoreDepreciationTime  : 00:00:02
PingInterval                        : 00:00:02
PingAvailabilityThreshold           : 0.333333333333333
PingFailureLimit                    : 3
PingPassLimit                       : 1
ThrottlingEnabled                   : True
RoutingRules                        : {DocRule}
ThrottlingRules                     : {}
MachinePools                        : {Machine Pool 1}
RoutingTargets                      : {SP1}
IsInitialized                       : True
TypeName                            : Microsoft.SharePoint.Administration.SPRequ
                                      estManagementSettings
DisplayName                         :
Id                                  : c44640c7-28d2-428c-b4e6-db7665accf62
Status                              : Online
Parent                              : SPWebApplication
                                      Name=intranet.adventure-works.com
Version                             : 9560
Properties                          : {}
Farm                                : SPFarm Name=SP2013_Config
UpgradedPersistedProperties         : {}
```

Workflow framework

SharePoint 2013 introduces a new, highly scalable workflow framework that is implemented by using the Workflow Manager, originally known as Windows Azure Workflow (WAW). In SharePoint 2013, the Workflow Manager farm is not installed by default. Therefore, a default installation of Share-Point 2013 can only use the same workflows that can be used in SharePoint 2010. When the Workflow Manager is installed, you can run both SharePoint 2010 and SharePoint 2013 workflows.

In SharePoint 2010, workflows run on the servers on which SharePoint is installed; that is, they run within the SharePoint farm. If your organization is a heavy user of workflows, this can have a detrimental effect on the performance of your farm because it is difficult to scale and distribute the SharePoint workflow components. SharePoint 2013 uses the same mechanism of managing Share-Point 2010 workflows as SharePoint 2010 and therefore suffers from the same limitations. There are no enhancements to SharePoint 2010 workflows in SharePoint 2013, you have the same actions and conditions as in SharePoint 2010, and they are built on Microsoft .NET Framework 3.5.

 Note The new workflow framework is not designed to work with Microsoft SharePoint Foundation 2013, and therefore with SharePoint Foundation you can only use and create SharePoint 2010 workflows.

A Workflow Manager farm can be installed on your SharePoint servers or on any servers, how-ever, it is not good practice to install it on domain controllers. With SharePoint 2013, if you are a heavy user of workflows, you should consider creating a Workflow Manager farm separate from your

SharePoint farm. Thus, you should install Workflow Manager on one or more servers that do not have SharePoint installed. However, be aware that SharePoint 2010 workflows will still run on your SharePoint 2013 servers in the legacy SharePoint workflow engine, also known as the SharePoint 2010 workflow host.

Only SharePoint 2013 workflows can make use of the Workflow Manager farm. Within SharePoint 2013 workflows, only those activities built on .NET Framework 4.5 and Windows Workflow Foundation 4 run within Workflow Manager. When a SharePoint 2013 workflow needs to use any Windows Workflow Foundation 3 artifacts, control is passed back to the SharePoint 2010 workflow host in SharePoint 2013. When the SharePoint Windows Workflow Foundation 3 process is complete, control returns to Workflow Manager.

SharePoint 2013 does not contain any SharePoint 2013 workflow templates only SharePoint 2010 workflow template. Using the browser, users create workflows from workflow templates, and instances of those workflows run against SharePoint objects, such as a SharePoint site, list item, or document. Therefore, when you first use SharePoint 2013, even if you have installed a Workflow Manager farm, it will not be used because your users will not be able to create any SharePoint 2013 workflows or run any SharePoint 2013 instances. SharePoint 2013 workflows and SharePoint 2013 workflow templates need to be created before you can take advantage of the Workflow Manger farm.

More Info You can read about creating workflows by using Microsoft SharePoint Designer 2013 or by using Visual Studio 2012 in Chapter 5, "Building composite solutions." That chapter also compares SharePoint 2010 workflows with SharePoint 2013 workflows.

Workflow Manager architecture

As with many of the other SharePoint 2013 enhancements, the driving force for the new workflow framework was designing it to support SharePoint online and multitenant applications, overcoming the significant challenges such environments pose in terms of isolation, scale, and resource management. The high-level architecture of the workflow is displayed in Figure 1-2.

The Workflow farm consists of two components: the Workflow Manager and a service bus that facilitates the communication among components within the farm by using the Open Authentication (OAuth protocol). The service bus is a messaging platform that has been running in Azure for some time that now can run on on-premises servers. The Workflow Manager uses the service bus as its core state management and messaging layer. All communication between SharePoint and the Workflow Manager is message based using a well-defined contract for events and management operations happening from SharePoint into the Workflow Manager using a series of Representational State Transfer (REST) HTTP calls. Therefore, the service bus is used for reliable message delivery and a message broker that also keeps the message state and workflow instance state consistent.

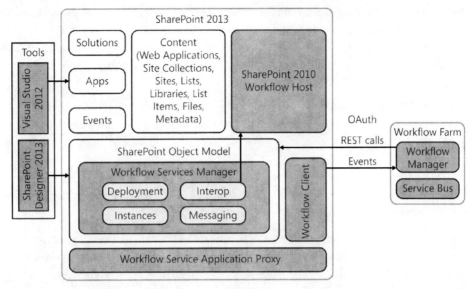

FIGURE 1-2 The workflow architecture is divided between the SharePoint 2013 infrastructure and the Workflow Manager infrastructure.

SharePoint 2013 contains a new component known as the Workflow Services Manager, which is the integration layer between SharePoint and the Workflow Manager. The Workflow Services Manager connects to other SharePoint services by using the Workflow Service Application Proxy and connects to the Workflow Manager via the Workflow Manager Client. You can install the Workflow Manager on the same servers as SharePoint, in which case the Workflow Manager Client is automatically installed as part of the Workflow Manager installation, known as the *colocated model.* You can also install Workflow Manager on servers that do not have SharePoint installed—the *federated model*—in which case you will need to install separately the Workflow Manager Client on SharePoint servers that are responding to web requests, so that they can communicate with the Workflow Manager. You can build a federated workflow farm to achieve high availability by joining three servers to the farm because they work like a mirror with a witness; that is, the servers need to achieve a quorum (you can do this with just two servers).

More Info To learn more about the service bus architecture, go to *technet.microsoft.com/ en-us/library/72646b45-646f-4dfb-ab52-e42f187655e7(v=azure.10).*

The Workflow Services Manager contains a number of services:

- **Deployment** This service manages workflow definitions. This is the service that deploys workflows you create in SharePoint Designer when you click the Publish command or when in the browser you associate a workflow template in the browser with SharePoint components, such as lists, libraries, content types, and sites.

- **Messaging**   This service takes events, such as when properties of a document change, and sends them as messages to the Workflow Manager. This Messaging service is also exposed to Apps. This makes it possible for Apps to have custom messages; for example, you can define a custom message from an external application that can be sent to a workflow and you can have a workflow that subscribes to that message.

- **Instance**   This service manages workflow instances. Therefore, it is this service that is used to obtain workflow instance status information, or if you wish to terminate a workflow instance.

- **Interop**   This service invokes SharePoint 2010 workflows.

The Workflow Manager farm uses new SharePoint REST endpoints to communicate back to the SharePoint farm by using the App model API. Therefore, SharePoint 2013 workflows use the same set of services as Apps to complete their tasks.

All communications with the workflow farm uses either the HTTP or HTTPS protocol. On servers within the workflow farm, within Internet Information Server (IIS) Manager, you will see one application pool, WorkflowMgmtPool, and one site, Workflow Management Site. A Workflow Manager server also contains the following four Windows NT services:

- Workflow Manager Backend

- Service Bus Message Broker

- Service Bus Gateway

- Windows Fabric Host Service

When a workflow farm is created, six databases are created on an SQL Server:

- Workflow databases:

  - WFManagementDB

  - WFInstanceManagementDB

  - WFResourceManagemetDB

- Service bus databases:

  - SBManagementDB

  - SbGatewayDatabase

  - SBMessageContainer01

The Workflow Manager farm provides no native support for high availability at the storage layer. You can use your own solution, such as SQL Server mirroring.

Installing a Workflow Manager farm

Before installing a Workflow Manager farm, you must have the following:

- Access to an SQL Server on which the Workflow Manager databases can be created, such as an instance of SQL Server 2008 R2 SP1, SQL Server Express 2008 R2 SP1, or SQL Server 2012.

- Relevant port numbers. The default ports numbers are 12290 and 12291.

- A mixed IPv4/IPv6 environment. The Workflow Manager installer available for SharePoint 2013 only works with IPv4 and not in pure IPv6 environments.

- A Workflow Manager installer that matches the build number of SharePoint 2013 with which you want to use it.

Note The Workflow Manager installer uses the Web Platform Installer (Web PI) to initiate the installation steps. You can find the Workflow Manager at *go.microsoft.com/fwlink/?LinkID=252092*. You can find the Workflow Manager Client, which is only needed on SharePoint servers that respond to web requests and do not have the Workflow Manager installed, at *go.microsoft.com/fwlink/?LinkID=258749*.

- Access to the Internet for the computers on which you are installing Workflow Manager; otherwise, you need to download and install the prerequisites prior to running the Workflow Manager installer.

- A service account known as the RunAs account, that must have read/write access to the SQL Server.

- An account to install and configure the Workflow Manager added to the local administrators group on each server that will be a node in the Workflow Manager farm.

Tip For the communication between SharePoint and the Workflow Manager using web protocols, you can use web debugging tools such as Fiddler. In such debugging scenarios it is helpful to use the same service account for the Workflow Manager as is used for the application pool ID for your web application. You can read more about debugging workflows with fiddler at *www.andrewconnell.com/blog/archive/2012/07/18/sharepoint-2013-workflow-advanced-workflow-debugging-with-fiddler.aspx*.

The Workflow Manager installer checks for any prerequisites and installs any that it does not find. After the binaries are installed, the Workflow Configuration Wizard starts (you can also start it manually at any time).

When you install the Workflow Manager on the first server, you create a workflow farm. You are asked which SQL server instance to create the farm databases, the service account, and to provide a Certification Generation Key, which has a similar function to the passphrase in a SharePoint farm. You will need this key when you join subsequent servers to the workflow farm. Each server within a work-flow farm is known as a *workflow node*.

When adding more than one server to a workflow farm, you need to edit the Domain Name System (DNS) and install load balancers so that any workflow node can respond to a request from your SharePoint farm.

After the workflow farm is created, you then need to register the farm with your SharePoint farm by running a Windows PowerShell cmdlet similar to the following on one of the servers in your SharePoint farm:

```
Register-SPWorkflowService -SPSite http://intranet.adventure-works.com -WorkflowHostUri
http://wmnlbname:12291 -AllowOauthHttp
```

In the preceding example, http://intranet.adventure-works.com can be any of the web applications that are created in the SharePoint farm. After this command is successfully executed, the Workflow Service Application Proxy will be started in the SharePoint farm, as illustrated in Figure 1-3.

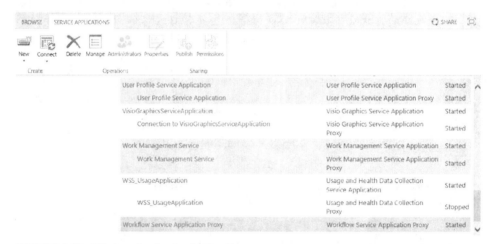

FIGURE 1-3 The Windows Service Application Proxy.

Note If the SharePoint server on which you run this command is not a workflow node in your workflow farm, you will need to install the client version of Workflow Manager to run the command successfully. The *–AllOAuthHttp* is only needed if you are using the HTTP protocol to communicate between the two farms. In a production environment, you should use HTTPS.

Monitoring a Workflow Manager farm

Typical ways to monitor the Workflow Manager farm are similar to other Microsoft products, includ-ing the following:

- **Performance counters** Each server on which Workflow Manager is installed contains the "Workflow Management" and "Workflow Dispatcher" counter sets.

- **Event Tracing for Windows (ETW)** Workflow Manager contains an ETW provider named Microsoft-Workflow and three ETW channels: Operational, Debug, and Analytic. You can find a complete list of events generated by Workflow Manager in the ETW manifest file located in the C:\Program Files\Workflow Manager\1.0\Workflow folder. You can use the Event Viewer to examine the logs, which you can find in the Microsoft-Workflow node under the Application and Services node, as depicted in Figure 1-4.

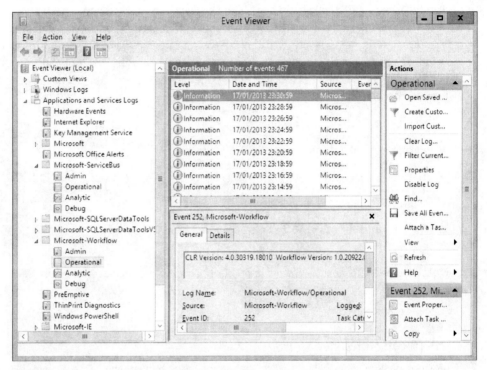

FIGURE 1-4 You can use the Event Viewer to exam Workflow Manager logs.

 Note If no event logs are visible within the Event Viewer, you might need to enable the analytic and debug logs. To do so, right-click in the event window, and then in the options menus that opens, click View and then click Show Analytic And Debug Logs.

- **Windows PowerShell** Like many other products, when Workflow Manager is installed, a shortcut is provided to a Windows PowerShell command window that automatically executes the relevant Windows PowerShell module so that the product-specific cmdlets are available. Workflow Manager is no different. Use the *Get-WFFarm* cmdlet to retrieve all details about your workflow farm.

- **Microsoft Workflow Manager Management Pack for System Center Operations Manager** This is available for download and supports both System Center Operations Manager (SCOM) 2012 as well as SCOM 2007 R2. Before you can import the Workflow Manager Management Pack into SCOM, both the SQL Server 2012 and Microsoft Service Bus Management Packs must be imported. You can find the Microsoft Workflow Manager Management Pack at *systemcenter.pinpoint.microsoft.com/en-US/applications/search?q=workflowmanager*.

UX improvements

Microsoft has redesigned the SharePoint UX to be clean and simple. If you use a browser that supports HTML5, you can now drag files to upload them. You can also perform bulk metadata edits, quickly access document previews and context, and take advantage of single-click tracking of documents so that you can monitor your most important work. Microsoft has also made infrastructure changes that affect the speed at which content pages are rendered in the browser. These changes include the following:

- Web server caching improvements

- Introduction of a minimal download strategy

- A new Theme engine

- Improved support for mobile devices

- Implementation of HTML5 and increased web browser support

 Note You can find details about other UX improvements, such as embedding and storing video and the rendering of images, in Chapter 3, "Enterprise Content Management."

Cache service improvements

In previous versions of SharePoint, each SharePoint server had its own cache. Commonly used information was stored in the server's memory. When a user requested content that used cache, the content was retrieved, for example, from the content database and saved in the memory of the SharePoint server that responded to the user's request. If the server subsequently responded to another request for the same content, the content was retrieved from memory, if it was still there, and no round trip to the content database was needed. However, if another server responded to the second request, the content would need to be retrieved from the content database, even though the content was still in the memory of the first server.

SharePoint 2013 uses a distributed caching mechanism that spans all of the SharePoint servers in the farm. Specific SharePoint components are programmed to take advantage of distributed cache; for example, social feeds, search, and authentication. Information related to these components is not cached on a per-server basis; the distributed cache mechanism is able to synchronize the data so that the same information is available across every web server. When content is saved in distributed cache, no round trip to the content database is needed for the second request.

SharePoint 2013 Distributed Cache Service (DCS) is based on the Windows Server AppFabric 1.1 caching model. You must use the version of AppFabric that ships with SharePoint 2013 and can be extended. In a default SharePoint 2013 installation, the DCS uses the following ports:

- Cache port: 22233

- Cluster port: 22234

- Arbitration port: 22235

- Replication port: 22236

Any firewalls configured between the servers must be configured accordingly for the distributed cache to work successfully.

Components in SharePoint 2013 that use distributed cache include the following:

- **Feeds**   This cache stores activities and conversations for use by the newsfeeds on a user's My Site. The primary use of this cache is for content that you follow and the Everyone feed. (You can find an overview of microblogging, newsfeeds, and distributed cache at *technet.microsoft. com/en-us/library/jj219700(office.15).aspx*.)

- **Logon tokens**   SharePoint uses the Security Token Service (STS) to create Security Asser-tion Markup Language (SAML) tokens. Both claims-based web applications and inter-farm communication use STS. The logon tokens cache stores the security token, known as a *claim* or a *FedAuth* token that is issued by STS for use by any web server in the server farm. Any web server that receives a request for resources can access the security token from the cache, authenticate the user, and provide access to the resources requested. Every time a user accesses a web server, the user needs to be authenticated, which can become an issue when using mul-tiple web servers. In SharePoint 2010, to ensure that the user stayed on the same web server, load balancing affinity—known as *sticky sessions*—was enabled. By caching the FedAuth token in the distributed cache, it is no longer necessary to enable sticky sessions, because the authen-tication token is now available from all web servers through the cache cluster.

- **Search**   This is used by the Content Search Web Part (CSWP), a new Web Part introduced with SharePoint 2013.

By using distributed cache for the microblog features and newsfeeds, SharePoint can provide the speed of broadcasting and quick information sharing that these two social computing com-ponents require. Distributed caching of newsfeeds removes the need for "activity gatherers" and timer jobs that used to do the role in SharePoint 2010 of gathering up events that were happening across SharePoint and delivering them to your newsfeed. All requests for newsfeeds are gathered on demand in real time, based on the current state of the social network. The social data is retrieved from the cached data, which has a life time of about a week, the My Site social databases and search index. Other than the CSWP, other Web Parts do not use distributed cache.

More Info You can learn more about social computing enhancements in SharePoint 2013 in Chapter 4, "Social computing."

The AppFabric Caching Service is a Windows service that runs on a SharePoint server, as shown in Figure 1-5. Microsoft recommends that you should not administer the AppFabric Caching Service from the Services window or the AppFabric Caching Services Properties dialog box. You should use either the Central Administration website or the SharePoint Windows PowerShell cmdlets because the implementation of distributed cache that uses the AppFabric Caching Services is specific to SharePoint 2013 and must be managed through SharePoint 2013.

FIGURE 1-5 The AppFabric Caching Service is one of the prerequisites when installing SharePoint 2013.

For SharePoint to use the caching service, in Central Administration, go to the Services On Server page and start the Distributed Cache service, as demonstrated in Figure 1-6.

A SharePoint server on which the Distributed Cache service is started is known as a *cache host*. A group of cache hosts is known as a *cache cluster*. To have Distributed Cache working on more than one server, the first server with Distributed Cache needs to have its firewall set to allow for inbound Internet Control Message Protocol. You can find information on how to create an inbound ICMP rule at *technet.microsoft.com/en-us/library/cc972926(v=WS.10).aspx*.

Services on Server ⓘ

Central Administration

Application
Management

System Settings

Monitoring

Backup and Restore

Security

Upgrade and Migration

General Application
Settings

Apps

Server: SP1 ▾ | View: Configurable ▾

Service	Status	Action
Access Database Service 2010	Started	Stop
Access Services	Started	Stop
App Management Service	Started	Stop
Business Data Connectivity Service	Started	Stop
Central Administration	Started	Stop
Claims to Windows Token Service	Started	Stop
Distributed Cache	Started	Stop
Document Conversions Launcher Service	Stopped	Start

FIGURE 1-6 To join a cache cluster, in Central Administration, on the Services On Server page, start the Distribute Cache service.

When a new SharePoint server is added to the SharePoint farm, upon running the Distributed Cache service, it joins the cache cluster. The cache cluster provides one distributed cache that spans all of the cache hosts, for which the total cache size is the total memory allocated to the Caching Service on each cache host. The memory allocation for the Distributed Cache service is set to a default value of 10 percent of total physical memory when SharePoint Server 2013 installs.

More Info To learn more about managing the Distributed Cache service, go to *technet. microsoft.com/en-us/library/jj219613/8v=office.159.aspx.*

Half of the memory allocation is used for data storage, known as the cache size, and the other half of the memory allocation is used for memory management overhead. When the cached data grows, the Distributed Cache service uses the entire 10 percent of the allocated memory.

The Distributed Cache service can run in one of the two following modes:

- **Dedicated mode**   The Distributed Cache service is started and all other services are stopped on the server. This is the recommended mode in which to deploy the Distributed Cache service. It is recommended that no more than 16 GB of memory should be allocated to the Distributed Cache service with at least 2 GB of memory reserve for other services. The TechNet article, "Plan for feeds and the Distributed Cache service (SharePoint Server 2013)," which is available at *technet.microsoft.com/en-us/library/jj219572(v=office.15).aspx*, states that if you allocate more than 16 GB of memory to the Distributed Cache service, the server might unexpectedly stop responding for more than 10 seconds.

- **Colocated mode** The Distributed Cache service is started along with other services on the server. However, it is not recommend that any of the following services or applications run on the same server as the Distributed Cache service:

  - SQL Server 2008 or SQL Server 2012

  - Search service

  - Excel Services in SharePoint

  - Project Server services

  It is recommended that when running the Distributed Cache in colocated mode, all non-essential services should be shut down to reduce the memory competition.

AppFabric provides administrative tools on the Start menu, as illustrated in Figure 1-7. You should not use these applications to manage the Distributed Cache service. Instead, use the SharePoint 2013 Management Shell.

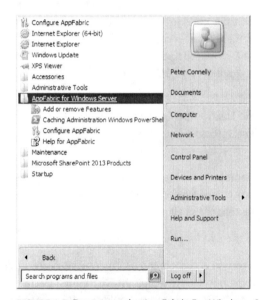

FIGURE 1-7 Do not use the AppFabric For Windows Server administration tools.

The Distributed Cache service can become unstable or enter an unrecoverable state when one or more servers experience an unplanned outage such as a power failure. Even a planned shutdown of a SharePoint server can affect the Distributed Cache service. It is therefore important to manage the service in SharePoint 2013, as described in the article at *technet.microsoft.com/en-us/library/jj219613(v=office.15)*.

There are seven SharePoint 2013 Windows PowerShell cmdlets with which you can manage the Distributed Cache service:

- *Add-SPDistributedCacheServiceInstance*

- *Clear-SPDistributedCacheItem*

- *Get-SPDistributedCacheClientSetting*

- *Remove-SPDistributedCacheServiceInstance*

- *Set-SPDistributedCacheClientSetting*

- *Stop-SPDistributedCacheServiceInstance*

- *Update-SPDistributedCacheSize*

Minimal Download Strategy

SharePoint 2013 is based on a very rich web interface that contains lots of "moving parts" and lots of customizable areas. In SharePoint 2010, many times when a user interacted with a page, the entire page was downloaded to the client computer, even when only a portion of the page changed. SharePoint 2013 includes a new navigation framework that improves page load performance by only downloading those portions of the page that have changed. This is known as the Minimal Download Strategy (MDS).

MDS is implemented as a new SharePoint feature, scoped at the web level. It works with the AjaxDelta control which is added to the head section of master pages. By default, the MDS feature is activated on the Team, Community, Wiki, Projects, App, and Blog site templates. When activated, it sets the web object *EnableMinimalDownload* property. It is not enabled on publishing sites.

By activating or deactivating the MDS feature or by using Windows PowerShell, you can switch MDS on or off. There are two other ways to disable MDS:

- If you place the *PageRenderMode* SharePoint control on a master page or content page and set the *RenderModeType* property to *Standard*, this will prevent the use of MDS. If the *PageRenderMode* control is absent from the page or the property is set to *MinimalDownload*, MDS is enabled.

- To render Web Parts or controls with MDS, the *MdsCompliantAttribute* must be set. All controls defined in the *Microsoft.SharePoint.dll* assembly have that attribute set; however, none of the controls in the *Microsoft.SharePoint.Publishing.dll* assembly have that attribute set.

Note If you have upgraded from SharePoint 2010, your custom controls or Web Parts will not automatically have the *MdsCompliantAttribute* attribute set and therefore will not be rendered by using MDS. If MDS is an important consideration on your website, you might need to have your developer edit, recompile, and reinstall the solution files for your custom controls and Web Parts.

When the site uses MDS and a page is requested, the address bar of the browser displays a URL similar to the following:

http://intranet.adventure-works.com/_layouts/15/start.aspx#/SitePages/Home.aspx.

The *start.aspx* file contains a JavaScript *asyncDeltaManager* object, which parses the URL and dynamically loads the page that follows the # sign. When subsequent requested pages contain the *querystring* parameter *AjaxDelta=1*, only the changed portions are downloaded to the client's browser.

The theme engine

In SharePoint 2010, themes reused the theme definition and format defined in the Office Open XML standard that was introduced with Microsoft Office PowerPoint 2007 to create new themes for slide decks. By using the browser on a SharePoint Server 2010 publishing site or on a site when the Publishing feature was enabled, you could create your own new themes or you could create a new *.thmx* file by using Word 2010, PowerPoint 2010, or Theme Builder. The *.thmx* file could then be uploaded into the Theme gallery.

In SharePoint 2013, the theme engine has changed so that themes are based on HTML5; therefore, users are not able to use the Office applications to create new themes. However, users can still change the look of a site or create new looks by using the browser (see Figure 1-8), changing the background image, colors, site layout (master page), and font. You can also preview and try out the theme before you apply it to your site.

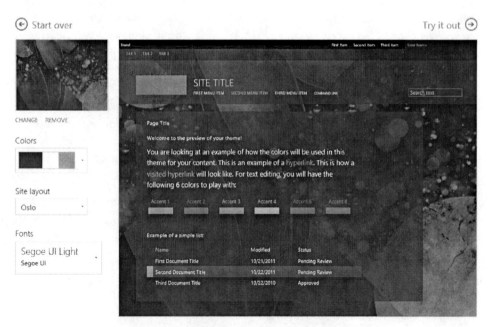

FIGURE 1-8 You can change the look of your site by using HTML 5 themes.

Note There is also a corresponding SharePoint 2013 Object Model API with which developers can create and apply a new theme programmatically.

In SharePoint 2013, 18 different looks are available. You can use any of these as a basis for a new look. The different looks displayed on the Change The Look page, are a combination of four components, background image, master page, color palette, and a font scheme. The color palette and font schemes are XML files that are stored at the top-level site of a site collection in the "15" folder, in a document library named Theme Gallery. This library has a URL of _catalogs/theme, to which you can navigate from the site settings page under Web Designer Galleries (see Figure 1-9). The two file types have the following extensions:

- *.spcolor* for color palettes files

- *.spfont* for font scheme files

FIGURE 1-9 The Theme Gallery 15 stores the theme files.

The four components are associated together to form a Composed Look. The information where to find the four components for each Composed Look is saved at the site level in a list named Composed Look, with a URL of _catalogs/design, as shown in Figure 1-10.

When a Composed Look is applied to a site, several images and CSS style sheets based on the .spcolor file are created. Then, a new folder is created in the Themes Gallery and the images and CSS style sheets are placed inside it, similar to how a theme was applied in SharePoint 2010.

FIGURE 1-10 You change the look of your site by choosing a Composed Look.

Support for mobile devices

SharePoint 2013 provides improvements in rendering content and location-aware lists that can aid in mobile application development. It also supports applications on mobile devices that should receive notifications from a SharePoint site.

Lists are made to be location-aware by using a new geolocation field. This field cannot be added when you create a list by using the browser; it must be inserted programmatically, and a new *.msi* package, *SQLSysClrTypes.msi*, must be installed on every SharePoint server that responds to web requests. This *.msi* package is part of the Microsoft SQL Server 2008 R2 SP1 Feature Pack for SQL Server 2008 or Microsoft SQL Server 2012 Feature Pack for SQL Server 2012 SP1.

> **Note** Although the geolocation field might be useful on mobile devices, it displays maps on other devices such as laptops. Also, you can create a geolocation column by using the browser, a script editor Web Part, and client-side code.

The improved mobile browser experience consists of the following three views:

- **Contemporary view**   An HTML5-optimized mobile browser experience, available to Mobile Internet Explorer 9.0 or later versions, for Windows Phone 7.5, Safari versions 4.0 or later versions, for iPhone 4.0, and the Android browser for Android 4.0 or later versions.

- **Classic view**   Identical to the mobile browser experience of SharePoint Server 2010. This uses HTML or similar markup languages such as CHTML or WML to provide backward compatibility for mobile browsers that cannot render the contemporary view.

- **Full-screen user interface**   A full-desktop view of a SharePoint site on a smartphone device.

The contemporary view is available on sites for which the new Automatic Mobile Browser Redirection site-level feature is activated. This feature checks if the mobile browser can handle HTML5 before sending the contemporary view to the mobile device; otherwise, the classic view is downloaded. By default, this feature is activated on the following site templates: Team Site, Blank Site, Document Workspace, Document Center, and Project Site.

On publishing sites, SharePoint 2013 includes device channels with which you can use different designs that target different devices, based on their user agent string.

The new stand-alone Office Web Apps Server product still provides mobile browser-based viewers: Word Mobile Viewer, Excel Mobile Viewer, and PowerPoint Mobile Viewer. These are optimized to render documents on phones.

More Info To read more about planning for mobile devices in SharePoint 2013, go to *technet.microsoft.com/en-us/library/gg610510(v=office.15).aspx*. For information on how to administer mobile device in SharePoint 2013, go to *technet.microsoft.com/en-us/library/ ff393820(v=office.15).aspx*.

Supported web browsers

SharePoint 2013 supports several commonly used web browsers. Internet Explorer 8, Internet Explorer 9, and Internet Explorer 10 (when in desktop mode) have full support for all collaboration actions in SharePoint 2013. Versions of Google Chrome, Apple Safari, and Mozilla Firefox (and 64-bit versions of Internet Explorer) offer limited support.

Internet Explorer 6 and Internet Explorer 7 are explicitly not supported; however, a designer of SharePoint 2013 Web Content Management (WCM) sites (also known as *publishing sites*) and the HTML markup they use to layout pages could create sites with which readers can view content by using any browser. Content authors on a publishing site would still need to use one of the supported browsers.

More Info To read more about browser support, see the TechNet article "Plan browser support in SharePoint 2013" at *technet.microsoft.com/en-us/library/cc263526(v=office.15). aspx* and "Supported mobile device browsers in SharePoint 2013" at *technet.microsoft.com/ en-us/library/fp161353.aspx*.

Service application improvements

From a service application perspective, the SharePoint 2013 architecture remains the same as that for SharePoint 2010. There are, however, new service applications available, service applications that have changed, and some that have been deprecated. This section details them all, but there are enhancements to the Business Intelligence (BI) services, such as Excel Services, PerformancePoint, and Visio Services, which are detailed in Chapters 5 and 6.

New service applications

SharePoint 2013 contains three new service applications:

- Machine Translation

- Work Management

- App Management

Of these three new service applications, only the Machine Translation service application can be used as a cross-farm service application; that is, it can be configured to be accessible from multiple SharePoint farms within your organization. The other two can only be used within a single farm.

Note No other service applications have been added or removed from the list of service applications that are shared across SharePoint farms. If you are using a service application farm in your SharePoint 2010 installation, you can upgrade this farm first before upgrading the consuming SharePoint farms.

The Machine Translation service application

This connects to the Bing cloud-based translation service by which users can employ machine translation on sites, files pages, and term sets located in the MMS. This cloud-based service doesn't understand context and keeps words in same order. This service can run in partitioned mode if you need to use it in a multitenant environment.

On the management page for the service application (see Figure 1-11), you can configure which file types to translate, the maximum file size (binary and text files), the maximum character count for Word documents, as well as other options, including specifying a web proxy server, number of translation processes created on each server, frequency of the throughput, maximum translation attempts, maximum synchronous translation requests, translation quota, and whether extra security checks are performed for Office 97-2003 documents. The Machine Translation service application processes translation requests asynchronously, synchronously (for instant translation), and via ad hoc translation. This service can be used as the primary translation engine not only for files, pages, and streams of bytes produced by programs, but it can also be used for variation's content.

FIGURE 1-11 You can configure the Machine Translation service application by using its management page.

There are a number of timer jobs for this service:

- Language Support, which runs weekly and updates the languages available to the Machine Translation service application.

- Machine Translation service application timer job that by default runs every 15 minutes and initiates the translation of documents that have been submitted to the Machine Translation service application. The frequency of this timer job is configured on the Service Application Management page.

- Translation Export Job Definition for each web application associated with a Machine Translation service application that exports pages and lists content to XLIFF for human translation or machine translation via the Machine Translation service application.

- Translation Import Job Definition for each web application associated with a Machine Translation service application that imports translated page and list content from XLIFF to the correct location in a site collection.

- Remove Job History removes the completed job history. The frequency of this timer job is configured on the Service Application Management page.

Full-trust solutions can be created to perform immediate or batch translations by using the REST API or Client-Side Object Model (CSOM) as well as server APIs. You can find information about writing custom solutions by using the Machine Translation service application at *msdn.microsoft.com/en-us/library/jj163145(v=office.15).aspx*.

Note The Machine Translation service application offers no user interface; therefore, any activity would need to be recorded by custom code.

The Work Management service application

The Work Management service application (WMSA) provides functionality to aggregate tasks. With it, users can view and track their to-do's and tasks from one central location: their My Site. Tasks are aggregated from a number of Microsoft products, including Microsoft Exchange 2013, Microsoft Project Server 2013, and SharePoint 2013.

The tasks are cached in the user's My Site with a two-way synchronization so that they can either be updated in the user's My Site or updated in the product where they were originated. Information concerning tasks held in Exchange 2013 is obtained by using the Work Management Synchronize with Exchange timer job, which runs every 5 minutes.

Exchange 2013 provides new and improved Exchange Web Services (EWS) and web service interfaces that can be used to access and manage information stored in Exchange. If you plan to use the Exchange 2013 integration capabilities with SharePoint, you need to install the Exchange Web Services Managed API, which can be downloaded from Microsoft's download site at *www.microsoft.com/en-us/download/details.aspx?id=35371*.

The WMSA is based on *Provider model* so that other systems can be integrated in the future.

The Central Administration website does not provide any management pages for this service application. Any integration with this service must be done programmatically.

Note The WMSA and the EWS Managed API must be installed if you want to use the social computing My Tasks to aggregate tasks from SharePoint, Exchange, and Project Server. You can read more about social computing in Chapter 4.

App Management Service

The App Management Service is used to access SharePoint Apps, which is a new application architecture for SharePoint 2013 (this is discussed later in this chapter).

Deprecated/changed service applications

This section discusses service applications that have changed or been deprecated.

The search service application

The search service application (SSA) is another area in which Microsoft has made major investments. SSA has been completely re-engineered from the ground up, built on functionality from SharePoint Server 2010 enterprise search and FAST Search for SharePoint 2010. Not only is FAST Search no longer a stand-alone product, but indeed, it is a dead one.

SharePoint 2013 enterprise search provides a powerful, scalable, and extendable service. It incorporates better support for in-context refinements and provides in-line previews. For example, you can find information about a document on the search results page without opening the document.

SharePoint 2013 search uses a single object model for all SharePoint 2013 products. This means that SharePoint Foundation 2013 and the Standard or Enterprise editions of SharePoint Server 2013 all have the same underlying search object model.

In SharePoint Server 2013 you can have multiple search schemas. The search schema contains the crawled properties, managed properties and their settings, and the mappings between the crawled and managed properties. In addition to the default search schema, site collection administrators and tenant administrators can also create search schemas specific to their site collection or tenant. Only unused managed properties that do not have crawled properties mapped to them can be reused.

SharePoint Search 2013 is not only used to help you locate content or people, it is also used in other components of SharePoint 2013, including eDiscovery, navigation, topic pages, and Internet-facing sites. Therefore, it should be one of the first service applications you should create. For example, you will not be able to create a successful Managed Metadata service application if a search service application is not installed.

 More Info You can read more about the improvements within enterprise search in Chapter 2, "Introducing the new search architecture."

MMS

MMS has become more robust. Tags can now have properties, and you can use these properties for site-based navigation. You can control how users create tags, and you can now "pin" terms to prevent accidental duplication of tags. MMS also includes improvements and additional capabilities in a multi-lingual environment, without the need to install language packs.

 More Info You can read more about using MMS terms for navigation in Chapter 3.

Office Web Apps

Office Web Apps is no longer a service application. It is now packaged as a separate product and installed on its own set of servers (farm). This way, you can scale, manage, and maintain Office Web Apps as a separate entity without affecting the installation of the SharePoint farm. It is also licensed separate from SharePoint licenses. Office Web Apps is used by Exchange 2013 and Lync 2013 as well as by SharePoint 2013, URL accessible file servers, and possibly in the future, third-party document stores, such as Oracle Universal Content Management (UCM) and EMC's Enterprise Content Management (ECM) Documentum products.

This means that even though you might not have SharePoint installed within your organization, you might want to install Office Web Apps so that you can use it with Exchange and Microsoft Lync to render documents. However, there are license implications in this scenario.

There is no licensing required for viewing documents in SharePoint 2013. But, if you want to create or modify documents by using Office Web Apps in SharePoint 2013, licenses will need to be purchased. You can read more about licensing Office Web Apps for editing Office files at *technet. microsoft.com/en-us/library/ff431682.aspx#license.*

Some improvements you will see if you use Office Web Apps in SharePoint 2013 include the following:

- You can view documents in full-screen mode or by using Web Parts. However, Microsoft Visio is not part of Office Web Apps, so you should use Visio Services to display Visio files.

- Not-so friendly URLs are removed.

- Multi-authoring is now available with PowerPoint and Word in addition to OneNote and Excel.

- When a user hovers over the item on the search results page in SharePoint, Office Web Apps displays a preview of the item's content.

The separation of Office Web Apps from SharePoint 2013 also frees the Office Web Application team to enhance the product independent of SharePoint.

Office Web Apps needs to be installed on either Windows Server 2008 R2 or Server 2012. It does not need access to an SQL Server, because it does not create any databases. Office Web Apps uses a shared XML configuration file called *Farm-Settings.xml* for the farm, and then each server in the farm has its own *Machine_Name.xml* file. You cannot install Microsoft Exchange, SharePoint, Microsoft Lync, SQL, or any version of the desktop Office programs on the same servers on which Office Web Apps is installed. If other products that are installed on the same servers as Office Web Apps use web services, they cannot use port 80, 443, and 809.

Warning After Office Web Apps is installed on a server, there are no visible signs on the Start menu that it is installed. Therefore, other administrators in your organization might incorrectly identify the server as a candidate for a clean install that they can use. To complete the installation of Office Web Apps, you use Windows PowerShell.

If you are using Office Web Apps with SharePoint 2013, after both farms are installed, you will need to bind the two together by using the Windows PowerShell *New-SPWOPIBinding* cmdlet on one of the servers in your SharePoint farm.

> **More Info** You can read more about Office Web Apps at *technet.microsoft.com/en-us/library/jj219456(v=office.15).aspx*, including how to use Office Web Apps with SharePoint 2013.

Web analytics

This is no longer a separate service application; it is now part of SharePoint's search engine. Search is a lot smarter in SharePoint 2013 and can be used to analyze individual actions by the end users as well as click through rates of sessions. This information is then used to provide relevance and suggestion information for users. SharePoint 2010 monitored who visited what and where they went. Now, search provides social analytics that also provides information on what users are doing. Microsoft has provided an extensible API.

You can find the analytic information for a site in an Excel file named *usage.xlsx*. To access this file, on the site settings page, in the Site Administration section, click Popularity Trends. The output in the file should look similar to that in Figure 1-12.

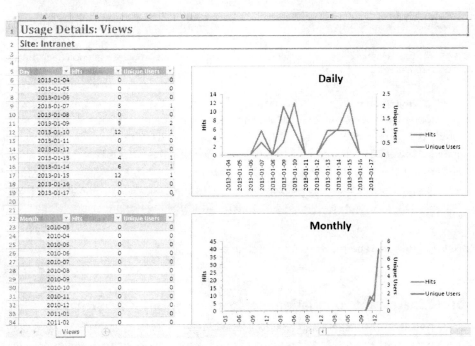

FIGURE 1-12 Site usage details as displayed in the *usage.xlsx* file.

To view search usage reports (see Figure 1-13), go to the Search Administration page, and then in the right navigation pane, in the Diagnostics section, click Usage Reports.

FIGURE 1-13 The Search Service Application conducts the analysis and reporting of analytical data. It is also used to report on search metrics.

You cannot upgrade the Web Analytics Service of SharePoint Server 2010 to the Analytics Processing Component in SharePoint 2013. When you upgrade to SharePoint 2013, you cannot attach and upgrade the SharePoint 2010 Web Analytics databases. You should turn off Web Analytics in the SharePoint Server 2010 environment before you copy the content databases that you want to upgrade to SharePoint 2013. Also, SharePoint 2013 does not support the Web Analytics Web Part. When a site is upgraded to SharePoint 2013, any pages that include the Web Analytics Web Part will render a message that informs the user that the Web Part is no longer supported.

More Info You can read more about search in Chapter 2.

Microsoft SharePoint Foundation Subscription Settings Service

This service provides multitenant functionality, and as you would expect, it gets better in SharePoint 2013. It still tracks subscription IDs and settings for service applications that are deployed in partitioned mode. All service apps in SharePoint 2013 can be partitioned. However, it still can only be deployed by using Windows PowerShell.

Most on-premises customers will probably not need to implement a multitenant environment; however, if you plan to use SharePoint Apps or host-named site collections, you will need to create this service application. SharePoint Apps are deployed in their own website in a special isolated domain such as AWApps.com or apps.adventure-works.com. The Microsoft SharePoint Foundation Subscription Setting Service is used to establish the domain/subdomain that hosts the websites for the SharePoint Apps. Similarly, the subscription service is used to establish the subdomain that host-named site collections use.

The User Profile service application

Most IT professionals had difficulties with the User Profile service application (UPSA) in SharePoint Server 2010, and problems after installing cumulative updates are infamous. Improvements include the following:

- Performance has been optimized. For example, indexes have been added to specific user properties to reduce full-table scans and batch import of data if you use the Business Connectivity Services.

- Compatibility with Common Directory Service configurations, including Forefront Identity Manager (FIM) and generic Lightweight Directory Access Protocol (LDAP) providers.

- Ability to monitor profile synchronization performance and stability.

- The User Profile Replication Engine (UPRE) was a separate download in SharePoint 2010. This is now part of SharePoint Server 2013. Using UPRE, you can replicate user profile information and some social information between multiple farms.

- Additional synchronization options (see Figure 1-14). You can use unidirectional Active Directory (AD) synchronization import as in SharePoint 2010, which still make use of FIM, plus SharePoint 2013 now includes the one-way AD Import, which was the only method available in Microsoft Office SharePoint Server 2007. In SharePoint 2013, you do not need AD replication permissions, even if you use FIM. You can filter on Organizational Units (OUs), users, and AD security groups by using LDAP filters for full or incremental imports, and you can switch between AD Direct and FIM.

 Note Switching from AD Direct to FIM import is not a trivial task. The consequences of switching can be dramatic. At a minimum, all of the synchronization connections and mappings need to be recreated. For more information on UPSA, read Chapter 4.

Configure Synchronization Settings

Use this page to manage the settings for profile synchronization of users and groups.

Synchronization Entities

Based on your selection, both users and groups, or only users will be synchronized across all synchronization connections.

Note: If you are upgrading from a previous version of SharePoint, it is recommended that you first do a Users only synchronization run, followed by a Users and Groups synchronization.

- Users and Groups
- Users Only

Synchronize BCS Connections

Select this option if you would like BCS (Business Connectivity Service) data to be imported. If you clear this selection, your AD and/or LDAP connections will be included in the profile synchronization run (full or incremental) but your BDC connections, if any, will be ignored. You can change this setting later to include the BDC data import.

☐ Include existing BCS connections for synchronization?

Synchronization Options

To use the full-featured SharePoint Profile Synchronization option, select 'Use SharePoint Profile Synchronization'.

To use the light-weight Active Directory Import option (with some limitations - see documentation), select 'Use SharePoint Active Directory Import'.

To use an external identity manager for Profile Synchronization, select 'Enable External Identity Manager'.

Note: Enabling external identity manager will disable all Profile Synchronization options and status display in SharePoint.

- Use SharePoint Profile Synchronization
- Use SharePoint Active Directory Import
- Enable External Identity Manager

FIGURE 1-14 The profile synchronization settings for users and groups.

Business Connectivity Service

Improvements to the Business Connectivity Service (BCS) in SharePoint 2013 include the following:

- An additional connection protocol, Open Data (OData), has been included. This is an industry-standard web protocol that is used to query and update data. OData applies web technologies such as HTTP, Atom Publishing Protocol (AtomPub), and JavaScript Object Notation (JSON) to provide access to information from a variety of applications, services, and stores. For years, SharePoint has been an OData provider, which means a SharePoint list can be consumed by using OData. In SharePoint 2013, you can now connect to an external data source by using OData. By using OAuth 2.0 with OData connections, you can also achieve more fine-grained permissions.

- Developers can create event receivers in SharePoint 2013 that are triggered when data in the external system has changed, as long as the external system provides a subscription and notifications interface. The application or user needs to subscribe to the external system for this to work.

- Support for SharePoint Apps has been added. Business Data Connectivity (BDC) information can be included within a SharePoint App. The BDC runtime then creates an External Content Type (ECT) that is scoped at the SharePoint App level. This limits use of the ECT to the SharePoint App. In SharePoint 2010, ECTs could only be scoped at the service-application level.

- SharePoint 2013 provides an event listener. This makes it possible for SharePoint users and custom code to receive notifications of events that occur in the external system. For example, developers can write custom code for external lists that trigger SharePoint events when data is changed. SharePoint users could then subscribe to alerts on external lists that are based on ECTs that make use of that custom code.

- External list performance improvements and the ability to export an external list to an Excel spreadsheet.

More Info You can read more about BCS in Chapter 5.

Access

There are now two service applications, as described here:

- **Access Services 2010** This mimics the Access service application on SharePoint 2010, by which the tables in your Microsoft Access database are stored as SharePoint lists on the site that was built from the Access web database site definition.

- **Access Services has been completely rebuilt** When Access 2013 databases are published to SharePoint 2013, an Access web app site is created and your data is now stored in a full-fledged SQL Server database, which is automatically generated in the SQL Server 2012 installation that was selected by a SharePoint administrator. The databases created will have a name, such as, db_<*guid*>, where <*guid*> is an automatically generated number. The tables, queries, macros, and forms are all stored in this database. Whenever you visit the Access web app site, enter data, or modify the design, you'll be interacting with this database behind the scenes. Therefore, SharePoint 2013 Access web app will not have the same limitations that SharePoint 2010 Access web databases had in terms of numbers of fields and sizes of tables.

  Advanced users who are familiar with SQL Server will be able to directly connect to this database for advanced reporting and analysis with familiar tools such as Excel, Microsoft Power View, and SAP Crystal Reports. Access web app site now has far more capabilities for rich forms and reports than were provided in SharePoint 2010.

  This does have implications for your database administrator as well as the operational-level agreements you might have with your business with regard to the maintenance of these Access 2013 web app databases.

More Info You can read more about Access in Chapter 5.

PowerPoint Automation Service

Although it's technically not a service application, but rather a SharePoint service because you only have to start the service by using the Services On Server page in the Central Administration web site, SharePoint 2013 includes the new PowerPoint Automation Service. Similar to the current Word Automation Service, it takes presentations and converts them into other formats such as HTML and PDF.

Web application and site collection improvements

Two important improvements in SharePoint 2013 include a change of Microsoft's recommendation that web applications should use claims-based authentication by default, and the use of host-named site collections.

Authentication

As with SharePoint 2010, with SharePoint 2013 you can create web applications to use either classic or claims-based authentication. With either type of web application, claims authentication is used for authentication flow within the farm. The authentication type of the web application only affects the authentication flow into and out of the SharePoint farm.

SharePoint 2013 has extended claims-based authentication via OAuth 2.0 and a dedicated server-to-server STS authentication, which together make it possible for your organization to use new scenarios and functionality for Exchange Server 2013, Lync Server 2013, apps in the SharePoint Store or App Catalog, and other services that are compliant with the server-to-server authentication protocol.

SharePoint 2013 supports user authentication based on the following claims-based authentication methods:

- Windows claims

- SAML-based claims

- Forms-based authentication claims

In SharePoint 2010 the recommendation was to create web applications by using classic-mode authentication because there were components that were not claims-aware, such as using the people picker and SQL Server 2008 R2 Reporting Services. Now, with the new, improved claims-based authentication in SharePoint 2013 being the default, Microsoft's recommendation is to use this authentication scheme for your web applications.

When using the Central Administration website, only claims-based web applications can be created. Classic-based authentication is now deprecated, and to create classic-mode web applications, you must use Windows PowerShell. If you are upgrading from SharePoint 2010 to SharePoint 2013, you can convert your classic-mode web applications to claims-based before upgrading.

SharePoint 2013 has much more logging to help you troubleshoot authentication issues. Examples of enhanced logging support include the following:

- Separate categorized claims-related logs for each authentication mode

- Information about adding and removing FedAuth cookies from the Distributed Cache Service

- Information about the reason why a FedAuth cookie could not be used, such as a cookie expiration or a failure to decrypt

- Information about where authentication requests are redirected

- Information about the failures of user migration in a specific site collection

Host-named site collections

Microsoft recommends that you create host-named site collections (HNSC) and not path-based site collection addressing. HNSC is a mechanism for consolidating web applications into individual site collections, yet letting them retain their existing URLs.

In SharePoint 2010, web applications contained one or more site collections and the common practice was to create them under wildcard-managed paths such as *http://intranet.adventure-works. com/sites/hr* or *http://intranet.adventure-works.com/sites/it*.

Using HNSC, each site collection can have its own top-level URL, so the equivalent site collection could be *http://hr.adventure-works.com* or *http://it.adventure-works.com*. Both of these site collections are created in the same web application and could be stored in the same content database; however, by looking at the URLs of these two site collections, users would not be aware of this. Using this technique you can reduce the number of web applications that you need in your SharePoint farm.

The web application that hosts the HNSC must have a default site collection at its root but does not need a template assigned to it, because it will not be used for anything. Also, for each HNSC you must update the DNS to point to the IP address for the web application that is hosting them or use a wildcard DNS entry.

Using HNSC suits a multitenant hosting environment such as Office 365 and was available in SharePoint 2010. However, in SharePoint 2013 Microsoft has overcome some key limitations and improved the scalability of HNSC, not just for cloud-based solutions, but it also scales much better for on-premises deployments. Microsoft is now recommending that HNSC should be the default for your URL site collection naming standards. However, there are still some limitations to this approach:

- HNSC cannot be extended or mapped. You need to set a different set of policies as per the URL.

- HNSC should not be hosted in multiple web applications. Although this is technically possible, it is complicated to achieve and manage. You should consider perhaps using HNSC in one web application, even though you can create HNSC and path-based site collections on the same web application that you use path-based site collections in other web applications. And, of course, it is very unlikely that you would use HNSC for personal sites.

HNSC cannot be created within Central Administration; you must use Windows PowerShell and you need to configure the DNS to send all requests for *http://*.adventure-works.com* to a web application. This web application must be extended with SharePoint and should not be bound to any specific host headers so that it handles all requests. After you have created an HNSC by using Windows Power-Shell, the HNSC appears on the View All Site Collection page for a specific web application within the Central Administration website, as shown in Figure 1-15.

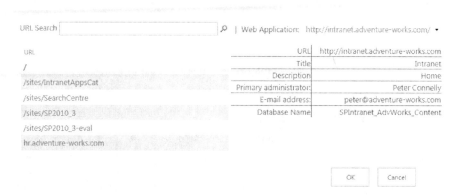

FIGURE 1-15 Use the Central Administration website to display both path-based and host-named site collections.

 More Info You can find more information about HNSCs on TechNet at *technet.microsoft.com/en-us/library/cc424952.aspx*.

Self-Service Site Collection Creation

As with SharePoint 2010, you can enable Self-Service Site Collection Creation (SSC) in SharePoint 2013; however, you have a number of new options, as shown in Figure 1-16, with which you can do the following:

- Allow users to create site collections by using the site collection signup page, *scsignup.aspx*.

- Provide users with a shortcut to create new Team sites at a defined location. When you select to prompt users to create either a Team site or a site collection, you can configure Site Classification Settings to be hidden from users, to be an optional choice, or to be a required choice.

 Note SSC is only applicable to path-based site collections, not HNSCs.

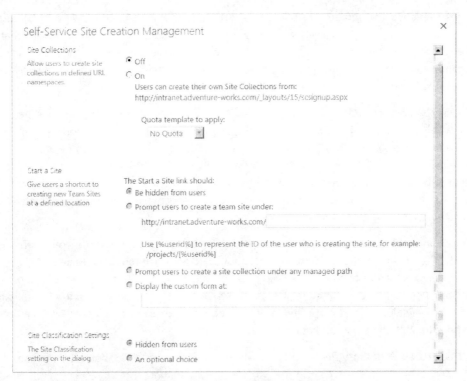

FIGURE 1-16 When enabling SSC, there are several options available.

If you use the Farm Creation Wizard, SSC is enabled by default.

Site collection and site administration

Site collection administrators can manage a number of new features that are introduced with SharePoint 2013. When you navigate to the site settings page at the top of a site collection, you see a number of new links that were not there in SharePoint 2010, such as the following:

- SharePoint App permissions at a site or site-collection level

- Term store management

- Popularity trends

- A large number of search-related links, including Search Result Sources, Search Result Types, Search Query Rules, Search Schema, Search Settings, Search Configuration Input, Search Configuration Export, Search Engine Optimization, and Popularity And Search Reports. Also, the FAST-related links have been removed.

- HTML Field Security

For organizations that upgrade from SharePoint 2010 to SharePoint 2013, they will need to decide which site collection administrators will want to use this new functionality. It might also mean that for some organizations the configuration of such functions will be kept internal to the IT department. Such organization will need to introduce new processes so that businesses can request the new functionality enabled by these links at a site-collection or site basis.

The Microsoft documentation states that in SharePoint 2013 a number of site templates are no longer available. This includes the Document Workspace, Personalization, Group Work, and all five of the Meeting Workspace site templates. Existing sites that were created by using any of these site templates in SharePoint 2010 will continue to operate in SharePoint 2013. Microsoft has stated that these site templates will be removed completely from the next major release of SharePoint, and sites that were created by using these site templates will not be supported. However in SharePoint 2013, you can create sites using these templates.

In SharePoint 2010, you could only create the PowerPoint Broadcast site at a site-collection level by using the Central Administration website or Windows PowerShell. It required Office Web Apps and the PowerPoint service application. Office Web Apps is now a separate server product that can serve multiple SharePoint farms, and therefore, in SharePoint 2013, sites created by using the PowerPoint Broadcast site definition are not supported. Any content in such sites must be moved and the sites deleted prior to upgrading any content databases that contain them.

The Visio Process Repository site template is available in SharePoint 2013; however, Microsoft has stated that it will be removed in the next major release of SharePoint.

SharePoint development changes

The application architecture is another area in which Microsoft has made a major investment. Everything within SharePoint is now called an app—custom code is an app, a document library is an app, your announcements list is an app, and access databases that you host within SharePoint are apps.

Microsoft has introduced a new API that runs in parallel with existing APIs. Any code that you created in SharePoint 2010 will continue to run. However, your developers now have the option of recomposing them as apps that can run on a different server or in the cloud, or can run on your SharePoint 2013 servers.

Using this new app model, you can now keep your SharePoint 2013 clean of custom code. With SharePoint 2010, to extend the out-of-the-box experience, you had to add custom code, and that custom code had to run on your SharePoint 2010 server. This added risk to your SharePoint installation. However, you cannot use all the same techniques when you try to extend SharePoint 2010 when it lives in the cloud.

The trend across the Internet with regard to services such as Facebook or LinkedIn is that when people add apps to those services, they are not adding code to the Facebook or LinkedIn servers. Apps are registered and published on those services. The app is run on other servers in the cloud, but they can integrate deeply with Facebook or LinkedIn. You can also have apps that are platform specific, so you can have iOS, Android, or web apps. On each of these platforms, the app is visually integrating with Facebook or LinkedIn services by running client-side code. This is code that is running on your tablet, mobile phone, or within your browser.

SharePoint 2013 application architecture provides the two approaches you will be familiar with when using SharePoint 2010—farm solutions and sandboxed solutions—plus it has an extended client-object model so that custom code can be created by using a similar apps model that is used by Facebook and LinkedIn. You can publish your SharePoint 2013 or Office 2013 apps uniformly whether your SharePoint installation is on-premises or in the cloud. SharePoint 2013 has support for the online SharePoint store, where you can use publically available apps which you might have to purchase or might be free. Alternatively, you can have an internal market place or you could use both the public store and an internal market place.

You will still need to create farm solutions in SharePoint 2013 for the same reasons you had to create them in SharePoint 2010; for example, to complete actions across site collection boundaries, to manage web applications, or the SharePoint farm. If your solution doesn't need to be a farm solution, then the question becomes should it be a sandboxed solution and SharePoint App? Microsoft's answer to that question is that you will not need sandboxed solutions. Sandboxed solutions will still work in SharePoint 2013; however, there are no improvements that Microsoft has made to them, other than they are tested for backward compatibility. But, if your organization is developing a new solution, your choices will be between farm solutions and SharePoint Apps.

Note SharePoint Apps do not work on web applications that use SAML. They do not support multiple zone; that is, alternative access mappings (AAM).

SharePoint Apps management

Using or developing SharePoint Apps when SharePoint is hosted in the cloud is slightly easier than when using or creating them for an on-premises installation of SharePoint 2013. The infrastructure to support apps is built for you. Also Microsoft has provided "Napa" Office 365 development tools with which developers can build apps for Office and/or SharePoint by using a browser window, with no need to install any other tool such as Microsoft Visual Studio. Before users can add a SharePoint App to their site and use it, SharePoint farm administration needs to complete a number of tasks to support SharePoint Apps in an on-premises installation of SharePoint 2013.

More Info You can find more information about creating apps for Office and SharePoint by using "Napa" Office 365 development tools at *msdn.microsoft.com/en-us/library/ jj220038(v=office.15).aspx*.

Using a SharePoint App

A site owner uses the Site Contents page or the Your Apps page to add a SharePoint App to a site. To navigate to the Your Apps page, click the Settings icon, and then in the menu that opens, click Add An App, as shown in Figure 1-17.

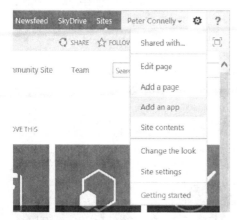

FIGURE 1-17 Use the Settings icon to display the Your Apps page.

SharePoint Apps are made available from one of three locations:

- **Apps You Can Add** On the Your Apps page, in the Quick Launch under Your Apps, click Apps You Can Add to be presented with a list of apps already available for your site. The list will contain the default apps, such as standard lists and libraries, as well as any apps that you might have added from the Microsoft's Online Marketplace.

- **The App Catalog** On the Your Apps page, in the Quick Launch, under Your Apps, click From Your Organization.

- **The Microsoft Online Marketplace** On the Your Apps page, in the Quick Launch, click SharePoint Store. You are then redirected to Microsoft's Online Marketplace, as illustrated in Figure 1-18. Apps that require a prerequisite that is not installed on a web application or tenancy appear dimmed and are unavailable. Some SharePoint Apps are free, whereas others you will need to purchase. When you purchase a SharePoint App, you must accept the license and you will need to agree to the permissions that the SharePoint App must have in order to execute, such as read access to lists or full control access to the site collection.

When you visit the SharePoint Store, you might notice that some of the apps are not available (they are displayed grayed out). These apps might require features that are not activated on your site; for example, when the app requires Internet-facing endpoints. You can activate Internet-facing endpoints by navigating to the Manage Web Applications page on the SharePoint Central Administration website. You can activate this feature on the Mange Web Application Features page, which you can navigate to by selecting the web application that you want to configure, and then on the Web Applications ribbon tab, in the Manage group, click Manage Features.

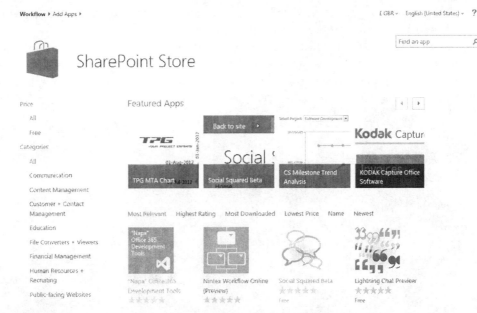

FIGURE 1-18 You can add SharePoint Apps to your site from the Microsoft Online Marketplace.

When you add a SharePoint App, a SharePoint App permission request is displayed, which you need to accept to use the SharePoint App. SharePoint Apps that have been added to a site from the Microsoft Online Marketplace then appear on the Your Apps page, in the Apps You Can Add section, on any site in the SharePoint farm. They can also be seen on the Site Contents page.

Identify and configure a SharePoint Apps URL

The Apps URL is used to identify SharePoint Apps. SharePoint App URLs are created when you first add a SharePoint App to any site in a site collection. They are configured in the following format:

<App Prefix>-<guid>.<App Domain Name>/<SharePoint App name>

For example, *apps-87e90ada14c175.AWapps.com/myapp*, where the *<App Prefix>* is apps, the *<App Doman Name>* is AWapps and *<guid>*, is an automatically generated number. Therefore, if you add a SharePoint App named myapp to a site that is within many different site collections, you will have multiple SharePoint App URLs of the format:

- apps-*<guid>*.AWapps.com/myapp, if the SharePoint App was added to a site in the root site collection of a web application.

- apps-*<guid>*.AWapps.com/*sites/hr*/myapps, if the SharePoint App was added to a site in a managed-path site collection, where *sites* is the managed-path name and *hr* is the top-level site of the site collection.

Because the App Domain is defined once per SharePoint farm, and a SharePoint farm can host many web applications with a variety of fully-qualified domain names (FQDNs), it is recommended to use an App domain name that is not tied to one of the FQDNs that you use for you web applications. For example, if you have web applications with FQDNs of *intranet.adventure-works.com*, *teams. adventure-works.com*, and *portal.contoso.com*, do not use a child domain name of *apps.adventure-works.com*; instead, use an isolated FQDN, such as *AWapps.com*.

Configure the App Domain Name as a wildcard DNS A record, as demonstrated in Figure 1-19.

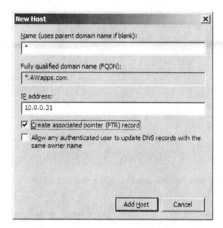

FIGURE 1-19 Configuring a wildcard DNS A host record for SharePoint Apps in the New Host dialog box.

The SharePoint App model uses OAuth access tokens, which describe who the current user and application are. To prevent any replay style of attack that would grant access to content by someone who was sniffing your network traffic, if you are using SharePoint Apps, you should be using Secure Sockets Layer (SSL). Using SSL prevents those scenarios from happening, and because you've seen the SharePoint Apps URLs are going to be different, you need a wildcard SSL certificate. You could use port 80 for a development or prototype environment.

To configure the App Prefix and App Domain name, use either Windows PowerShell or the Central Administration website.

The PowerShell commands will be similar to the following:

```
Set-SPAppSiteSubscriptionName -Name "app" -confirm:$false
Set-SPAppDomain "AWDomain.com"
```

Using the Central Administration website, you can display or configure the App Prefix and App Domain name by using the Configure App URLs page, as shown in Figure 1-20. In the Quick Launch, Click Apps, and then under App Management, click Configure App Urls.

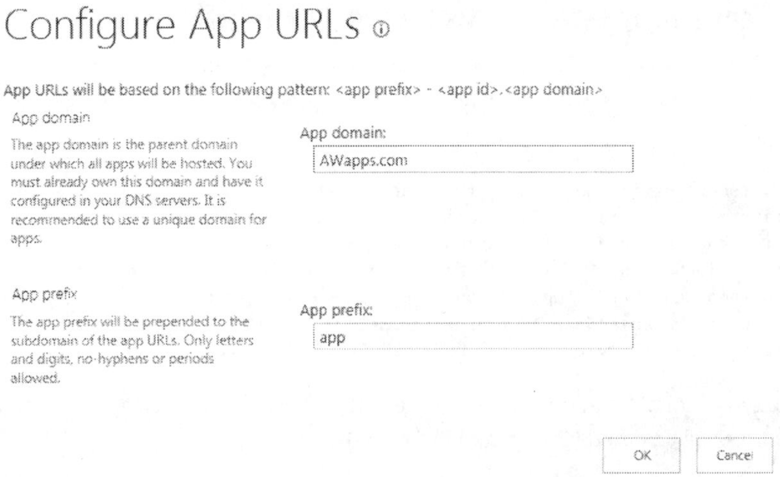

Configure App URLs ⓘ

App URLs will be based on the following pattern: <app prefix> - <app id>.<app domain>

App domain

The app domain is the parent domain under which all apps will be hosted. You must already own this domain and have it configured in your DNS servers. It is recommended to use a unique domain for apps.

App domain:

```
AWapps.com
```

App prefix

The app prefix will be prepended to the subdomain of the app URLs. Only letters and digits, no-hyphens or periods allowed.

App prefix:

```
app
```

OK   Cancel

FIGURE 1-20 Use the Configure App URLs page in the Central Administration website to set the App Domain and App prefix.

Start SharePoint Apps-related service instances

Using the Central Administration website, start the Microsoft SharePoint Foundation Subscription Settings Service and the App Management Service instances, if they're not already started (see Figure 1-21).

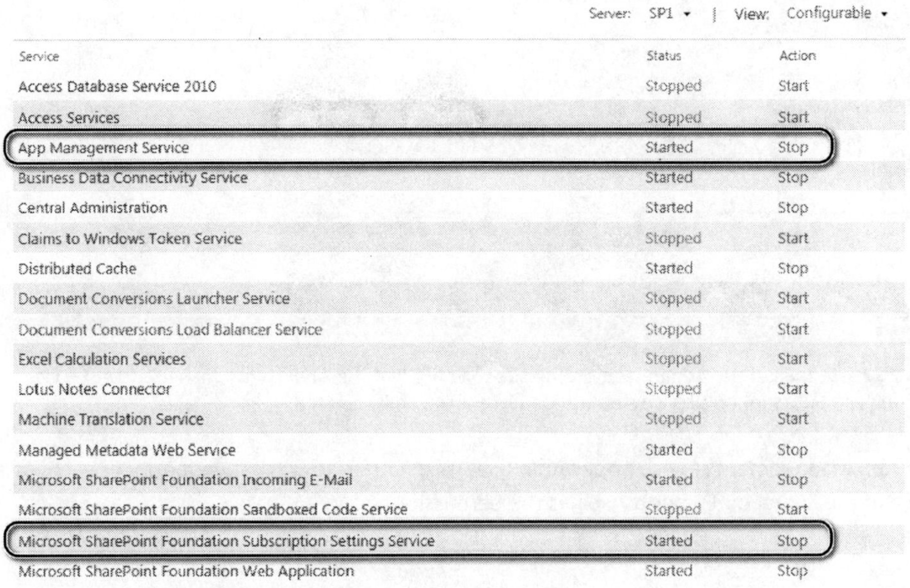

Server: SP1 ▾ | View: Configurable ▾

Service	Status	Action
Access Database Service 2010	Stopped	Start
Access Services	Stopped	Start
App Management Service	Started	Stop
Business Data Connectivity Service	Started	Stop
Central Administration	Started	Stop
Claims to Windows Token Service	Stopped	Start
Distributed Cache	Started	Stop
Document Conversions Launcher Service	Stopped	Start
Document Conversions Load Balancer Service	Stopped	Start
Excel Calculation Services	Stopped	Start
Lotus Notes Connector	Stopped	Start
Machine Translation Service	Stopped	Start
Managed Metadata Web Service	Started	Stop
Microsoft SharePoint Foundation Incoming E-Mail	Started	Stop
Microsoft SharePoint Foundation Sandboxed Code Service	Stopped	Start
Microsoft SharePoint Foundation Subscription Settings Service	Started	Stop
Microsoft SharePoint Foundation Web Application	Started	Stop

FIGURE 1-21 Start the Subscription Setting Service and App Management Service.

Create SharePoint Apps-related service applications

Use Windows PowerShell to create the Application Management Service Application and the Subscription Service Application, if one does not already exist, by using commands similar to the following:

```
$appPool= Get-SPServiceApplicationPool -Identity "SPServiceApps"
$app = New-SPSubscriptionSettingsServiceApplication -ApplicationPool $appPool '
   -Name SettingsServiceApp -DatabaseName SettingServiceDB
$proxy = New-SPSubscriptionSettingsServiceApplicationProxy -ServiceApplication $app
$appServ = New-SPAppManagementServiceApplication -ApplicationPool $appPool '
   -Name AppManServiceApp -DatabaseName AppManServiceDB
$appProxy = New-SPAppManagementServiceApplicationProxy -ServiceApplication $appServ
```

You can use the Central Administration website to check that these two service applications and their proxies were successfully created, as depicted in Figure 1-22.

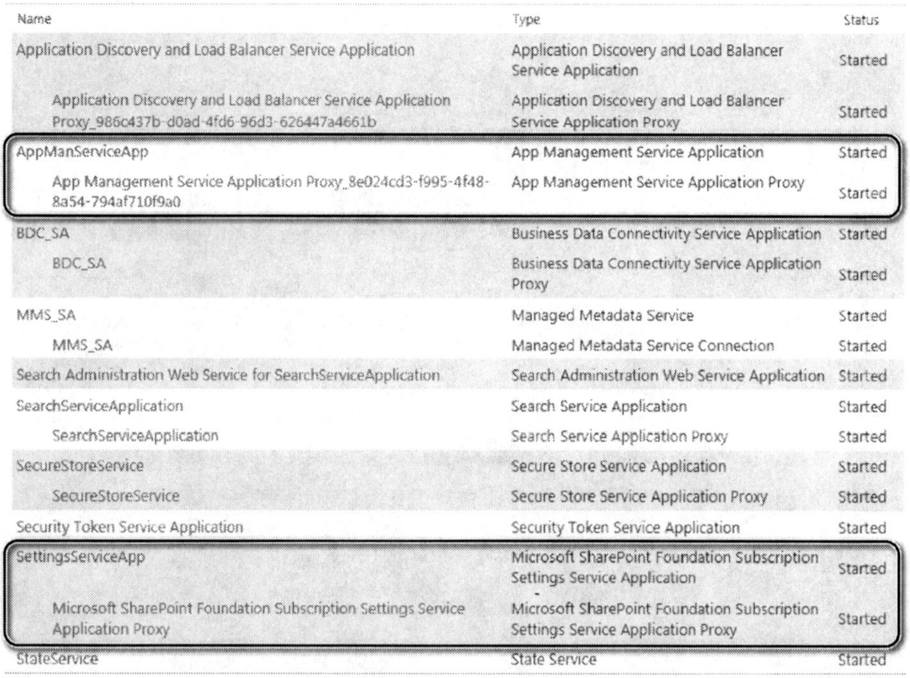

Name	Type	Status
Application Discovery and Load Balancer Service Application	Application Discovery and Load Balancer Service Application	Started
Application Discovery and Load Balancer Service Application Proxy_986c437b-d0ad-4fd6-96d3-626447a4661b	Application Discovery and Load Balancer Service Application Proxy	Started
AppManServiceApp	App Management Service Application	Started
App Management Service Application Proxy_8e024cd3-f995-4f48-8a54-794af710f9a0	App Management Service Application Proxy	Started
BDC_SA	Business Data Connectivity Service Application	Started
BDC_SA	Business Data Connectivity Service Application Proxy	Started
MMS_SA	Managed Metadata Service	Started
MMS_SA	Managed Metadata Service Connection	Started
Search Administration Web Service for SearchServiceApplication	Search Administration Web Service Application	Started
SearchServiceApplication	Search Service Application	Started
SearchServiceApplication	Search Service Application Proxy	Started
SecureStoreService	Secure Store Service Application	Started
SecureStoreService	Secure Store Service Application Proxy	Started
Security Token Service Application	Security Token Service Application	Started
SettingsServiceApp	Microsoft SharePoint Foundation Subscription Settings Service Application	Started
Microsoft SharePoint Foundation Subscription Settings Service Application Proxy	Microsoft SharePoint Foundation Subscription Settings Service Application Proxy	Started
StateService	State Service	Started

FIGURE 1-22 Use the Central Administration website to verify that the Application Management Service Application and Subscription Service Application were successfully created.

The App Management service application uses its database to track the identity of each installed instance of the SharePoint Apps as well as the permissions.

Create a farm-wide default web application

Use Windows PowerShell to create the SharePoint farm-wide default web application that maps to the wildcard DNS entry. This web application will be used to redirect requests to the correct site collection, based on the SharePoint App URL. Do not create a site collection to this web application or bind it to any host name.

> **Note** You will need to either stop or delete the default IIS website that is created when the Windows Server Web Application role is added to the SharePoint server.

Creating and managing App Catalogs

In SharePoint 2013, each web application has its own App Catalog. Therefore, if you have multiple web applications, and you want the same apps to be available in all web applications, you need to create an App Catalog for each web application and upload all the apps into all the App Catalogs.

Use the Central Administration website to create an App Catalog for each web application for which you want to use SharePoint Apps. In the Quick Launch, click Apps, and then under App Management, click Manage App Catalog to display the Manage App Catalog page, as illustrated in Figure 1-23. To the right of Web Application, select the appropriate web application, select the Create A New App Catalog Site option, and then click OK.

Manage App Catalog ⓘ

Web Application: http://cthub.adventure-works.com/ ▾

App Catalog Site

The app catalog site contains catalogs for apps for SharePoint and Office. Use this site to make apps available to end users. Learn about the app catalog site.

The selected web application does not have an app catalog site associated to it.

⦿ Create a new app catalog site
◯ Enter a URL for an existing app catalog site

[OK]

FIGURE 1-23 Use the Manage App Catalog page to create an App Catalog for each web application.

When you click OK, a new site collection is created in the web application using the App Catalog Site (APPCATALOG#0) site template. The App Catalog site contains a list, named App Request, and two libraries, Apps For Office and Apps For SharePoint. It is in these two libraries that you upload your .*app* files.

After an App Catalog site is created, you can also use the View Site Settings on the Manage App Catalog page to navigate to the site settings page of an App Catalog site for a specific web application.

After an App Catalog for a web application is created, the next task is to configure whether users can get SharePoint apps from the SharePoint Store and/or apps for Office from the Office Store. To configure these settings on the SharePoint Central Administration website, navigate to the Apps page. In the SharePoint And Office Store section, click Configure Store Settings. If users cannot purchase apps, they can still browse the SharePoint Store and request an app.

When users request an app for SharePoint from the SharePoint Store, users can request a specific number of licenses and provide a justification for the purchase of the app for SharePoint. Submitted requests are added to the App Requests list in the App Catalog of the web application that contains the user's site collection. Farm administrators and the App Catalog site owner can view and respond to app requests.

Upgrading to SharePoint 2013

Upgrading to SharePoint 2013 from SharePoint 2010 is in many ways similar to upgrading from SharePoint 2007 to SharePoint 2010, as pointed out in the following:

- You are only able to upgrade from the previous version of SharePoint; that is, you can only upgrade to SharePoint 2013 from SharePoint 2010. If you are still using Windows SharePoint Services 3.0 or Microsoft Office SharePoint Server 2007, you must first upgrade to Microsoft SharePoint Foundation 2010 or Microsoft SharePoint Server 2010, as detailed at *technet. microsoft.com/en-us/library/cc303420.aspx*.

- You can upgrade to SharePoint 2010 by using the database attach upgrade method. Even though you might have been through the database attach process with the previous versions, you might find your experience with SharePoint 2013 to be different. When you upgraded previous versions of SharePoint, you mainly had to consider content in lists and libraries. However, like most organizations, you now have a larger amount of content stored in content databases, and you would have used other SharePoint capabilities—for example, MMS, Excel Services, InfoPath Services—or Business Intelligence functionality, such as Power Pivot or PerformancePoint Services (PPS).

  The methods for upgrading these other services are different from migrating content. The following service application databases support the database attach upgrade method:

  - BDC

  - MMS

  - PPS

  - Secure Store Services (SSS)

- User Profile (Profile, Social, and Sync databases)

- Search Administration

  You might also find that some components—for example, if you have deployed PowerPivot v1.0—will block a database attach. This is when you might need to consider the next method.

- Create a clean SharePoint farm with new services and web applications and then use a third-party tool to incorporate content from SharePoint 2010 lists and libraries.

- Some components will require separate migrations; for example, Power Pivot, Excel Services, InfoPath Forms Service.

- Content migration is still supported using services and client code.

However, the upgrade process differs from the upgrade to SharePoint 2010 in the following aspects:

- In-place upgrade is not available. This means that you can no longer install SharePoint 2013 on the same hardware on which SharePoint 2010 is installed.

- The SharePoint 2013 upgrade process upgrades the database schema and content but not the site collections, which remain in SharePoint 2010 mode, also known as the SharePoint 2010 compatibility level. SharePoint 2013 is able to support both SharePoint 2010 and SharePoint 2013-mode site collections within the same web application, and requests are redirected as necessary to one of two root directories: the 14 hive, the SharePoint 2010 mode folder and the 15 hive, the SharePoint 2013 mode folder. This makes it possible for legacy solutions to work with SharePoint 2010-mode site collections; therefore, you can deploy your SharePoint 2010 solutions to the SharePoint 2013 farm, and in most cases they will work without needing any changes. However, it is likely that you will need to modify those solutions if you want them to work with SharePoint 2013-mode site collections.

- The Visual Upgrade option in SharePoint 2010 is replaced with an optional SharePoint 2013-mode snapshot of the site collection that you can use to evaluate new functionality and discover any upgrade issues.

- You can use a Site collection health check on SharePoint 2010 and SharePoint 2013-mode site collections, which completes checks similar to the pre-upgrade option in SharePoint 2010.

The next section describes these new upgrade options. You can find more information on the upgrade process on TechNet at *technet.microsoft.com/en-gb/sharepoint/fp142375*.

Using compatibility levels to create site collections

SharePoint 2010-mode site collections are not limited to those sites that were created on your SharePoint 2010 farm and included into your SharePoint 2013 when you completed a database attach. By default, any SharePoint 2013 farm allows users to create a new site collection as either SharePoint 2010 mode or SharePoint 2013 mode, as shown in Figure 1-24.

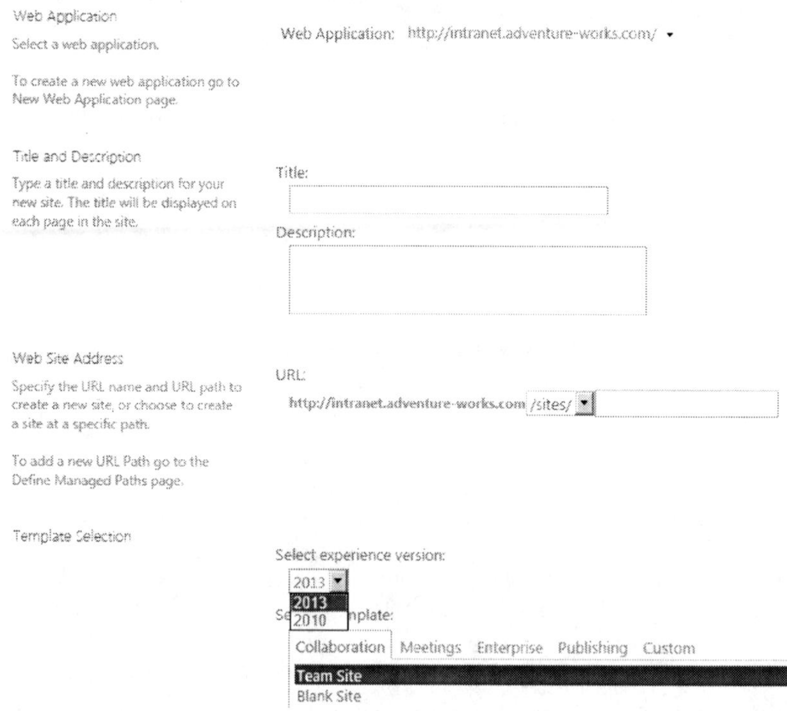

Web Application
Select a web application.

To create a new web application go to New Web Application page.

Web Application: http://intranet.adventure-works.com/ ▾

Title and Description
Type a title and description for your new site. The title will be displayed on each page in the site.

Title:

Description:

Web Site Address
Specify the URL name and URL path to create a new site, or choose to create a site at a specific path.

To add a new URL Path go to the Define Managed Paths page.

URL:

http://intranet.adventure-works.com /sites/ ▾

Template Selection

Select experience version:

2013 ▾
2013
2010

Select template:

Collaboration   Meetings   Enterprise   Publishing   Custom

Team Site
Blank Site

FIGURE 1-24 You can create a new site collection in either 2010 or 2013 mode.

A user can create a site collection in either mode, with SharePoint 2013 being the default. To create only SharePoint 2013 site collections, use the following Windows PowerShell commands, substituting your web application URL for *intranet.adventure-works.com*.

```
$webapp = Get-SPWebApplication http://intranet.adventure-works.com;
$webapp.CompatibilityRange = [Microsoft.SharePoint.SPCompatibilityRange]::NewVersion;
$webapp.Update();
```

To display compatibility settings, use the following command:

```
$webapp.CompatibilityRange
```

This generates the following output:

MaxCompatibilityLevel	MinCompatibilityLevel	DefaultCompatibilityLevel	Singular
15	15	15	True

By using this setting, when you go to the site collection page, in the Template selection, there will be no drop-down menu; instead, the text "2013 experience version will be used" is displayed. When you want site collections created only in SharePoint 2010 mode, set the *SPComability Range* value to *OldVersions*, or use *AllVersions* to create site collections in either SharePoint 2013 or SharePoint 2010 mode.

Upgrading from a SharePoint 2010-mode site collection

In SharePoint 2010 mode, sites are displayed as they would be on a SharePoint 2010 farm and only SharePoint 2010 features are enabled. You can allow site collection administrators to upgrade their site collection or a farm administrator can upgrade site collections by using Windows PowerShell.

If you have any SharePoint 2010-mode sites that you upgraded from Microsoft Office SharePoint Server 2007 and are still using the SharePoint Server 2007 user interface, you cannot upgrade them to SharePoint 2013 mode. In SharePoint 2010 you could upgrade the SharePoint Server 2007 user interface to the SharePoint 2010 user interface by using the visual upgrade feature. This feature is not available in SharePoint 2013; therefore, sites that use the SharePoint Server 2007 user interface must either move to the SharePoint Server 2010 user interface before the content databases that contain those sites are attached to SharePoint 2013 or the upgrade process will force a visual upgrade.

> **Note** If you are upgrading from SharePoint Server 2010 and use My Sites, ensure that the web application where you host your My Sites and its content database are ready for users to upgrade their My Sites successfully before you allow users to access their My Sites upgrade the My Site Host site collection.

The site collection administrator upgrade process

By default, site collection administrators can upgrade their own site collections. A pink status bar is visible at the top of each page, as illustrated in Figure 1-25. You can click the "X" at the right end of the status bar to make it disappear; however, when you redisplay the page, the status bar is redisplayed.

FIGURE 1-25 A status message displayed at the top of SharePoint 2010-mode site collection pages.

Remind me notifications and links If you click Remind Me Later, the status bar message is hidden from the site collection administrator for 30 days. This value can be changed by modifying the web application *UpgradeReminderDelay* property by using the following Windows PowerShell commands, where *15* is the number of days for the new notification setting for the web application. Substitute your web application URL for intranet.adventure-works.com.

```
$webapp =Get-SPWebApplication http://intranet.adventure-works.com;
$webapp.UpgradeReminderDelay = 15;
$webapp.update();
```

Note You can provide an additional link on the status bar to another page on which you could provide additional information; for example, you could give notifications about your organization's upgrade plans and training program. No default page exists for such information, and then the link is not present. If you want to use this option, first create your page in a location where site collection administrators can access and then use Windows PowerShell to edit the web application *UpgradeMaintenanceLink* property.

Site collection upgrade page   On the status bar message, when Start Now is clicked, you are redirected to the Site Collection Upgrade page, as shown in Figure 1-26. You can also navigate to it from the Site Settings page by clicking Site Collection Upgrade in the Site Collection Administration section.

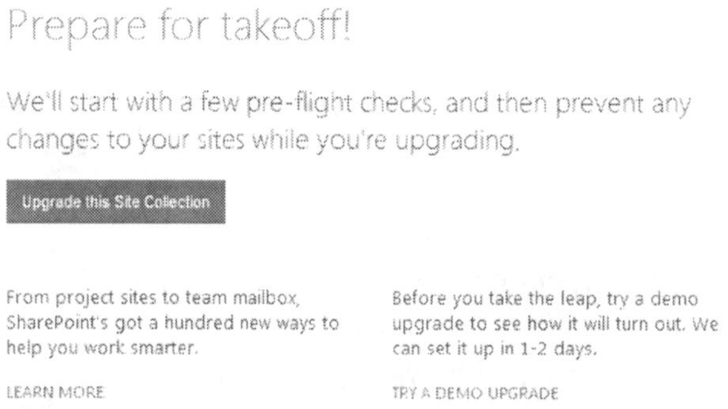

Prepare for takeoff!

We'll start with a few pre-flight checks, and then prevent any changes to your sites while you're upgrading.

    Upgrade this Site Collection

From project sites to team mailbox,   Before you take the leap, try a demo
SharePoint's got a hundred new ways to   upgrade to see how it will turn out. We
help you work smarter.   can set it up in 1-2 days.

LEARN MORE   TRY A DEMO UPGRADE

FIGURE 1-26 The Site Collection Upgrade page is where you can upgrade the site collection, learn more about the upgrade process, or try a demo upgrade.

When you click Try A Demo Upgrade, a dialog box opens, in which you can create an upgrade evaluation site collection.

Note You can prevent site collection administrators from creating an upgrade evaluation site collection by setting the web application *AllowSelfServiceUpgradeEvaluation* property to *0*. The Try A Demo Upgrade link will no longer be displayed. The *AllowSelfServiceUpgradeEvaluation* property is also available at the site-collection level, so you can decide on a per-site collection level whether to allow site collection administrators to create upgrade evaluation site collections.

Click Upgrade This Site Collection to display the Just Checking dialog box, as depicted in Figure 1-27, and then click I'm Ready to start the upgrade process. After you or the site collection administrator has started the upgrade process, there is no going back.

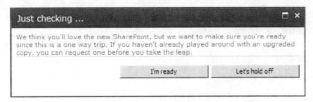

FIGURE 1-27 Click I'm Ready to start the site collection upgrade process.

When you click I'm Ready, the Upgrade Status page appears, and the message in the pink status bar changes to "We're doing work to improve this site. Please bear with us if you experience temporary delays or glitches". A site collection health check is run in repair mode to ensure that the site collection is healthy enough to upgrade successfully. If the health check is successful, the remainder of the upgrade process occurs. The page automatically updates as the upgrade progresses and displays upgrade process information, including, errors or warnings, upgrade start time, and where you can find the upgrade log file.

Note You can also view the upgrade status by clicking Site Collection Upgrade on the site setting page and then clicking Review Site Collection Upgrade Status.

After the upgrade process has concluded successfully, the Upgrade Status page displays, as shown in Figure 1-28.

Home ✎ EDIT LINKS

Site Settings › Site Collection Upgrade › Upgrade Status

Upgrade Completed Successfully

- Status: Upgrade Completed Successfully
- Errors: 0
- Warnings: 1
- Upgrade Started: 9/13/2012 6:42 PM
- Last Updated: 9/13/2012 6:42 PM
- Upgrade Completed: 9/13/2012 6:42 PM
- Log File: 20120913-184202-492.txt

FIGURE 1-28 The Upgrade Status page displays the results of the upgrade process.

Each site collection administrator has an upgrade log (.*txt*) for their site collection. These files comply with the Unified Logging System (ULS) conventions. The .*txt* files are created in the evaluation site in the _catalogs/MaintenanceLogs folder. Thus, when the evaluation site is deleted, these files will also be deleted, so you might want to save these files to another location. When you upgrade a site collection, the same .txt files are created in the same folder.

You can also find the upgrade status for a site collection by using Windows PowerShell commands as shown in the following example, together with its output:

```
$site = Get-SPsite http://intranet.adventure-works.com/sites/sp2010_2
$site.UpgradeInfo
```

```
Status       : Completed
UpgradeType  : VersionUpgrade
Errors       : 0
Warnings     : 1
RequestDate  : 13/09/2012 22:05:07
StartTime    : 13/09/2012 22:05:07
LastUpdated  : 13/09/2012 22:05:25
RetryCount   : 1
LogFile      : _catalogs/MaintenanceLogs/20120913-230507-692.txt
ErrorFile    : _catalogs\MaintenanceLogs\20120913-230507-692-error.txt
```

Note As with SharePoint 2010, you must take care when using Windows PowerShell with objects that implement the *IDisposable* interface, such as sites, site collections, and the site administration objects. Therefore, if you run code similar to that shown in the preceding example, use *$site.Dispose()* or the *SPAssignment* cmdlets.

Managing site collection upgrades

When a web application is created, an Upgrade Site Collection timer job is created for that web application, which is scheduled to run once every minute. When a site collection administrator clicks the I'm Ready button in the dialog box, or the farm administrator uses Windows PowerShell to start a site collection upgrade, the site collection is placed in an upgrade queue, which gives the Upgrade Site Collection timer job the ability to run parallel upgrades when possible. The site collections are upgraded in the order in which they are added to the queue.

Also, to prevent site collection upgrades from affecting the performance of the SharePoint server as it gets on with other tasks, the timer jobs are throttled to only allow a maximum number of site collection upgrades at one time. Using Windows PowerShell, a SharePoint farm administrator can do the following:

- Modify the upgrade throttling settings for a web application or content database

- Add a site collection to the upgrade queue

- Remove a site collection from the upgrade queue

- View the upgrade queue and use filters to see which site collections are currently being upgraded

Modifying the upgrade throttling settings There are four settings, three web application throttles and one at the content database throttle, that you can change to affect the number of site collections that will be upgraded in parallel:

- The web application *AppPoolConcurrentUpgradeSessionLimit* throttle (default, 5) and the content database *ConcurrentSiteUpgradeSessionLimit* throttle (default, 10) work together to limit the number of concurrent upgrades that can take place at any one time.

  - The *AppPoolConcurrentUpgradeSessionLimit* is the number of site collections that can be upgraded per SharePoint server for the web application.

  - The *ConcurrentSiteUpgradeSessionLimit* limits the maximum number of site collections that can be upgraded per content database across all SharePoint servers.

  For example, if an upgrade queue for a web application contains 12 site collections, all site collections are contained within one content database, and the farm consists of two SharePoint servers, only 10 site collections will be taken off the upgrade queue to be processed. The two remaining site collections will remain on the queue for the next execution of the timer job on one of the servers.

- The two web application throttles, *UsageStorageLimit* (default, 10 MB) and *SubwebCountLimit* (default, 10 sites), limit those site collections that can be upgraded by site collection administrators (known as self service). If a site collection is greater than *UsageStorageLimit* or contains more than *SubwebCountLimit* sites, those site collections must be upgraded by the SharePoint farm administrator.

You can view the upgrade throttle settings for a web application, by using Windows PowerShell commands, as shown in the following example, together with its output:

```
(Get-SPWebApplication '
    http://intranet.adventure-works.com).SiteUpgradeThrottleSettings
```

```
AppPoolConcurrentUpgradeSessionLimit : 5
UsageStorageLimit                    : 10
SubwebCountLimit                     : 10
Name                                 :
TypeName                             : Microsoft.SharePoint.Administration.SPSi
                                       teUpgradeThrottleSettings
DisplayName                          :
Id                                   : 20ab6845-aa50-42f6-9b24-87d5b1f3c6f3
Status                               : Online
Parent                               : SPWebApplication
                                       Name=intranet.adventure-works.com
Version                              : 9203
Properties                           : {}
Farm                                 : SPFarm Name=SP2013_Config
UpgradedPersistedProperties          : {}
```

To view the throttle settings for all content databases, use the following commands:

```
Get-SPContentDatabase | select Name, ConcurrentSiteUpgradeSessionLimit
```

Name	ConcurrentSiteUpgradeSessionLimit
CTHub_Content	10
SPIntranet_AdvWorks_Content	10
MySitesAdvWorks_Content	10
Portal_Content	10
TeamsAdvWorks_Content	10

Upgrading site collections   Microsoft does not recommend that you upgrade all site collections as part of the initial upgrade process and that site collection administrators should be left to upgrade their site collections. Microsoft does state that there are circumstances for which you might need to upgrade site collections, such as the following:

- Extremely important sites

- Very large sites

- Highly customized sites

However, after a period of time you might want to upgrade those site collections that are still in SharePoint 2010 mode. You can use the following Windows PowerShell command to upgrade a site collection:

```
Upgrade-SPSite -VersionUpgrade http://intranet.adventure-works.com/sites/sp2010
```

Note You can use the *Upgrade-SPSite* command to repair failed upgrades.

There are number of parameters that you might want to use on this command:

- **-QueueOnly**   This places the site collection on the upgrade queue.

- **-Unthrottled**   Use this parameter to start the upgrade immediately; the site collection is not placed in the upgrade queue.

- **-Email**   Use this to specify whether to send an email upon completion of the site collection upgrade.

Note To prevent site collection administrators from upgrading site collections, set the site collection *AllowSelfServiceUpgrade* property to *false*.

Removing a site collection from the upgrade queue   To remove a site collection from the upgrade queue, stop the appropriate web application site collection upgrade timer job and then remove the site from the queue by using the Windows PowerShell *Remove-SPSiteUpgradeSessionInfo* cmdlet. Next, restart the timer job to resume the upgrade process for the remaining sites in the queue.

 Note   A site collection cannot be removed from the queue if it is currently being upgraded.

Viewing the upgrade queue   To view all site collections in the upgrade queue for each content database in the SharePoint farm, use the following command:

```
Foreach ($db in Get-SPContentDatabase) {
   Get-SPSiteUpgradeSessionInfo $db -ShowInProgress -ShowCompleted -ShowFailed | ft
}
```

To view all site collections in all upgrade queues for a SharePoint farm, use the following command:

```
foreach ($site in (Get-SPWebApplication).Sites) { '
   $site.url; '
   Get-SPSiteUpgradeSessionInfo -Site $site; '
}
```

Using an evaluation site

Before a site collection owner decides to upgrade, he can ask for a demo upgrade site, also known as an upgrade evaluation site collection. This is a copy of his site collection but in SharePoint 2013 mode. Using the evaluation site, he can review the new interface and functionality and then determine what works. Any solutions will need to be reactivated. The site collection administrator should also consider asking advance users to check on the evaluation site for any customizations and solutions that they have created. He should also ask them to use the evaluation site to try their favorite approaches to creating so that they start to learn the new interface, new features, or discover any limitations.

The evaluation site is created by the Create Upgrade Evaluation Site Collection timer job that is scheduled to run daily. There is one timer job for each web application in farm. When a site collection owner clicks the Create An Evaluation Site Collection link a second time, before the timer job has run, the message box shown in Figure 1-29 opens.

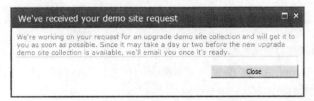

FIGURE 1-29 A message box appears when you click Create An Evaluation Site Collection a second time.

Note You can use PowerShell to determine if a site collection is an evaluation site by displaying the site collection property *IsEvalSite*.

If you click Try A Demo Upgrade and an evaluation site already exists, the message box depicted in Figure 1-30 appears.

FIGURE 1-30 A message box indicating that an upgrade demo site already exists.

The evaluation upgrade site is created either by snapshot if you are using the Enterprise version of SQL Server or by backing up the site collection and restoring it to the new URL. It is created by default in the same content database as the original site collection with a URL similar to the copied site collection, but with *-eval* appended to the URL. For example, if the original site had a URL of *http://intranet.adventure-works.com/sites/SP2010*, the evaluation site will have a URL of *http://intranet.adventure-works.com/sites/SP2010-eval*. A pink status bar is displayed at the top of each page, as demonstrated in Figure 1-31.

FIGURE 1-31 The evaluation site warning message informs the user when the evaluation site will be deleted; by default the expiration period is 30 days.

After the evaluation site collection is created, it coexists alongside the original site collection; however, changes to the original site collection are not replicated to the evaluation site after the snapshot is taken.

The evaluation site collection is deleted by the web application's timer job, Delete Upgrade Evaluation Site Collection job, which is scheduled to run daily. Evaluation sites are deleted by default 31 days after they have been created. This value can be changed by modifying the web application *UpgradeEvalSitesRetentionDays* property.

Running the site collection health checker

To run the health checker, on the Site Settings page, click Site Collection Health Checks (see Figure 1-32) to go to the Site Collection Heath Checks page and then click Start Checks.

FIGURE 1-32 Use the Site Collection Health Checks link on the site settings page to navigate to the Site Collection Health Checks page.

The Site Collection Health Check Results page displays, similar to that illustrated in Figure 1-33.

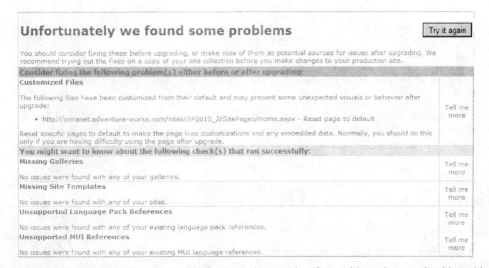

FIGURE 1-33 The Site Collection Health Check Result page identifies problems that you should consider fixing, either before or after upgrading.

The health check can be run on SharePoint 2010-mode and SharePoint 2013-mode sites. In Share-Point 2013, when running the health check on a site collection created from the Publishing Portal SharePoint 2013 site template, it reported problems that a number of files are customized by default when the site was created, as shown in Figure 1-34. Because such a site was not created from an upgraded SharePoint 2010 site, you should not reset those files.

Site Settings › Site Collection Health Check Results

Unfortunately we found some problems

You should consider fixing these before upgrading, or make note of them as potential sources for issues after upgrading. We recommend trying out the fixes on a copy of your site collection before you make changes to your production site.

Consider fixing the following problem(s) either before or after upgrading:

Customized Files

The following files have been customized from their default and may present some unexpected visuals or behavior after upgrade:

- http://intranet.adventure-works.com/_catalogs/masterpage/WelcomeSplash.html - Reset page to default
- http://intranet.adventure-works.com/_catalogs/masterpage/CatalogArticle.html - Reset page to default
- http://intranet.adventure-works.com/_catalogs/wfpub/Collect Feedback - SharePoint 2010/ReviewFeedback_1033.xoml.wfconfig.xml - Reset page to default
- http://intranet.adventure-works.com/_catalogs/masterpage/oslo.html - Reset page to default
- http://intranet.adventure-works.com/_catalogs/masterpage/CatalogWelcome.html - Reset page to default
- http://intranet.adventure-works.com/Pages/default.aspx - Reset page to default
- http://intranet.adventure-works.com/_catalogs/masterpage/startermaster.html - Reset page to default
- http://intranet.adventure-works.com/_catalogs/masterpage/ArticleLinks.html - Reset page to default
- http://intranet.adventure-works.com/Translation Packages/Forms/Translation Package/template.dotx - Reset page to default
- http://intranet.adventure-works.com/_catalogs/masterpage/ArticleRight.html - Reset page to default
- http://intranet.adventure-works.com/_catalogs/masterpage/EnterpriseWiki.html - Reset page to default
- http://intranet.adventure-works.com/_catalogs/wfpub/Approval - SharePoint 2010/ReviewApproval_1033.xoml.wfconfig.xml - Reset page to default

Tell me more

FIGURE 1-34 SharePoint 2013-mode sites by default can contain problems reported by the health check.

You can also start the site collection health check by using the Window PowerShell *Test-SPSite* cmdlet, and you can use *Repair-SPSite* to repair issues found. You cannot add additional health checks; however, you can extend the health rules included in the health checks.

Licensing in SharePoint 2013

With both Microsoft Office SharePoint Server 2007 and SharePoint Server 2010, there were two versions of SharePoint Server: a Standard edition and an Enterprise edition. In a SharePoint farm your organization would decide to install one or the other. For example, you would install one or more servers running SharePoint Server Enterprise and purchase SharePoint Server Enterprise client access licenses (CALs). All users who accessed that server could use the full Enterprise feature set. There was no way to mix both standard and enterprise CALs on one farm; the only way to ensure that only users who had an Enterprise CAL accessed Enterprise features was to have separate Enterprise and Standard farms.

With SharePoint Server 2013, you still have to purchase a server license for each server, and that server license is now the same whether you want to use Standard or Enterprise CALs. However, now, within one SharePoint Server farm, you can assign either Standard or Enterprise CALs to users and enable license checks. With this new functionality, you can ensure that only users with the appropriate license can use a specific feature. You can purchase SharePoint Server CALs or a CAL suite which includes Exchange and Lync. SharePoint Server CALs can also be purchased as user CALs or device

CALs. Many of the functionality that was only included in the Enterprise edition of SharePoint Server 2010, require Enterprise CALS, such as the Business Intelligence service applications and InfoPath Form Services.

By default, SharePoint Server CAL licensing is disabled and can be enabled and managed by using the following new Windows PowerShell cmdlets:

- *New-SPUserLicenseMapping*

- *Add-SPUserLicenseMapping*

- *Remove-SPUserLicenseMapping*

- *Get-SPUserLicenseMapping*

- *Enable-SPUserLicensing*

- *Disable-SPUserLicensing*

- *Get-SPUserLicense*

 More Info You can find an introduction to User License enforcement in SharePoint Server 2013 at *blogs.technet.com/b/wbaer/archive/2012/11/12/introduction-to-user-license-enforcement-in-sharepoint-server-2013.aspx*.

Summary

Cloud computing is definitely a theme of SharePoint 2013 and will continue to be going forward. The core architecture of SharePoint 2013 has remained the same as that of SharePoint 2010. However, SharePoint 2013 includes a number of performance improvements at the architectural level such as shredded storage, whereby versions of the same file are saved as deltas of the original file; SharePoint farm-level cross-server caching, whereby the same information is synchronized across every web server; and a new Workflow Framework that can be hosted on servers on which SharePoint 2013 is not installed.

SharePoint 2013 includes three new service applications: Machine Translation, Work Management, and App Management. It also features a number of changed service applications—in particular a unified search service application that has been developed from the ground up, which is the combination of SharePoint Server 2010 enterprise search and Fast Search for SharePoint 2010. This service application is now so crucial to a SharePoint farm that it should be the first service application you should create. The functionality of two service applications has been redesigned to such an extent that they do not exist as entities. The Web Analytics functionality is now incorporated into search, and Office Web Apps is now a separate product that cannot be installed on the same servers as SharePoint 2013, but needs its own servers if you want to use it.

Web Applications and site collections from an architectural perspective are much as they were in SharePoint 2010. Claims-based authentication is now the default and HNSCs are now fully supported. Many of the additional functions that has been added to the SharePoint 2013 services can be configured at the site-collection and site level, giving site collection and site owners more options regarding how they prefer to use SharePoint.

A new application framework has been added to SharePoint 2013 that facilitates the development of applications for Office and SharePoint, both in the cloud and on-premises. Organizations can use the Application Management Service Application to host their own Apps Catalogs rather than to publish their internal Office and SharePoint Apps to Microsoft's online market place.

The SharePoint 2013 upgrade process only supports the database attaches and separates the upgrade of the database schema and content from the site collections.

CHAPTER 2

Introducing the new search architecture

Searching in Microsoft SharePoint 2013 is another area in which Microsoft has made major invest-ments. SharePoint 2013 incorporates a new search engine that was in development with FAST when SharePoint acquired it. Much of the new search platform might indeed have the same names as some of the components from search engines of SharePoint 2010 and Microsoft FAST Search Server for SharePoint 2010, but the only component that has been carried forward from those search engines is the SharePoint crawler. Technologies and ideas from Microsoft Research, Microsoft Bing, and elsewhere have been included to provide a comprehensive set of enterprise search capabilities that provide plenty of room for you to customize.

> **Note** Although Microsoft FAST Search Server for SharePoint 2010 is supported as a stand-alone product until 2020, the other FAST stand-alone products are still available and have varying support end dates. You can find more details at *support.microsoft.com/lifecycle/search/default.aspx?sort=PN&alpha=fast*.

No matter which SharePoint 2013 products you are using, whether it is SharePoint Foundation 2013 or SharePoint Server 2013, there is just one SharePoint 2013 search engine. SharePoint 2010 pro-vided both a basic search function in SharePoint Foundation 2010 as well as an enterprise search that was used by SharePoint Server 2010. But, you could also opt to purchase a third search engine: FAST Search Server for SharePoint 2010. Now, all SharePoint 2013 products also have the same underlying search object model.

SharePoint 2013 enterprise search provides a powerful, scalable, and extendable service. It incor-porates better support for in-context refinements and provides in-line previews. For example, you can find information about a document on the search results page without opening the document. You can see this core technology used in a variety of ways within SharePoint 2013, such as eDiscovery.

If you are familiar with search in SharePoint 2010, many of the terms are the same and have similar functionality, for example, connectors and protocol handlers still gather information from content sources, IFilters—now called format handlers—are still part of indexing, index files are stored in folders on the server, and crawled and managed properties must be mapped to one another. However, the crawling/gathering and indexing parts of the search engine in SharePoint 2013 are now performed in very separate components.

Custom ranking models are managed through Windows PowerShell by using XML files, as it was in SharePoint 2010. You create the search architecture within SharePoint 2013 as you would in SharePoint 2010 by creating one or more search service applications (SSAs). However, in SharePoint 2013, you can only implement the search architecture by using Windows PowerShell. You cannot use the Central Administration website as you could in SharePoint Server 2010 to distribute components across several servers in the farm. The SSA can be consumed by applications within the SharePoint farm and from other farms. You can also host it in a multitenant hosting environment.

Search is now so important for other SharePoint 2013 components, for example, that the Managed Metadata Services (MMS) term store and the User Profile Service Application (UPSA) cannot be installed unless the SSA is created. An SSA should be one of the first, if not *the* first, service application that you should create in any SharePoint 2013 deployment.

As with SharePoint Server 2010, for small deployments—such as one you might create for developers or for demonstration purposes—a fully functional SharePoint 2013 enterprise search topology can be created by running the Farm Configuration Wizard. However, most organizations will create their own search topology that suits their specific needs and will host search components that crawl and index content on separate application servers.

As with SharePoint 2010, you can create your search topology by using Windows PowerShell; however, in SharePoint 2013 the search administration pages on the Central Administration website do not allow you to scale out the default topology. So, for at least SharePoint 2013, you will need to use Windows PowerShell. Before you do so, though, you should have a good understanding of the SharePoint 2013 architecture and topology and the new features that are now included in search. The aim of this chapter is to introduce you to the SharePoint 2013 search architecture and new search functionality that needs to be configured by a SharePoint server administrator.

Architecture and topology

Search in SharePoint 2013 has been completely redesigned, boasting a new logical and physical architecture. With the new search components, you can configure within a single farm greater redundancy and scalability. The search architecture incorporates a number of search components and databases. The SSA contains the components on application servers, and a server running either Microsoft SQL Server 2008 R2 or Microsoft SQL Server 2012 is host to the search databases.

Logical architecture

The logical architecture can be divided into the following three components (see also Figure 2-1):

- Capturing and analyzing content

- Querying the content captured

- Administrating the search functionality

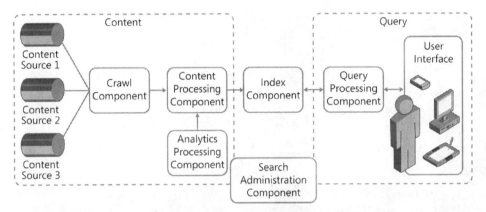

FIGURE 2-1 The logical architecture of SharePoint 2013 search, which consists of Search crawls, capture, and analyses content, which users can then query.

The architecture consists of the following six components, which you can place on different servers, thereby scaling out your farm:

- Crawl

- Content Processing

- Analytics Processing

- Index

- Query Processing

- Search Administration

Note The crawl component is implemented in the SharePoint Server Search 15 (*mssearch. exe*) Windows NT service. The other five search components are implemented in *noderunner.exe*. A separate instance of *noderunner.exe* is executed for each of these components.

Crawling and content architecture

The crawl and content processing architecture includes the crawl component, crawl database, and content processing component, as illustrated in Figure 2-2. The crawl and content processing components can be scaled out based on crawl volume and performance requirements.

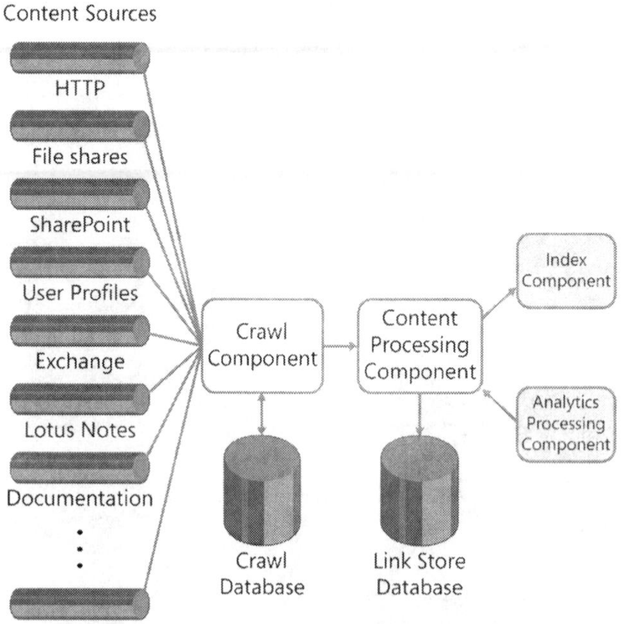

Content Sources

FIGURE 2-2 The crawl and content processing components obtain information from content sources and stores information into the crawl database, index files, and the link store database.

Crawl component

The crawl component completes no processing at this stage; the content is simply acquired by using index connectors. It is the index connector that knows how to connect to content sources, what to crawl, and how to crawl it. SharePoint 2013 still has protocol handlers for sts3, sts4, sps3, and so on, which are based on custom interfaces running unmanaged C++ code.

Index connectors   SharePoint 2013 provides a new connector framework, based on the Business Connectivity Services (BCS) framework that was introduced in SharePoint 2010. The new SharePoint 2013 indexing connector framework provides a simpler approach to developing indexing connectors. SharePoint 2013 uses both protocol handler-based indexing connectors and BCS indexing connectors to crawl content. By default, SharePoint 2013 provides the following index connectors:

- Protocol handlers:
  - SharePoint content.
  - People Profile Connector to include the information stored in the People Profiles databases. This connector is only available with SharePoint Server 2013.

- HTTP. In SharePoint 2013, this connector can also be used to crawl anonymous websites.

- File Shares.

■ BCS connectors:

- Exchange public folders.

- EMC Documentum.

- Lotus Notes.

- Taxonomy Connector. This requires that the Term Store associated with a MMS service application is configured for crawling. MMS is a SharePoint SSA; therefore, this type of BCS connector is only available with SharePoint Server 2013.

- Custom index connectors that use one of the Business Data Connectivity (BDC) content source types: Line of Business (LoB) data (database, or web services indexing connectors) or custom repository (.NET Framework and BCS custom indexing connectors).

- In SharePoint 2013, BCS connectors can retrieve claims information for content stored in content sources. SharePoint 2013 also provides improved exception capturing and logging to help troubleshoot errors which you might encounter when crawling content sources that use BCS connectors. When binary large object (BLOB) data is stored in a SQL database, you can use a BCS connector to crawl BLOBs. It is expected that Microsoft partners and other companies will produce other connectors.

 More Info You can read more about building custom index connectors at *msdn.microsoft. com/en-us/library/ee556429(v=office.15).aspx.*

Content sources SharePoint 2013 content sources are similar to those in SharePoint 2010, as outlined in the following:

■ All addresses within a content source must be accessed by using the same protocol handler or BCS connector.

■ A single content source can contain up to 500 starting addresses and an index server can support up to 500 content sources.

■ When the crawl component retrieves a SharePoint page that contains out-of-the-box Web Parts that renders the content asynchronously in the browser, the crawler gets a "classic"-type rendering of the page in order to index them.

■ You can use crawler impact rules to throttle or specify the number of simultaneous requests that the crawl component can use to request content from a content source.

- You can independently configure crawl schedules for each content source. For each content source, you can specify a time to perform full crawls and a different time to do incremental crawls. You can also start a crawl manually.

One new option for SharePoint content sources is the ability to configure continuous crawls on the Edit Content Source page, as demonstrated in Figure 2-3.

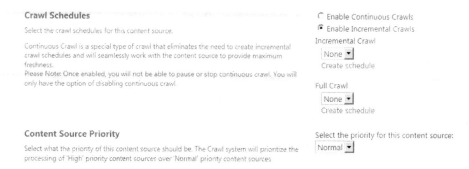

Crawl Schedules

Select the crawl schedules for this content source.

Continuous Crawl is a special type of crawl that eliminates the need to create incremental crawl schedules and will seamlessly work with the content source to provide maximum freshness.
Please Note: Once enabled, you will not be able to pause or stop continuous crawl. You will only have the option of disabling continuous crawl.

○ Enable Continuous Crawls
◉ Enable Incremental Crawls
Incremental Crawl
[None ▾]
Create schedule

Full Crawl
[None ▾]
Create schedule

Content Source Priority

Select what the priority of this content source should be. The Crawl system will prioritize the processing of 'High' priority content sources over 'Normal' priority content sources

Select the priority for this content source:
[Normal ▾]

FIGURE 2-3 Continuous crawl is a new crawl option for SharePoint content sources.

A continuous crawl by default starts every 15 minutes, which you can change by using the Windows PowerShell *Set-SPEnterpriseSearchCrawlContentSource* cmdlet. The crawl component pushes the content from the SharePoint sites to the Content Processing Component and then onto the Index component. Therefore, a document can appear in the index within seconds of going through the content processing component. It also means that you can get the latest changes even while a full crawl is starting, so you can see results before a full crawl completes. Enabling continuous crawl offers the following advantages:

- The search results are very fresh because the SharePoint content is crawled frequently to keep the search index up to date.

- The search administrator does not need to monitor changing or seasonal demands for content freshness. Continuous crawls automatically adapt as necessary to the change rate of the Share-Point content.

You should be using this feature for search-driven applications for which it's important that new content appears immediately after it has been created. The Newsfeed in My Sites and Team Sites are examples of such SharePoint Apps that could benefit from continuous crawl.

Microsoft recommends that you plan to install SharePoint Server For Internet Sites (FIS) in a medium-farm topology; that is, one that meets the following criteria:

- Optimized for 3,400,000 items

- Processes 240 documents per second

- Can handle a usage pattern of 85 page views per second

- Corresponds to 129 queries per second

Then, you enable continuous crawl with an interval of one minute, instead of the default interval of 15 minutes.

> **Note** You can use the Crawl Health Reports to monitor crawl performance. You can find the link to the Crawl Health Reports on the Quick Launch of the Search Administration pages on the Central Administration website. The health reports available are: crawl rate, crawl latency, crawl queue, crawl freshness, content processing activity, CPU and memory load, and continuous crawl.

Crawled properties The crawl component stores the crawled items—both the actual content as well as their associated metadata, known as crawled properties—in a crawl database before passing the crawled items to the content processing component.

Examples of crawled properties are Author, Title, and Creation Date. Any new crawled properties will be discovered automatically and are grouped into categories that are based on the IFilter or protocol handler of the crawled item. The following are example categories:

- **Office** This includes crawled properties from Microsoft Word documents, Microsoft Excel worksheets, and so on.

- **Business Data** This includes crawled properties that were obtained by using a BCS connector to external systems such as databases.

- **Web** This includes crawled properties from websites.

> **Note** Multiple crawl components can be deployed to improve the rate of crawling, which leads to an improved *index freshness*. Index freshness is a term that describes the latencies involved during the crawling and indexing processes. *Retrieval latency* is the lag time between content modification and when the data was crawled. *Indexing latency* is the time lag required for crawled content to be indexed.

Crawl database

The crawl component uses one or more crawl databases to temporarily store information it retrieved from the content sources about crawled items as well as to track crawl history. This database holds information such as the last crawl time, the last crawl ID, and the type of update during the last crawl.

Content processing component

The content processing component is between the crawl component and the index component; hence, why it is sometimes known as the *indexing pipeline*. The SharePoint 2013 content processing component looks very similar to the FAST pipeline and seems to have inherited important FAST-like features.

The content processing component completes operations such as document parsing by using *format handlers*. File formats are automatically detected, and content processing no longer relies on using file extensions. Out of the box, there are format handlers for HTML, DOCX, PPTX, TXT, Image, XML, and PDF formats. IFilter is still supported. It maps crawled properties to the managed properties of crawled items to transform them into objects that can be stored in the index files. In addition, both the content processing component as well as the query processing component performs linguistics processing such as language detection and entity extraction. It also produces the phonetic name variations for people search, which no longer relies on the Microsoft speech server engine but is natively incorporated into Search for SharePoint 2013.

The SharePoint 2013 entity extractors are very similar to the FAST entity extractors, which can be used to create custom refiners. Importantly, there is a capability to call out to web services and perform custom content processing tasks, known as "Content Enrichment Web Service." This makes it possible for organizations to add a custom step to content processing to modify the managed properties for crawled items before they are indexed. You could use this mechanism to cleanse the data, tag or classify it, or partition large technical documents into "sensibly searchable chunks," thereby enhancing the productivity of a user when she searches for information.

More Info You can read more about Content Enrichment Web Service at *msdn.microsoft.com/en-us/library/sharepoint/jj163968(v=office.15)*.

The content processing component also writes information about links and URLs to the Link Store database. This information can be subsequently used by the analysis processing component to calculate link popularity statistics and provide relevancy weighting possibilities. Anchor text within links can also contribute to page content for ranking purposes. These are core techniques used by Google and Bing. Applying these techniques to private data sets, in which most documents are not interlinked, will need to be done with some thought. In turn, the analytics processing component writes information related to the relevance of these links and URLs to the search index via the content processing component.

Analytics architecture

The analytics architecture consists of the analytics processing component, analytics reporting database, and the Link Store database, as shown in Figure 2-4. It is this part of the search architecture that provides the replacement functionality for the SharePoint Server 2010 Web Analytics service application and solves the limitations of that service application.

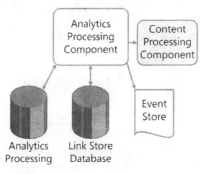

Analytics
Processing
Component

Content
Processing
Component

Event
Store

Analytics
Processing

Link Store
Database

FIGURE 2-4 The analytics processing component analyses crawled items and stores the results in the analytics processing database.

> **Note** With the SharePoint Server 2010 Web Analytics service application, there was no concept of item-to-item recommendation based on a user's behavior; that is, when a user viewed content, there was no way to tell him that other users who viewed that content also viewed some other content. Nor could you promote search results based on an item's popularity, commonly known as *link popularity*. (Link popularity is basically the number of links that point to an item or page. It is considered by many search engines as a factor for relevancy.) The Web Analytics service application required a very powerful SQL Server, significant storage, and a disk infrastructure that supported high input/output operations per second (IOPS). There was also a problem scaling the Web Analytics service application.

The analytics processing component

The analytics processing component analyzes the crawled items (search analytics) and how users interact with the search results (usage analytics). It also provides a way for additional context to be introduced during the indexing process, which can later be used to customize relevancy ranking as well as for other purposes. It then provides the crawl processing component (using a partial update) with additional information to include in the index files, such as view counts, so that they are included in the search results, and users can sort on them.

Input to the analysis process is provided by the Link Store database and the Event Store, with the results from usage analytics stored in the analytics reporting database.

The Link Store database

The Link Store database contains unprocessed information extracted by the content processing component. It also contains information about search clicks—the number of times people click on a search result from the search result page. The analytics processing component performs the analysis on data stored in this database.

The Event Store

The analytics processing component analyzes the events in the Event Store by using the following techniques:

- **Special Event Handling**   Certain types of events are written to the *.usage* files.

- **Filtering Out Events**   This prevents non-relevant events from being included in the usage analytics. As an example, requests from robots are not included in the usage analytics.

- **Normalize Events**   The event information is stored in such a way so that it can be counted along with other types of page requests; for example, when a user uses the Office Web App to read a document stored in a SharePoint library, that should be counted as reads against the document.

- **Allowed To Pass**   This is the normal method for including a page request in usage analytics.

- **Custom Events**   You can configure up to 12 custom events in addition to the events provided by SharePoint 2013.

- **Calculation**   The analytics process calculates the sum or average across events.

- **Reports**   SharePoint 2013 provides a number of default reports, including the following:

  - Top queries.

  - Most popular documents in a library or site.

  - Historical usage of an item, including the number of view counts for the last history as well as for all time.

The analytics reporting database

The analytics reporting database stores the results of usage analysis.

Index and query architecture

The index and query architecture consists of two components: the index component and a set of search index files, as depicted in Figure 2-5. These sit between the crawl processing component and the user interface.

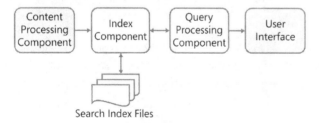

Search Index Files

FIGURE 2-5 The index component updates the index, which the query processing component uses to return result sets to the user.

The index component

The index component can be scaled out based on content and query volume and performance requirements. It completes the following tasks:

- Receives process items from the content process and writes them to a search index file that is stored on a server hard disk on which the index component is running.

- Receives queries from the query processing component, retrieves information from the search index, and returns result sets to the query processing component.

The SharePoint 2013 index architecture is based on the rows and columns concepts in FAST Server for SharePoint 2010. This will be new to you if you only used SharePoint 2010 enterprise search. *Index partitions* (columns) make it possible for the index to be split between servers, thereby providing the ability to scale both data volumes and query loads. *Index replicas* (rows) provide a level of redundancy with groups of servers.

Index partitions   If the indexing component runs on one server, the number of items it can index per second and the total number of items it can include in the index is limited by the size of hard disk space assigned to the index files on that server. To scale out so that you can have more than one server, you divide the index into discrete portions, called index partitions, each partition holding a separate part of the index. The search index is the aggregation of all index partitions.

Index replicas   The index files are also accessed to respond to users' queries. When a partition is hosted by one server, you are limited to the number of queries per second (QPS) to which it can respond. If you find that you need to handle more QPS than one server can provide, or you need to provide fault tolerance so that SharePoint can return search results from data in all index partitions, even when one of the servers is no longer available, you should consider hosting replicas of partitions on other SharePoint servers.

Each index partition has one primary index replica and zero or more secondary index replicas. Each secondary index replica contains the same information as the primary index replica. Therefore, to spread the query load for one index partition over three servers, you need one primary index replica on one server, and the other two servers contain a secondary index replica. The updates from the content processing engine are sent to the primary replica, which is responsible to push those updates to the secondary replicas. This is very different from SharePoint 2010 for which all replicas received updates directly.

The index component is also responsible for moving the index replicas when the topology changes by the search administration component.

> **Note** A server can host many primary index replicas and many secondary index replicas. However, keep in mind the search performance will be degraded if the server is indexing multiple index partitions while it is simultaneously executing queries against the index replicas.

The query processing component

When a user enters one or more keywords in the search box, a query is sent to the query processing component, which processes the query by sending it to the appropriate search providers to retrieve results. A search provider can be a local SharePoint 2013 search index component or a remote source. After the results are collected from the search providers, the query processing component performs additional processing and then returns the results so that they can be displayed. The query processing component can interface with two search providers:

- Federated search (the query is forwarded to an external search engine)

- SharePoint 2013 index component

The query processing component performs linguistic processing at query time, such as word breaking, stemming, spell checking, and the thesaurus.

With SharePoint 2013, the new query processing component provides options to enhance the user's query to improve precision, recall, and relevancy. The query processing component includes the following:

- Query spelling correction suggestions.

- Query rules, which can trigger search requests automatically, spawn multiple queries which are then aggregated, or trigger a "best bet," which in SharePoint 2013 is called a promoted result. The query processing component also makes it possible for the results sets returned by the search engine to be processed, according to rules, before being displayed to the user.

- Query conditions cause rules to be triggered; for example, a condition could be that specified words are included in the query.

- Ranking models that can be configured to suit different groups of users, which can be chosen at query time. Ranking models for search queries can be created from an XML file by using the Windows PowerShell *New_SPEnterpriseSearchRankingModel* cmdlet. The ranking model can then be used in the query builder.

> **Note** You can use the query health reports to monitor query performance. To access the link to the query health reports, go to the Central Administration website and then look in the Quick Launch of the Search Administration pages. The health reports available are: query latency trends, overall query latency, default SharePoint flow query latency, federation query latency, local SharePoint search flow query latency, people search flow query latency, and index engine query latency.

The search index files

The search index consists of a set of flat files in folders on a server that represent an inverted catalog. The search index is the center of search. What is in the search index determines what users find when they look for information by entering search queries or by interacting with Internet or intranet pages. In addition to various full-text indexes, there are separate indexes of the managed properties that are marked as retrievable and those that are marked as queryable. There is also a separate index for attribute vectors, and there are numeric indexes.

To include the contents and metadata of crawled properties in the search index, you must map crawled properties to managed properties. Both crawled and managed properties are written to the search index. Some crawled properties automatically generate new managed properties and the mapping; for example, one such crawled property type that does this is site columns in SharePoint libraries. When you create a site column in a list or library, and when the list or library is crawled, a crawled property, a managed property, and a mapping between the crawled and managed property is automatically created for the site column.

The search administration component and database

The search administration component (the SharePoint Search Host Controller service—hostcontrollerservice.exe) runs the system processes for SharePoint 2013 search and adds and initializes new instances of search components. It also manages search topology changes.

A search administration component is created for each search service application that you create. You can see the component on the Central Administration website, on the Manage Service Application page, as illustrated in Figure 2-6. It does not require a service application proxy, because it does not need to communicate directly with web servers.

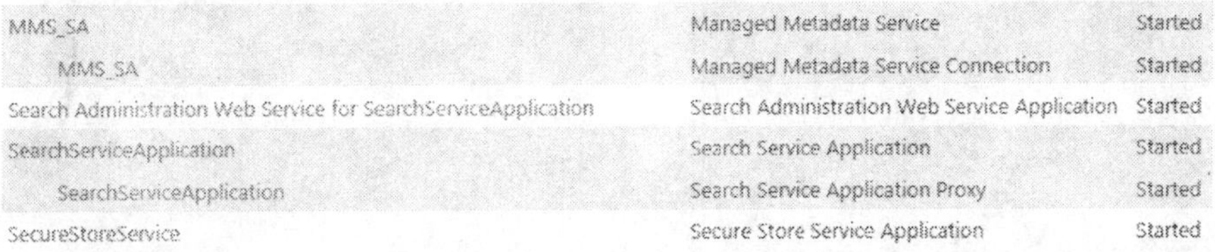

MMS_SA	Managed Metadata Service	Started
MMS_SA	Managed Metadata Service Connection	Started
Search Administration Web Service for SearchServiceApplication	Search Administration Web Service Application	Started
SearchServiceApplication	Search Service Application	Started
SearchServiceApplication	Search Service Application Proxy	Started
SecureStoreService	Secure Store Service Application	Started

FIGURE 2-6 Each Search Service Application has a Search Administration Web Service Application.

The administration component stores information in the Search Administration database about search and how it is configured, including the search schema. You can configure SharePoint 2013 via the Central Administration website, SharePoint 2013 Windows PowerShell cmdlets, or programmatically.

The search schema contains the mapping from crawled properties to managed properties and the settings on the managed properties. Managed properties define what users can search for and how, what users can refine on and how, in what order search results appear, and more. It contains the following:

- The mapping between crawled properties and managed properties. This includes the order of priority in which values are copied from crawled to managed properties. You can set the managed property to include content from the first crawled property that is not empty or to include content from all crawled properties that are mapped to the managed property.

- How the managed properties should be written to the search index. For example, to which full-text index the values of the managed properties should be written and to which weight group (context).

- The settings for the different managed properties. For example, whether you can search on, query on, or refine search results by particular managed properties.

Search schema updates are propagated through the search system every minute. In addition to the default search schema, site collection administrators and tenant administrations can also create search schemas specific to their site collection or tenant. Only unused managed properties that do not have crawled properties mapped to them can be reused. For example, if you created a site-specific content type with site columns that generates crawled properties, you could create a new managed property that maps to one of those crawled properties.

Search topology

With SharePoint 2010, many organizations created a two-server farm for purposes of resiliency and high availability, in which all services were spread across the two servers. Going forward, because of the importance of the search service application and the load it can place on the web servers, it will be the norm to see at a minimum four-server farms (see Figure 2-7): two web servers and two application servers explicitly for running search services, thereby providing a highly available and resilient solution.

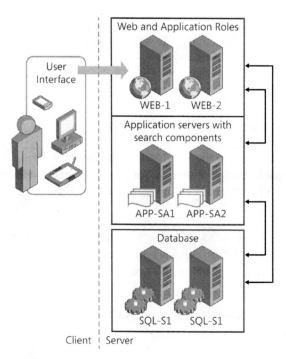

FIGURE 2-7 A four-server SharePoint 2013 farm provides high availability at both the web-server and application layers.

Note A user-facing server is a server on which the Microsoft SharePoint Foundation Web Application Service is started. An application server is a server that is designed not to be user facing. It might or might not have the Microsoft SharePoint Foundation Web Application Service started; it might be hosting just Windows Communication Foundation (WCF) endpoints.

One of the properties of an SSA is *PerformanceLevel*. There are three performance levels: *Reduced*, *PartlyReduced*, and *Maximum*. The *Reduced* performance level specifies the relative number of threads for the indexer performance. The *PartlyReduced* and *Maximum* values have the same maximum thread counts. The difference is that when the *PerformanceLevel* is set to *PartlyReduced*, the threads have a normal priority, but when set to *Maximum*, the threads have an above normal priority.

When you create an SSA, it is configured to run at maximum performance level, which suits a SharePoint 2013 topology that contains application servers that host only search components. If you do not have dedicated search application servers, you might consider reducing the performance level to *PartlyReduced*, or for a development environment to *Reduced*. You can use the Windows PowerShell *Get-SPEnterpriseSearchService* cmdlet to display the performance level and the *Set-SPEnterpriseService* cmdlet to change the performance level.

More Info You can read more about the planning that you need to do to deploy search in SharePoint 2013 at *technet.microsoft.com/en-us/library/cc263400(v=office.15).aspx*. For examples of topologies, see the technical diagrams enterprise search architectures for SharePoint Server 2013, which you can find at *www.microsoft.com/en-us/download/details. aspx?id=30383* and Internet sites search architectures for SharePoint Server 2013 at *www. microsoft.com/en-us/download/details.aspx?id=30464*.

Search user interface enhancements

SharePoint 2013 makes it easy to customize the appearance—known as the *look and feel*—of the search results user interface (UI). Not only did Microsoft redesign the SharePoint 2013 search content and query architecture, but it included a new results framework and UI.

Search result pages

With SharePoint 2013, similar to SharePoint 2010, you can specify an enterprise search center at the search service-application level. When you use the drop-down list from the search box and select Everything, People, or Conversations, you are redirected from the page and site you are on, and the search results are displayed on the enterprise search center. You can also register a search center at the site-collection and site level. Out of the box, when you search for information on a site, the search results are displayed by using the _layouts/15/osssearchresults.aspx page. This means that you are not redirected to the enterprise search center.

For lists and libraries, an additional search box displays. This is an awesome new feature for Share-Point 2013, and when you use this input box for your search query, you are not taken to a search results page, but instead, the result items are shown in list view. This means that users can find a specific item in a list or library without searching the site or everything, which is known as *In Line Search*.

The Navigation displayed in the Quick Launch control on search pages and as a drop-down lists from the search box can be configured at the site and site-collection level by using the Search Setting page, to which you can navigate from the Site Settings page. It can also be set at the search service application level.

Search Web Parts

The new Web Parts on the search results page of an enterprise search center (see Figure 2-8) are as follows:

- **RefinementScriptWebPart**   Helps users refine search results.

- **SearchBoxScriptWebPart**   Displays the search box with which users can search for information.

- **SearchNavigationWebPart**   Helps users to navigate among search verticals.

- **ResultScriptWebPart**   Displays the search results and the properties associated with them. This Web Part replaces the SharePoint Server 2010 Core Results Web Part. This Web Part also provides you with a hover card that contains information about the result item and possibly a thumbnail of the result items.

With SharePoint 2010, the search results page contained a number of Search Web Parts that were based on the Data View Web Part. To change how search results were displayed in SharePoint 2010, you customized or created new custom XSLT code that those Web Parts used. Now, in SharePoint 2013, you can customize the appearance of important types of results by using display templates and result types, which are critical to the new search platform and are explained later in this chapter.

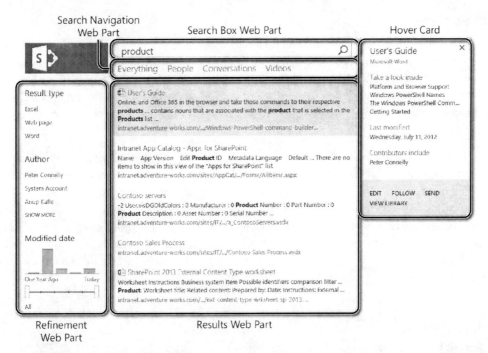

FIGURE 2-8 The Search Web Parts and the Hover card on the results page of an enterprise search center.

There are a number of other search-related Web Parts:

- **Taxonomy Refinement Panel Web Part** Users can refine search results on term-set data.

- **Search-Driven Content Web Parts** Examples include the Articles Web Part, Catalog-Item Reuse Web Part, Items From A Catalog Web Part, Items Matching A Tag Web Part, Pictures Web Part, Popular Items Web Part, and Recently Changed Items Web Part. A number of these are described in Chapter 3, "Enterprise Content Management," because they are related to Web Content Management sites.

- **Content Search Web Part (CSWP)** This is a new Web Part introduced in SharePoint 2013. It is a new content rollup Web Part similar to the Content Query Web Part (CQWP); however, it uses search queries and display templates, client-side script, and not server-side XSLT. When you add the Web Part to the page it shows recently modified items from the current site. This setting can be changed to show items from other sites or lists. This Web Part is used extensively in search-driven applications, including the massive change of emphasis in the implementation of Enterprise Content Management (ECM) within SharePoint 2013, such as the new Web Content Management (WCM) publishing model and the Cross-Site Publishing feature that is discussed in Chapter 3.

Hover cards

When you hover over a result item, a hover card is displayed. If the result item is a Microsoft Office document, the hover card includes the headings "Take A Look Inside," "Last Modified," "Contributors Include," and at the bottom of the block there are links labeled Follow (social feature), Open, View Library, and Send. Under the Take A Look Inside heading, there are links to headings within the file. When you click these links, the document opens and you are brought to the section you clicked within that file.

If the result item is an Office document and your SharePoint 2013 farm is linked to an Office Web Apps farm, you are also provided with a thumbnail preview. Using these previews, you can browse through the entire document, see all the pages, animations, and zoom in. Users therefore can find the exact content they are looking for from the search results page, without clicking the document link and waiting for the document to open in a new browser window or the office client applications. This functionality only worked out of the box with FAST Search for SharePoint 2010. With SharePoint 2013, this functionality only works on web applications that use claims authentication. It will not function on web applications that use classic Windows authentication.

Display templates

Display templates define the visual layout and behavior of a result type by using HTML, CSS, and JavaScript. You can customize the existing display templates or create display templates by using an HTML editor, such as Adobe Dreamweaver, Microsoft SharePoint Designer, Microsoft Visual Studio, or even Notepad. The new or modified display template is then uploaded into the display templates gallery by a site collection administrator. You can include the following four types of components in a display template:

- Managed properties that will identify the properties you want to display from the returned search result items. These will be referenced in the HTML you include in the display templates.

- Any JavaScript or CSS files that you want used with your display template must be externalized so that you can add them to your display template. When you upload a display template, SharePoint extracts these files into the display template gallery from the HTML file.

- Inline JavaScript, below the first <div> in your display template.

- HTML to render the results. You need to incorporate placeholders where you want the values from the managed properties to be displayed.

 Note Display templates are HTML files.

You can find the out-of-the-box display templates in your Master Page Gallery, in the Display Templates folder, as shown in Figure 2-9. You can find the display templates that are used for search in the Search folder.

Master Page Gallery ▸ Display Templates ⓘ

	Type	Name	Modified	Modified By	Checked Out To	Compatible UI Version(s)
☐	📁	Content Web Parts	8/3/2012 4:34 PM	☐ System Account		
	📁	Filters	8/3/2012 4:34 PM	☐ System Account		
	📁	Language Files	8/3/2012 4:34 PM	☐ System Account		
	📁	Search	8/3/2012 4:34 PM	☐ System Account		
	📁	Server Style Sheets	8/3/2012 4:34 PM	☐ System Account		
	📁	System	8/3/2012 4:34 PM	☐ System Account		

FIGURE 2-9 Display templates are new to SharePoint 2013. You can use them to dynamically display search results.

Result Types

Display templates are invoked based on a set of rules defined in Result Types. A Result Type consists of:

- **Rules**   These determine when to apply a Result Type, based on the specified conditions. A rule can consist of multiple conditions. Rule conditions can be joined by using equality, comparison, and logical operators. You can use them to identify specific predefined types of content, such as an email, a PDF, a Word document or, a SharePoint Wiki. You can also use them to specify a result source or any managed property as part of the criteria for a rule. For example, you can specify that the rule is only applicable when the user property field, Job Title, contains "Director."

- **Properties**   Determines the list of managed properties for the result. You must add managed properties to the list before you map the managed property to a display template.

- **Display templates**   Defines the visual layout for the Result Type.

A Result Type can apply to the entire search service application, site collection, or site; no custom coding is required. The out-of-the-box Result Types cannot be changed; however, you can create a copy of them and then modify that copy. The new version of the Result Type is created from your copy, and your copy of the Result Type will be used in preference to the version of the Result Type provided when SharePoint 2013 was first installed.

There is an inheritance hierarchy to Result Types. When the display template framework identifies Result Types that are applicable to a set of search results, the Result Types from the current site, the site collection, and SSA are retrieved. The Result Type that matches and has the highest priority is the one that is used to render the result items that are returned.

To create a Result Type at the top-level site of a site collection, navigate to the Site Settings page, and then under Site Collection Administration, click Search Result Types to display the Manage Result Types page, as shown in Figure 2-10.

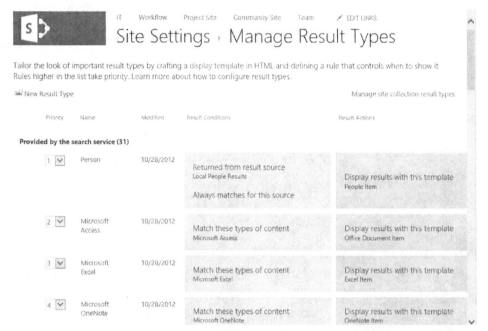

FIGURE 2-10 Use the Manage Result Types page to create new Result Types. The order determines which rules are checked first. SharePoint applies the first match it finds.

At the top of the page, click New Result Type to display the Add Result Type page, as demonstrated in Figure 2-11.

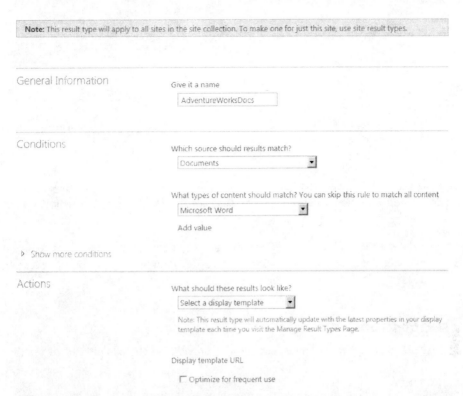

General Information

Give it a name

AdventureWorksDocs

Conditions

Which source should results match?

Documents

What types of content should match? You can skip this rule to match all content

Microsoft Word

Add value

▷ Show more conditions

Actions

What should these results look like?

Select a display template

Note: This result type will automatically update with the latest properties in your display template each time you visit the Manage Result Types Page.

Display template URL

☐ Optimize for frequent use

FIGURE 2-11 Provide a name for the Result Type, specify the condition, and select the display template to use.

Search refinements

Search refinements are provided by the Refinement Web Part on the search results page. There are two different modes for the Refinement Web Part:

- **Search Results** The refinement data works essentially the same as it did in SharePoint Server 2010, except that it now works with display templates.

- **Faceted Navigation** This uses a term from the Term Store to filter what kind of data should be displayed. You can configure different refiners for different terms in a term set. Refiners are based on managed properties from the search index. To use a managed property in this manner you need to set Refinable to Yes - Active, as shown in Figure 2-12. For example, in the Term Store you define the term "Camera" and have the managed properties Megapixel Count, Color, and Manufacturer as refiners for the term Camera. This provides users with options to narrow or refine their query.

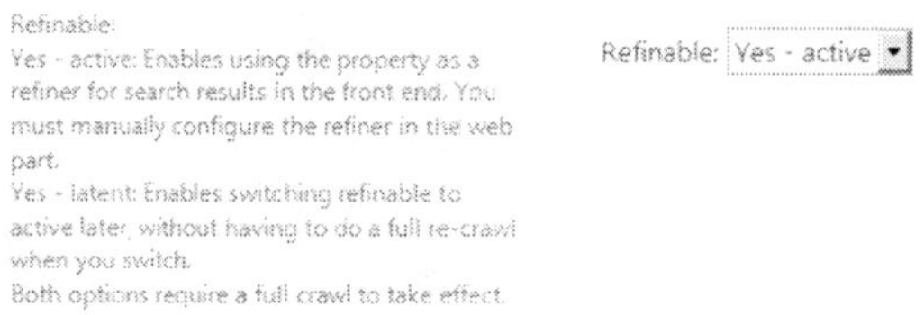

Refinable: Yes - active

FIGURE 2-12 To use faceted navigation, you need to map a term in the Term Store with a managed property that is configured as Refinable.

Note In SharePoint 2013, to configure Managed Properties, on the Central Administration website, go to the Search Administration pages and then, in the Quick Launch, click Search Schema.

Refinement is different with SharePoint 2013 in that you can define display templates to use for rendering different kinds of refinement. With SharePoint 2010, you had to write your own custom refiner.

Query suggestions

SharePoint 2013 greatly improves the query suggestions provided in SharePoint 2010 via the following:

- Personal SharePoint activities are used in query suggestions; that is, a user has a personal query log.

- It includes weighting based on sites that a user has previously visited.

- It uses the most frequent queries across all users that "match" the search terms.

The behavior of the query suggestions turns into more of a "browse and find" kind of experience. Suggestions are provided to the user as she types search keywords and also once the search results have been displayed. Thus, users will see suggestions before and after the query process has completed. The suggestions provided to the user after the result items are displayed consist of links that the user has clicked through at least twice before, and the content displayed for that content matches the user's search criteria.

Server administrators can use the link in the Quick Launch on the Search Administration page to add inclusion and exclusion lists for suggestions. You can use the Windows PowerShell *Import-SPEnterpriseSearchPopularQueries* cmdlet to import search suggestions to a site from a file that contains a comma-separated list of suggested queries.

Configuring and managing SharePoint 2013 search

SharePoint 2013 search architecture is implemented by creating, configuring, and managing SSAs. Creating the SSA is the same as in SharePoint 2010, using Windows PowerShell or the Central Administration website. You can configure and manage SharePoint 2013 search by using the same two tools.

The configuration of search at the service-application level will look similar to those available with SharePoint Server 2010. However, many of the configuration changes you can make are no longer limited to the SSA. Changes can also be made at the site collection, and some can even be made at the site, as discussed earlier in this chapter.

This section details some of the administrative tasks that are either new or have changed at the service-application level.

Managing search at the SSA level

As with SharePoint 2010, you use the Search Administration pages in SharePoint 2013 to manage search at the SSA level. Use the following procedure to navigate to the Search Administration home page:

1. On the home page of the Central Administration website, under Application Management, click Manage Service Applications.

    The Manage Service Application page opens.

2. Click to the right of the name of the SSA and then, on the Service Applications ribbon tab, in the Operations group, click Manage.

    The Search Administration page opens.

As with SharePoint 2010, the Search Administration page in the Central Administration website provides a summary of the system status for an SSA and the Quick Launch (see Figure 2-13) provides links to pages on which you can complete search-related administrative tasks.

Central Administration

Farm Search Administration

Search Administration

Diagnostics
Crawl Log
Crawl Health Reports
Query Health Reports
Usage Reports

Crawling
Content Sources
Crawl Rules
Server Name Mappings
File Types
Index Reset
Crawler Impact Rules

Queries and Results
Authoritative Pages
Result Sources
Query Rules
Query Client Types
Search Schema
Query Suggestions
Search Dictionaries
Search Result Removal

FIGURE 2-13 Use the links in the Quick Launch of the Search Administration page to carry out search-related administrative tasks.

Here are the links in the Quick Launch that are new for SharePoint 2013:

- **Diagnostics**   Within this group, you can now access Crawl Health Reports, Query Health Reports, and Usage Reports. Some of this data was available in the search reports in Share-Point 2010. These reports were briefly described earlier in this chapter. You can find more information on search diagnostics at *technet.microsoft.com/en-us/library/jj219611(v=office.15).aspx.*

- **Crawling**   No new links.

- **Queries and Results**   New links in this group include Result Sources (replaces the Feder-ated Locations and Scopes links), Query Rules, Query Client Types, Search Schema (replaces Metadata Properties link), Query Suggestions, and Search Dictionaries. Search Schema was discussed earlier in this chapter. The other links are discussed in the next section.

Changing the search topology

When you use the Central Administration website—either the Configuration Wizard or the New Search Service option on the Service Application page—all six search components are running on the server that is hosting the Central Administration website. This is known as the default topology. When you configure an SSA by using Windows PowerShell, you can place the components where you like.

You can view the status of the search topology of an SSA by using the Search Administration home page in the Central Administration website. The Search Application Topology is displayed at the bottom of this page, as shown in Figure 2-14.

Search Application Topology

Server Name	Admin	Crawler	Content Processing	Analytics Processing	Query Processing	Index Partition 0
SP1	✓	✓	✓	✓	✓	✓

Database Server Name	Database Type	Database Name
sql1.adventurew.com	Administration Database	SearchServiceApplication_DB_98b2845583fd43fbb289d60a3b0689df
sql1.adventurew.com	Analytics Reporting Database	SearchServiceApplication_AnalyticsReportingStoreDB_9371504bf46d4d9e88202d419132790f
sql1.adventurew.com	Crawl Database	SearchServiceApplication_CrawlStoreDB_dd3e3b160fd7474cae20f08982572b1c
sql1.adventurew.com	Link Database	SearchServiceApplication_LinksStoreDB_025c1ab7852845aabd7a3e2eef6c7539

FIGURE 2-14 You can use the Search Administration page on the Central Administration website to view the Search Application Topology for an SSA.

To get the same information by using Windows PowerShell, type the following command:

```
Get-SPEnterpriseSearchServiceApplication | Get-SPEnterpriseSearchTopology –Active |
    Get-SPEnterpriseSearchComponent
```

Unfortunately, unlike SharePoint 2010, SharePoint 2013 does not provide any mechanism within the Central Administration website to change the search topology; you must use Windows PowerShell to complete that task.

If you want to scale the search components over a number of servers, you cannot modify the active topology. You must first clone the active search topology and then complete the following tasks:

1. On the application server on which you want to add the search components, start the search service instance.

2. Modify the cloned topology to add, move, or remove search components. You cannot remove index partitions. To create an index replica, add a new index component, providing the partition number of the index partition that you want to clone.

3. Activate the new topology.

More Info You can read more about managing the search topology at *technet.microsoft. com/en-us/library/jj219705(v=office.15).aspx#Proc9.*

Result sources

Results Sources effectively combine Search Scopes and Federated Locations from SharePoint 2010 into one interface. However, they add a number of new features regarding how you can build the queries that make up the Result Source.

When an SSA is first created, there are a number of result sources available out of the box, such as Local SharePoint Results, Popular, and Items Matching a Content Type (see Figure 2-15). To navigate to this page, on the Search Administration page, in the Quick Launch, under Queries and Results, click Result Sources.

SearchServiceApplication: Manage Result Sources

By using search federation, users can simultaneously search content in the search index of this search service, as well as in other sources, such as internet search engines.
You can define a new source by clicking on **New Result Source**.
To enable users to search content in the source in the Search Center, specify the source in the properties in one of the web parts enabled for federation.
Result Sources replace the Search Scopes, which are deprecated in the current version. You can access the read-only list of previously configured search scopes by clicking on **Search Scopes**.

New Result Source

Name	Creation Date	Default	Status
Custom			
Company Intranet Site	9/20/2012 2:47:43 PM		Active
System			
Conversations	7/22/2012 9:26:47 PM		Active
Documents	7/22/2012 9:26:47 PM		Active
Items matching a content type	7/22/2012 9:26:47 PM		Active
Items matching a tag	7/22/2012 9:26:47 PM		Active
Items related to current user	7/22/2012 9:26:47 PM		Active
Items with same keyword as this item	7/22/2012 9:26:47 PM		Active
Local People Results	7/22/2012 9:26:46 PM		Active
Local Reports And Data Results	7/22/2012 9:26:47 PM		Active
Local SharePoint Results	7/22/2012 9:26:46 PM	√	Active
Local Video Results	7/22/2012 9:26:47 PM		Active

FIGURE 2-15 The default Result Sources that are created when you create an SSA.

In SharePoint 2010, you could only choose one of two sources: Local Search and OpenSearch 1.1. With SharePoint 2013, there are two additional sources: Remote SharePoint servers and Exchange, as shown in Figure 2-16.

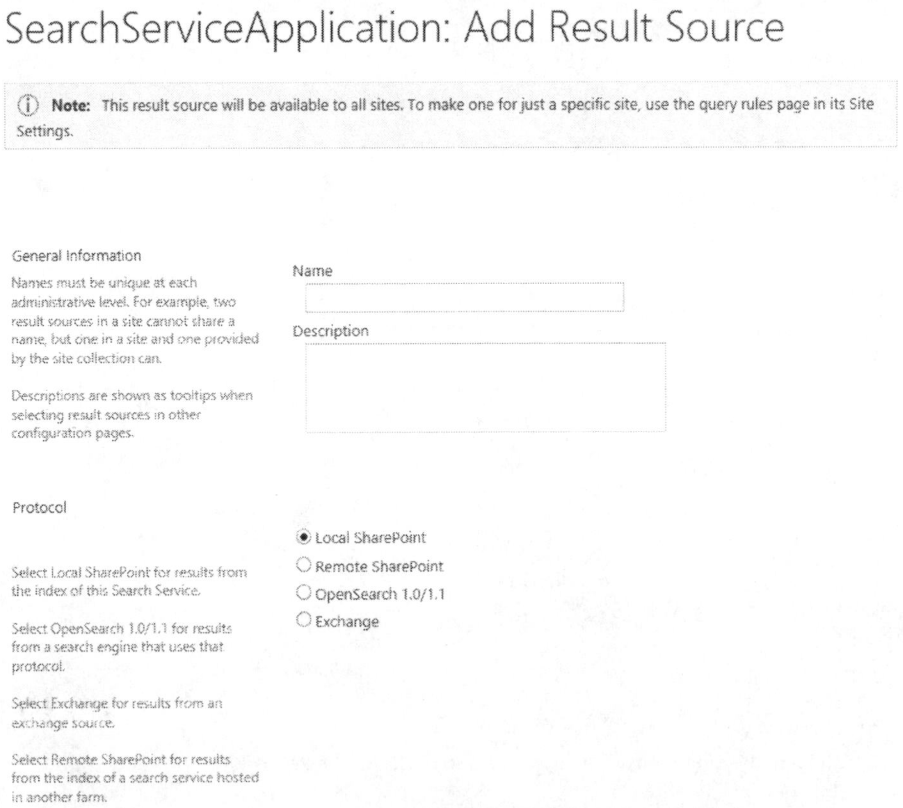

SearchServiceApplication: Add Result Source

> (i) **Note:** This result source will be available to all sites. To make one for just a specific site, use the query rules page in its Site Settings.

General Information

Names must be unique at each administrative level. For example, two result sources in a site cannot share a name, but one in a site and one provided by the site collection can.

Descriptions are shown as tooltips when selecting result sources in other configuration pages.

Name

Description

Protocol

Select Local SharePoint for results from the index of this Search Service.

Select OpenSearch 1.0/1.1 for results from a search engine that uses that protocol.

Select Exchange for results from an exchange source.

Select Remote SharePoint for results from the index of a search service hosted in another farm.

- ● Local SharePoint
- ○ Remote SharePoint
- ○ OpenSearch 1.0/1.1
- ○ Exchange

FIGURE 2-16 When you create a new Result Source, choose the protocol and type.

Because SharePoint and People Search results are served by the same search index (which was not the case for FAST Search for SharePoint 2010), when you create a new Result Source or edit an existing Result Source, you need to choose which of the two Result Types you want. Also, at the bottom of the Result Source page, you specify a query transformation and configure credential information, as shown in Figure 2-17.

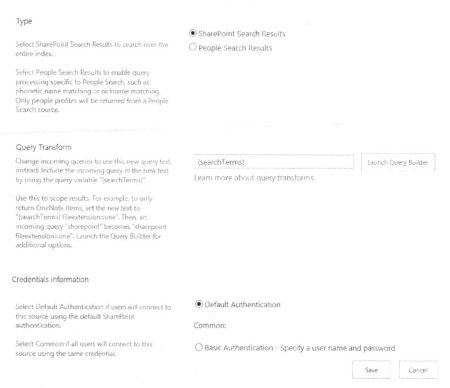

Type

Select SharePoint Search Results to search over the entire index.

Select People Search Results to enable query processing specific to People Search, such as phonetic name matching or nickname matching. Only people profiles will be returned from a People Search source.

◉ SharePoint Search Results
◯ People Search Results

Query Transform

Change incoming queries to use this new query text instead. Include the incoming query in the new text by using the query variable "{searchTerms}".

Use this to scope results. For example, to only return OneNote items, set the new text to "{searchTerms} fileextension=one". Then, an incoming query "sharepoint" becomes "sharepoint fileextension=one". Launch the Query Builder for additional options.

{searchTerms}   Launch Query Builder

Learn more about query transforms.

Credentials Information

Select Default Authentication if users will connect to this source using the default SharePoint authentication.

Select Common if all users will connect to this source using the same credential.

◉ Default Authentication

Common:

◯ Basic Authentication - Specify a user name and password

Save   Cancel

FIGURE 2-17 Configure the query transformation and credentials for the Result Type.

When you click Launch Query Builder, the Build Your Query Wizard starts (see Figure 2-18), with which you can quickly construct a query; for example, to restrict the return results or add a prefix to the user's search terms.

FIGURE 2-18 Use the Build Your Query Wizard to build and test your queries for Result Sources.

The Build Your Query Wizard consists of three tabs:

- **Basics** Use this tab to build queries via the Keyword Query Language (KQL) to add keyword filters and property filters. Both kinds of filters can contain dynamic variables. The dynamic variables are replaced with actual values when the user types a query.

  - Keyword filters query the full-text search index; that is, all the managed properties in the search index that are set to "Searchable." This includes the body of the document.

  - Property filters are used to query the content of managed properties that are set to "Queryable."

- **Sorting** Use this tab to change the sort order and the relevance rank of the search results. To determine how search results for the query are sorted, you can either use the relevance rank based on the rank model, or you can select any managed property that is set to "Sortable" from the drop-down list. To change the rank of search results, you can define which rank model should be used for the query that you are building or define dynamic ranking rules to promote or demote particular results based on keywords, content types, file name extensions, and more.

- **Test** Use this tab to test the query that you built. This gives you an opportunity to experiment to see whether changing variables would have the effect that you want on the query.

 Note With SharePoint 2013, KQL contains three new operators, XRANK, NEAR, and ONEAR, that were only previously available in FAST query language (FQL). In Search for SharePoint 2013, SQL syntax is not supported, and although you can still construct FQL queries, because FQL is deprecated, you should wherever possible use KQL queries. FQL was originally designed for complex query construction and intended for creating queries programmatically.

Query rules

Query rules are new in SharePoint 2013 search, and their aim is to try to get SharePoint 2013 search to react intelligently to what the user might be trying to find by transforming the queries to improve the relevance of search results. For each query rule, a condition or conditions are specified that cause the query rule to run. For each condition, one or more actions are specified. You can create query rules that apply to all site collections in a web application that consumes a particular SSA. Alternatively, you can create rules that apply per site or per site collection so that they supplement query rules that are at the SSA level.

A query rule can spawn more queries, each with its own transformation. You can display the results of each of these queries in a separate result block on a search results page, or you can transform the original query by specifying conditions and actions. Using query rules, you can have search requests from a user that trigger multiple queries and multiple result sets. All matching query rules can generate results and the query component will organize the results for rendering to the user. Use query rules to promote important results, show blocks of additional results, or to fine tune ranking.

Query client types

Query client types are also new in SharePoint 2013 search. They are used in relation to query throttling. A query client type identifies applications that send queries to SharePoint search. Each query client type can be associated with one of three tiers: Top, Middle, or Bottom. When the resource limit is reached, query throttling is enabled and SharePoint search processes queries from client applications in the Top tier first, the Middle tier next, and then finally from the Bottom tier. The query client types available out of the box include: Client-Side Object Model (CSOM), PeopleResultsQuery, SEOSiteMapQuery and WebService.

Search dictionaries

To access the MMS Term Store (see Figure 2-19), on the Search Administration page, in the Quick Launch, click Search Dictionaries.

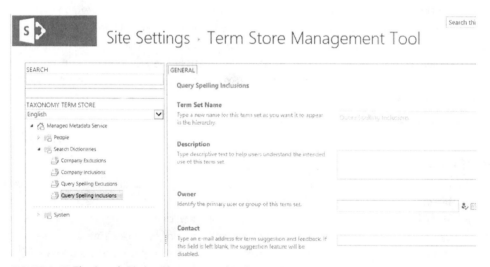

FIGURE 2-19 The Search Dictionaries are stored in the MMS Term Store.

You can use the Term Store to define query spelling corrections. This adds a customizable "did you mean" functionality. Also included in the Search Dictionaries are Company Exclusions and Inclusions with which you can extract company names from documents, out of the box.

Note In SharePoint 2013, when a profile import from Active Directory (AD) is completed, it automatically populates a special MMS term set named People and creates three term sets from the AD properties: Department, Job Title, and Location. The terms in these term sets are the unique values across all users for each of these AD properties.

Search processes

The search processes include the Host Controller, which is a Windows NT service that manages various processes called *NodeRunners*. When you first install SharePoint 2013, you see a *NodeRunner.exe* process for each of the Content Processing, Analytics Processing, Index, Query Processing, and search administration components that are created in your farm. The *mssearch.exe* process contains the Crawl component. To discover which NodeRunner is running which search component, type the following Windows PowerShell command:

```
$ID=(Get-process hostcontrollerservice.Id);
Get-WmiObject -Class Win32_Process -Filter "ParentProcessID=$ID" |
    Format-List -Property ProcessName, ProcessID, CommandLine
```

Note You can see which NodeRunner process is running which search component by using Task Manager. On the Processes tab, from the View menu, click Select Columns, and then in the Select Process Page Columns dialog box, scroll down and click Command Line. Remember to click Show Processes From All Users to display the *noderunner.exe* processes.

Site level search admin summary

Site collection administrators can now manage the following search-related functionality:

- Create and/or override Query Rules, including promoted results, Result Types, display templates and result resources, either for remote locations or as a custom search vertical.

- Create refiners.

- Start a local crawl. This can be done down to the list level—a very significant enhancement.

- Create managed properties.

Site owners can complete all the above tasks, except for creating managed properties. They can view managed and crawled properties, but they cannot create or modify them. Search configurations can be exported and imported at both the site and site-collection level.

Deprecated search functionality

SharePoint 2013 contains all the search features that were contained in SharePoint 2010 enterprise search as well as new functionality.

Host distribution rules

With SharePoint Server 2010, host distribution rules were used to associate start addresses with a specific crawl database. By default, start addresses are load-balanced across crawl databases, based on space availability. However, with SharePoint Server 2010, you could assign a start address to a specific crawl database for availability and performance reasons. Due to changes in SharePoint 2013 search architecture, host distribution rules are removed. SharePoint administrators used the host distribution rules to overcome the 25 million items per start address support limit in SharePoint 2010. Whereas SharePoint 2013 does not have this limitation, therefore host distribution rules are not needed.

The SharePoint Search API

The SharePoint Search API has been expanded greatly; however, the following options have been removed or deprecated:

- SQL Syntax has been removed. This was a deprecated option in SharePoint 2010.

- The search web service, *_vti_bin/search.asmx,* is deprecated but not removed. If you need to remotely access search, your developers should use the query CSOM or the query REST Service.

Summary

The new SharePoint 2013 search architecture consists of six components: Crawl, Content Processing, Analytics Processing, Index, Query Processing, and Search Administration. Each SSA you create will contain these six component as well as four databases: Crawl, Link, Analytics Reporting, and Search Administration. You can scale out your search topology by placing these components on separate servers.

The index for an SSA is stored in files on the servers that host the SSA's index component. You can create many index components associated with one SSA, thereby splitting the index across many servers. There are two ways of splitting your index: index partitions and index replicas. The search index for the service application is the aggregation of all index partitions. You can spread the query load on an index partition by creating index replicas, which provide a level of redundancy.

SharePoint 2013 also includes a new search user interface with new Search Web Parts that can be customized by using Result Types and display templates. The hover card is prevalent throughout the user interface. It displays information about the returned result item, and if your SharePoint 2013 installation is linked to an Office Web App farm, it displays graphical previews of the content of Office documents.

CHAPTER 3

Enterprise Content Management

Microsoft has invested greatly in Enterprise Content Management (ECM). The result is a significant improvement in records management and Web Content Management. This has included new site templates, such as the Discovery Center and the Product Catalog, and new Web Parts.

With the powerful Web Content Management functionality added to Microsoft SharePoint 2013, organizations can quickly develop and adapt over time the categories and taxonomies upon which their sites are built. Site collection boundaries are no longer an issue for publishing content. Key to these improvements is search and metadata which has facilitated the introduction of a new publishing model for Web Content Management. This makes it possible for site navigation to be defined by terms that are stored in the Term Store of the Managed Metadata Service (MMS). Publishing pages can then be aggregated from a number of sources by using the new Content Search Web Part.

Microsoft has also optimized SharePoint 2013, not only in terms of the code deployed but also with regard to optimizing the site for the visitors, for search engines, for performance, for web designers, and content authors. This chapter explores these content management improvements.

Records management and compliance

Electronic discovery—more commonly known as *eDiscovery* (and also shortened to Discovery)—is the process of identifying and delivering electronic information that can be used as evidence in legal proceedings. Many organizations have pre-existing content management systems that they want to make available within SharePoint and use the Discovery functionality. SharePoint 2013 includes built-in support for the Content Management Interoperability Services (CMIS) standard for interoperability. This makes it possible for an organization to interact within SharePoint with non-SharePoint repositories that adhere to the CMIS specification.

The Discovery Center

The Discovery Center (see Figure 3-1) has been completely redesigned in SharePoint 2013 and is a new type of site collection. It has been specifically re-engineered for managing Discovery cases and *holds*. A hold is a method to preserve content. In SharePoint 2010, you could place documents, pages, and list items on hold, which prevented users from deleting or editing them. SharePoint 2013 has provided In-Place Holds, which can be used to preserve sites and Exchange mailboxes. An In-Place Hold also makes it possible for users to continue to edit or even delete preserved content.

A Discovery Center can be deployed as a single, centralized enterprise-wide portal in which individual users who have access rights are able to create and manipulate discovery cases across multiple SharePoint farms and Microsoft Exchange. All of the data managed by the Discovery Center can be exported into the industry-standard Electronic Data Reference Model (EDRM) XML format so that it can be imported into a review tool.

FIGURE 3-1 The Discovery Center home page.

Note A Discovery Center must be created in a web application that supports claims authentication.

The following are the two primary components of an eDiscovery case:

- **eDiscovery set** These are used to find content and apply a hold. Each set contains the following:

  - Sources Locations to be searched, such as Exchange mailboxes, SharePoint sites and files shares. Any content that is indexed by the Search Service Application (SSA) can be discovered from the Discovery Center. These sources must be crawled by the SSA that is associated with the web application that contains the Discovery Center. If you want to discover content held in Microsoft Lync you must configure Lync to archive content to Exchange and then configure the SSA to include Exchange as a result source, if it is not already defined as one.

Note If you archive content from Lync in Exchange, you can also discover Lync content.

- **A filter** This defines what you are searching for and can include search terms, a date range, and an author's name.

- **An option** This applies an in-place hold when the content in a source matches a filter.

■ **eDiscovery query** This finds content and exports it. An export can contain documents and their versions, lists as a comma-separated values (CSV) file, SharePoint pages as MIME HTML (*.mht*) files, Exchange objects, crawl log errors, and an XML manifest file that provides an over-view of the exported information. Each query contains:

- **Query filters** These define what you are searching for. Similar to an eDiscovery set filter, with the addition that query filters can also use *stemming*. Stemming is a method of mapping a linguistic stem to all matching words. For example, in English, the stem "buy" matches bought, buying, and buys.

- **Sources** Defines the location to be searched.

Planning Discovery Centers

The key to planning the number of Discovery Centers needed is the link between an SSA and the content that the SSA crawls. If an SSA does not crawl all the content that you want to electronically discover, you might need to create multiple Discovery Centers, as shown in Figure 3-2.

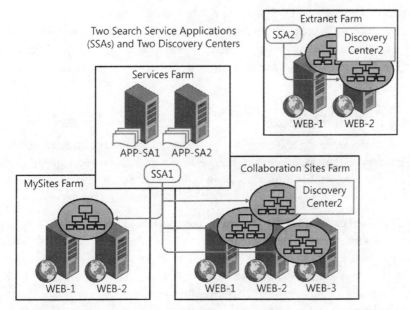

FIGURE 3-2 You create Discovery Centers in a web application such that all the content you want to discover is crawled by the SSAs linked to that web application.

Note You can configure one SSA to crawl content in more than one SharePoint farm. When using such a configuration, you would only need one Discovery Center.

An SSA in an on-premises SharePoint farm cannot crawl content in the Microsoft Office 365 SharePoint Online multitenant platform. In such a scenario, you would have two Discovery Centers, as depicted in Figure 3-3.

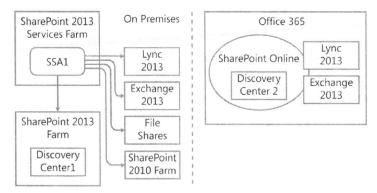

FIGURE 3-3 Creating a separate Discovery Center for each isolated SSA.

Note For a SharePoint 2013 Discovery Center to locate content in Exchange Server, it must be an Exchange Server 2013 and each web server in the SharePoint 2013 farm must have installed the Exchange Web Service (EWS) Managed API. The Exchange Server 2013 must be added as a Result Source. You can obtain the EWS Managed API 2.0 from the Microsoft download site at *www.microsoft.com/en-us/download/details.aspx?id=35371*. For more information about Result Sources, go to Chapter 2, "Introducing the new search architecture."

Unified Discovery and Site Mailboxes

SharePoint 2013 also supports searching and exporting content from file shares as well as exporting content from SharePoint and Exchange. This means that you can inspect content for legal or auditing reasons, but you can also export that content so that it can be retained for legal or compliancy reasons.

A new feature within SharePoint 2013 is Site Mailboxes, also sometimes referred to as Team Folders, which provide seamless integration with Exchange 2013 and SharePoint 2013. Each Site Mailbox has an email address by which a user can use SharePoint 2013 or Outlook 2013 to view the content of that Site Mailbox. Site Mailboxes also provide links to SharePoint libraries in Microsoft Outlook 2013; thus, users can drag content into a SharePoint library from within Outlook.

The content can include emails that are stored in Exchange Server 2013 and documents that are stored in SharePoint libraries. The aim is to keep content where it belongs. Exchange Server stores the emails, providing users with the same message views for email conversations that they use every day. SharePoint stores the documents, offering document coauthoring, versioning, metadata tagging, and other document management features.

For those emails that really are more like documents, such as status reports that are final and you don't expect to have further conversations about them, you can, for instance, drag them into Share-Point libraries by using Site Mailboxes—in essence "docifying" them. You might want to do that for very important business records so that they can be made immutable and can take advantage of consistent retention policy that you apply to other records. Compliance on Site Mailboxes happens in the background, without getting in the way of end users. For instance, when end users create a site, they are asked to pick a lifecycle policy that determines how long the site and its accompanying Site Mailbox should be kept.

Therefore, teams can manage both the documents and the emails together that are produced for a project. Site Mailboxes can only be accessed and edited by site members.

Before you can use Site Mailboxes, the following conditions must be satisfied:

- The User Profile Service Application (UPSA) must be configured

- You are using Exchange 2013

- SharePoint must have Secure Sockets Layer (SSL) configured

- An EWS-Managed API must be installed on each SharePoint application server

- You have Establish OAuth Trust and Service Permissions on SharePoint Server 2013

- Exchange Server 2013 is configured for Site Mailboxes

The preceding tasks are detailed in the TechNet article "Configure Site mailboxes in SharePoint Server 2013," which you can read at *technet.microsoft.com/en-us/library/jj552524(v=office.15).aspx*.

After you have met these requirements, you can then use Site Mailboxes by activating the Site Mailbox feature at the site level.

> **More Info** You can read more about using Site Mailboxes on the Exchange Team Blog at *blogs.technet.com/b/exchange/archive/2012/08/22/site-mailboxes-in-the-new-office.aspx*.

In-place holds

With SharePoint 2010, users could not change or delete content when it was on hold. However, Share-Point 2013 introduces a new concept of an in-place hold that is applied at the site level. When an in-place hold is applied, a copy of the content as it was at the time the hold was initiated is preserved. The content is preserved in its original location or when a user attempts to modify or delete content, on first modification because a hold was applied, a copy is preserved in a preservation hold library. This gives users the ability to still work with the content in its original location. They do not even have to know that their content is on hold.

The preservation hold library is only visible to site collection administrators and users, who at the web-application level, have been given permissions to see all content in all site collections within the web application. The search crawler also has special permissions to crawl content in the preservation hold library.

The Information Management Retention timer job runs periodically. All the content in the preservation hold library is compared to the eDiscovery set filters that put the site on hold. The content from the preservation hold library is deleted by the timer job when the content does not match at least one of the filters.

Site-level retention polices

With SharePoint 2013, site policies have been improved to include retention policies for sites and Site Mailboxes. You can a define policies on when sites are deleted, and if needed, what workflows are to be executed. For example, you might want to archive a site as part of your organization's clean-up process.

The concept at the heart of this new functionality is *site closure*. When you close a site, it does not appear in the places that aggregate open sites to site members, such as Outlook, Outlook Web Access and Project Server, will trim links to the site. The site might still be accessed via its URL and it can still be modified. When you specify to delete a site after it has closed, by closing a site you have started a countdown to its deletion. Closing a site collection, however, makes the site collection and all subsites read-only. Also, if the closed site has any subsites, when the closed site is deleted, all its subsites will be deleted, whether they are in a closed state or not. Site owners do have the option of postponing the deletion of a closed site, depending on the configuration of the site policy.

Note A site owner can re-open a closed site. To do so, on the Site Settings page, click Site Closure And Deletion.

Creating a Site Policy

Site policies are created at the site-collection level, but are applied at the site level, including the top-level site of a site collection. To create a new site policy, perform the following procedure:

1. Navigate to the site collection where you would like to create the site policy.

2. Click the Settings icon to display the Site Settings page, and then under Site Collection Administration, click Site Collection Features.

   The Site Collection Features page opens.

3. To the right of Site Policy, click Activate, if the site collection feature is not already activated, as shown in Figure 3-4.

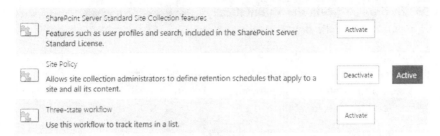

SharePoint Server Standard Site Collection features

Features such as user profiles and search, included in the SharePoint Server Standard License.

Activate

Site Policy

Allows site collection administrators to define retention schedules that apply to a site and all its content.

Deactivate   Active

Three-state workflow

Use this workflow to track items in a list.

Activate

FIGURE 3-4 Activate the Site Policy Site Collection feature if it is not already activated.

4. Navigate back to the Site Settings page and then, under Site Collection Administration, click Site Policies (Not Site Collection Policies).

5. Click Create to display the New Site Policy page and type the name for the policy. Select Close And Delete Sites Automatically. The page displays four options, as described below and shown in Figure 3-5.

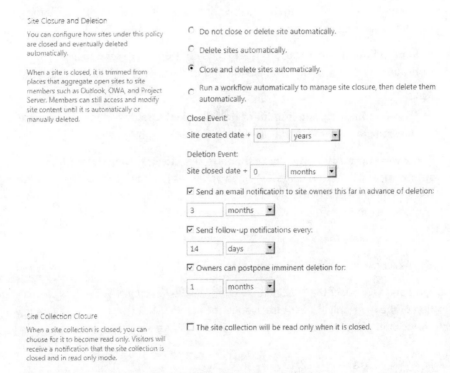

Site Closure and Deletion

You can configure how sites under this policy are closed and eventually deleted automatically.

When a site is closed, it is trimmed from places that aggregate open sites to site members such as Outlook, OWA, and Project Server. Members can still access and modify site content until it is automatically or manually deleted.

○ Do not close or delete site automatically.

○ Delete sites automatically.

◉ Close and delete sites automatically.

○ Run a workflow automatically to manage site closure, then delete them automatically.

Close Event:

Site created date + [0] [years ▼]

Deletion Event:

Site closed date + [0] [months ▼]

☑ Send an email notification to site owners this far in advance of deletion:

[3] [months ▼]

☑ Send follow-up notifications every:

[14] [days ▼]

☑ Owners can postpone imminent deletion for:

[1] [months ▼]

Site Collection Closure

When a site collection is closed, you can choose for it to become read only. Visitors will receive a notification that the site collection is closed and in read only mode.

☐ The site collection will be read only when it is closed.

FIGURE 3-5 You can automate the closure and deletion of sites.

- **Do not close or delete site automatically**   Use this condition when you want the site owner to manually delete the site.

- **Delete sites automatically**   Use this condition when you want to manually close the site, but the site will be deleted automatically. This option offers the same choices, as the next option with regard to deleting the site automatically, and also requires you to specify how long after its creation time the site will be closed.

- **Close and delete sites automatically**   Use this condition when you want to automate site closure and deletion. You are provided with five configuration options:

  - **Close event**   Use this option to specify how long to wait after a site is created before closing the site. You can specify the length of time in Days, Months, or Years.

  - **Deletion event**   Use this option to specify how long to wait after a site is created before deleting the site. You can specify the length of time in Days, Months, or Years.

  - **Send an email notification to site owners this far in advance of deletion**   Use this option to send an email to the site owner at a specified length of time before the site is scheduled to be deleted.

  - **Send follow-up notifications every**   Use this option to send recurring follow-up notifications warnings of the site deletion and to specify the intervals at which they are to be sent.

  - **Owners can postpone imminent deletion for**   Use this option to allow site owners to postpone the deletion of the site for a specified length of time.

- **Run a workflow automatically to manage site closure, then delete them automatically**   Use this condition when you want to add custom logic to the closure process. You specify the name of the workflow, how long after the site is created to run the workflow, and whether to rerun the workflow periodically until the site is closed.

6. Click OK to create the new policy.

   The new policy is created and appears in the Site Policies listing.

You can optionally select the The Site Collection Will Be Read Only When It Is Closed check box. A notification of the read-only state is displayed in the status bar at the top of every page within the site collection, including application pages, as illustrated in Figure 3-6.

This site is read only at the site collection administrator's request.   ✕

FIGURE 3-6 A message displays on all pages within a site collection when you close the top-level site of a site collection and select to make it read-only.

You can close the notification message by clicking the "X" at the far right of the message; however, when you return to the page the notification is redisplayed.

Note When you define site policies in a site collection, which is a content-type hub you can publish and share those site policies across site collections.

Using a Site Policy

You can use a site policy with any site within that site collection where the site policy is created as follows:

1. Navigate to the Site Setting page for the site to which you want to apply the site policy.

2. Under Site Administration, click Site Closure And Deletion.

3. On the Site Closure And Deletion page, in the Site Policy section, select the appropriate site policy, as shown in Figure 3-7.

FIGURE 3-7 Select a site policy for the site.

4. Click OK to apply the site policy to the site.

You can use the Site Closure And Deletion page to do the following:

-   Apply, select, or remove a site policy. You cannot change the selected site policy of a closed site. You must first open the site, and then select a different policy. To remove all site policies, select No Site Policy.

-   View the site policy details such as the date and time that the site was closed and when the site will be deleted.

-   Manually close a site; however, before you can manually close a site, you must apply a site policy for which the Do Not Close Or Delete The Site Automatically condition has been selected.

-   Open a closed site.

The CMIS producer

The CMIS producer was introduced as part of the SharePoint 2010 Administrator's Toolkit. The CMIS producer has been completely redesigned and is included in SharePoint 2013. You use it on a site-by-site basis by activating the site feature: Content Management Interoperability Services (CMIS) Producer. It works in most authoring environments where SharePoint list web services work. For example, once activated, Adobe users can, via the Adobe Bridge file share, use basic document-management operations such as creating, updating, deleting, checking in and checking out, and managing the versions of documents and document metadata; and then within a program (such as Photoshop), all document versions and metadata are exposed. Unfortunately, this site feature is not available in Office 365.

Web Content Management

Microsoft has invested heavily in Web Content Management (WCM) in SharePoint 2013. With SharePoint 2010, WCM functionality was largely unchanged from Microsoft Office SharePoint Server 2007. WCM pages, known as *publishing pages*, were based on page layouts which contained field controls that were responsible for retrieving content from a site's Pages library and displaying it to the users. Content was structured into pages within sites, and that structure was the basis for navigation and the organization information architecture (IA). Content authors usually added static content to pages or dynamically displayed data from lists or libraries by using the Content Query Web Part (CQWP); however, those lists and libraries had to be stored within sites in the same site collection.

With SharePoint 2013, the emphasis is now on displaying content based on search as well as the structure of the site, and the way the navigation is organized can be based on managed metadata. WCM pages can contain content that rolls up other content from anywhere within your SharePoint implementation, including external content.

The new publishing model

You can now truly develop a user experience (UX) wherein the content on pages is dynamically displayed as the result of indexing the content and how the content is tagged. A visitor to your site need not know the location of where the content resides, nor should it concern him. Visitors land on pages—known as *landing pages* or *detailed pages*—that only need to be configured once because they dynamically obtain their content, based on the properties of the Web Parts and controls that they contain. Of course, the content that dynamically populates those pages might need to be structured for ease of use for WCM authors and setting permissions. However, the number of locations where content is created and maintained can be consolidated and streamlined. You could decide to store all of the content in a single Pages library, or for a multilingual solution, a Pages library for each language. Changing the structure of the authoring site has no impact on UX for a visitor to your site.

The introduction of this new publishing model does not prevent organizations from using the methods that they used with SharePoint 2010. However, it does mean that organizations can take advantage of the content they have already created. And they can reuse that content not only within the sites where the content is located, but across sites, site collections, and web applications.

The key advantages of having a search-driven publishing model are the following:

- It breaks down site collection boundaries.

- It eliminates large list thresholds.

- It facilitates a more flexible and dynamic publishing model.

- It provides friendly URLs.

- It offers flexible site hierarchy and navigation.

SharePoint 2013 introduces managed navigation, which also works with variations. Structured navigation—based on the SharePoint website structure—also still works; it synchronizes the content and structure between the source and target variations labels.

Friendly URLs

One of the great improvements in SharePoint 2013 for WCM is the separation of URLs and site hierarchy. When you browse to a SharePoint 2013 publishing site for the first time, you might notice that the URL format has changed. Instead of an address with a */Pages/default.aspx* extension, the page URL ends with only /. This is known as a friendly URL (FURL). Such URLs are also Search Engine Optimization (SEO)-friendly and friendly URLs will appear in search results.

With Managed Navigation, you can use friendly URLs, shorter URL formatted addresses, sometimes specified in the SharePoint 2013 interface as FURLs. This means that you will not see "HTTP response status 302 Moved Temporarily" redirections. Managed Navigation provides a scheme for friendly URLs that is consistent across site, category, and item pages.

The Managed Navigation provider is what makes this experience possible. When you navigate to the root of any site that uses the managed navigation provider, the Site Welcome Page setting controls the page that's loaded and displayed in the browser, but the URL you see (and that appears in search results) is rewritten to this friendlier format.

Any page, including your site's Welcome Page, can have a friendly URL. Depending on how you configure your site, most pages are automatically assigned a friendly URL. Friendly URLs can be localized.

SharePoint 2013 also automatically generates a canonical URL for each page. This is a URL that uniquely identifies the content of the page. It is also the URL that is stored in the index of most search engines. Configuring a canonical URL prevents the same content from being stored in the index of search engines multiple times.

Cross-site collection publishing

SharePoint 2013 introduces a cross-site collection publishing (XSP) feature with which you can reuse content across multiple site collections. It uses the built-in search capabilities of SharePoint 2013. SharePoint 2013 does not just break down the site collection boundaries, or the web application boundaries. You can now design sites for which content is obtained from other SharePoint farms; thus, your WCM content can span the boundaries between intranets and the Internet.

You can now have one authoring site collection that feeds multiple publishing site collections, with each site collection having a different Internet domain that is optimized for search engines and crawled by Internet search engines. Microsoft has designed XSP for exactly this scenario and others like it, without requiring the use of content deployment. It specifically had some common scenarios in mind, including being able to accomplish the following:

- Share an item list or a Page library as a publishing catalog

- Consume a catalog from search

- Combine XSP with the variations feature to enable authoring of multilingual sites from a common authoring site collection

When working with XSP, you do not need WCM pages. All of the content can be located in the search index and retrieved dynamically by using catalog URLs. Your WCM solution could consist of one page layout which is used by one WCM page that is then used by Managed Navigation as a Template Page to display content dynamically by using search.

To use XSP, the Cross-Site Collection Publishing site collection feature must be activated. Using this feature, you can share lists and libraries—including the Pages library—as catalogs so that other sites and site collections can use the catalog content on their pages. For example, content is stored in libraries and lists in an authoring site collection, which can then be reused across three separate publishing site collections by using the Content Search Web Part (CSWP), as demonstrated in Figure 3-8.

Of course, there will be some scenarios in which XSP is not efficient or appropriate, such as the following:

- When you crawl external data with a non-SharePoint connector, you cannot use XSP; however, if you use Business Connection Services (BCS), you can use it.

- You have a Variations site collection which is consuming data from another Variations site or site collection and you want to publish content from that site to a publishing site that has variations enabled.

- If you have one Variations site that depends on metadata from another Variations site to drive site navigation, and you use XSP to publish content to the target site, the navigation metadata transfer might not work as expected.

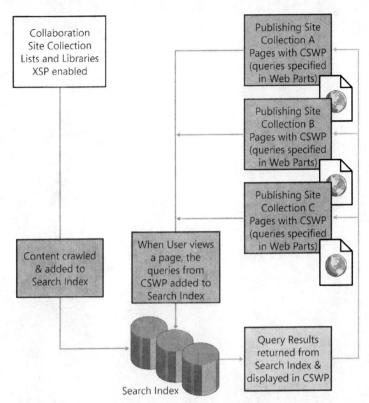

FIGURE 3-8 With XSP, search, and the use of the CSWP, you can create content in one site collection and reuse it across three site collections.

Catalogs

SharePoint 2013 introduces catalogs on WCM sites. You can use catalogs to publish content across site collections; that is to say, without catalogs you cannot use XSP. Out of the box, there are a number of Web Parts with which you can create a truly dynamic search-driven experience; however, as with everything related to SharePoint, your developers can write custom code to populate catalogs, connect a product catalog to a site, and curate individual pages with custom page layouts and HTML content that appears only in the defined context.

When you enable the XSP site collection feature, on the list or library Settings page, under General Settings, there is a new link named Catalog Settings that displays the Catalog Settings page, as shown in Figure 3-9.

> **Note** Before using this page to configure the list or library as a catalog, you should add a column to the list or library so that you can tag items from a MMS term set. You should add at least one item to the list or library and then tag it against one of the terms from the term set using the column you just created, before publishing the item.

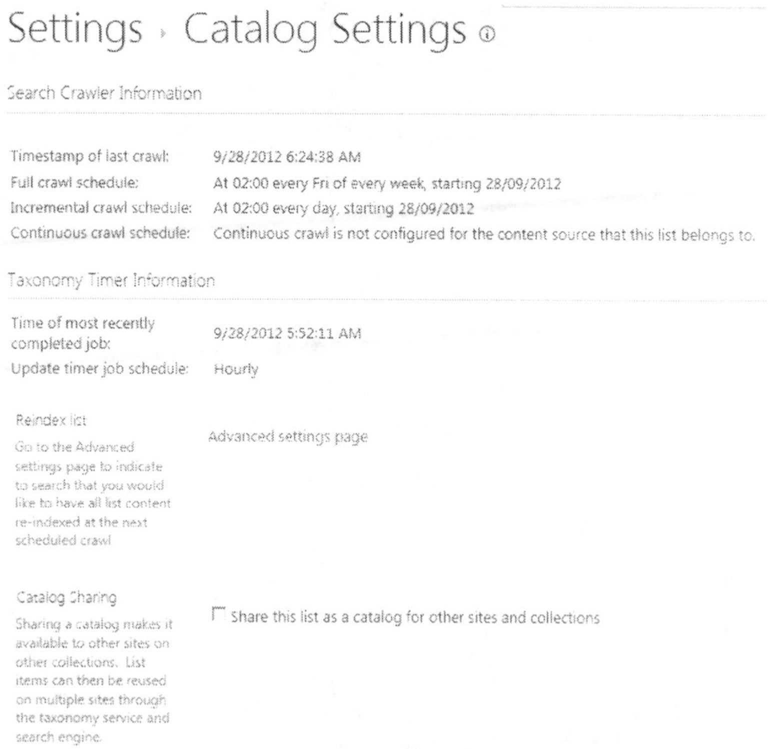

Settings › Catalog Settings ⓘ

Search Crawler Information

Timestamp of last crawl:	9/28/2012 6:24:38 AM
Full crawl schedule:	At 02:00 every Fri of every week, starting 28/09/2012
Incremental crawl schedule:	At 02:00 every day, starting 28/09/2012
Continuous crawl schedule:	Continuous crawl is not configured for the content source that this list belongs to.

Taxonomy Timer Information

Time of most recently completed job:	9/28/2012 5:52:11 AM
Update timer job schedule:	Hourly

Reindex list

Go to the Advanced settings page to indicate to search that you would like to have all list content re-indexed at the next scheduled crawl

Advanced settings page

Catalog Sharing

Sharing a catalog makes it available to other sites on other collections. List items can then be reused on multiple sites through the taxonomy service and search engine.

☐ Share this list as a catalog for other sites and collections

FIGURE 3-9 You use the Catalog Settings page to share a list or library as a catalog.

Using the Catalog Settings page, you can suggest how the friendly URLs are created so that they point to a single item in the list or library. You can choose up to five columns in the list or library that, when combined together, uniquely identify an item in the list. In the Catalog Navigation section, select the column you created earlier that maps to a term set. You can also choose to enable anonymous access.

After you shared a list or library as a catalog and SharePoint 2013 has subsequently crawled the list or library, you can then manage your catalog connections on the Manage Catalog Connections page. To access this, on the Site Settings page, in Site Administration section, click Manage Catalog Connection. It is the configurations on the Manage Catalog Connection page that sites use to render content from the catalog. For example, you can specify whether to auto create the category page or specify an existing page.

SharePoint Server 2013 includes a new publishing site collection template, the Product Catalog Site Collection, as demonstrated in Figure 3-10.

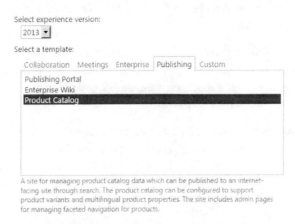

Template Selection

Select experience version:

2013 ▾

Select a template:

Collaboration   Meetings   Enterprise   **Publishing**   Custom

Publishing Portal
Enterprise Wiki
Product Catalog

A site for managing product catalog data which can be published to an internet-facing site through search. The product catalog can be configured to support product variants and multilingual product properties. The site includes admin pages for managing faceted navigation for products.

FIGURE 3-10 Use the Product Catalog Site Collection to store and maintain data that is used in catalog scenarios.

By default, the XSP site collection feature is automatically activated in the Product Catalog Site Collection. However, you must still configure the catalog settings to share content with other site collections, just as you would with lists and libraries on other sites.

When a catalog-enabled list or library is connected to a publishing site collection, a *Result Source* is automatically created for the list or library. Result Sources are a combination of the Federated Search and Search Scopes from SharePoint 2010, both of which are detailed in Chapter 2, "Introducing the new search architecture." Basically, they are used to narrow the scope from which the search results can be retrieved; therefore, the Result Source created for a library or list is limited to content within the library or list. You can also copy a Result Source or change it to specify an even narrower search result scope.

Category pages

Category pages are page layouts that are used for displaying structured content such as catalog data. You use category pages to aggregate content that meets certain criteria or parameters that are closely tied to Managed Navigation.

As with SharePoint Server 2010, you created page layouts to provide a set of pages with a uniform layout. So too is the purpose of catalog pages; however, you do not need to create as many category pages as you had to do with page layouts. They will still define how and where the content is to be presented—for example, a title in bold, followed by other information—but because they are search driven, using search and catalog-related Web Parts, you will not need as many.

Category pages can be auto created or you can create them yourself. Web Parts that you will use to create category pages include the following:

- **Catalog Item Reuse Web Parts**   You use this Web Part to reuse or republish the content of an item from a catalog.

- **Items from a Catalog**   Use this to show items from the site's lists or libraries that have been configured as a catalog. When this Web Part if added to a page, by default it displays items from the default catalog that match the page's navigation context. You can edit the Web Part's properties to modify the search criteria.

- **CSWP**   Although not specially linked to catalogs, with this Web Part, you can show content that is the result sets of a search query that you specify as a Web Part property. When added to a page, the default configuration of the Web Part is to display recently modified lists and library content from the current site. This Web Part is especially powerful when it is used in combination with Managed Navigation and category pages.

- **CQWP**   This was the most-used content rollup Web part in SharePoint 2010. With the introduction of the CSWP in SharePoint 2013, this will no longer be true. However, Microsoft has made a minor improvement to the CQWP. Similar to the CSQP, the CQWP now has the ability to filter the content results by the page navigation term, as shown in Figure 3-11.

Navigation Context:

☐ Filter by page navigation term

FIGURE 3-11 Select the Filter By Page Navigation Term check box to use the CQWP with Managed Navigation.

CSWP and the CQWP

In SharePoint 2007 and 2010, most WCM sites, whether they were intranet or Internet websites, made use of the CQWP to dynamically roll up content. The CQWP uses Extensible Stylesheet Language Transformations (XSLT) to render content. SharePoint 2013 still uses XSLT; unfortunately, it is still limited to only being able to find content within a site collection.

The CSWP and other SharePoint 2013 search-related Web Parts use a JavaScript-based display template. JavaScript is client-side code; that is, it is sent from the SharePoint Server to the user's device, where the browser interprets and executes it. Although this reduces the load on the SharePoint servers and simplifies implementing custom solutions, it also introduces challenges with Internet websites, where the devices of the site's visitors are numerous and cannot be controlled or dictated by an organization. Many of the new default display templates used by the search-related Web Part rely on JavaScript to render the content. Users can disable the use of JavaScript, and therefore the browser would display SharePoint 2013 pages as blank pages. The CSWP does provide a property, *AlwaysRenderOnServer*, which when set to *true* uses server-side XSLT-based rendering, instead. The number of visitors to a SharePoint 2013 site who have JavaScript disabled might be few, but it is something to keep in mind when developing solutions.

> **More Info** You can read more about Request Management in Chapter 1, "Architectural enhancements."

Managed navigation

SharePoint 2010 introduced the MMS as a repository of hierarchical terms for tagging purposes. SharePoint 2013 uses the terms in the Term Store of MMS to provide a navigation framework for dynamically generated pages and associated SEO-friendly URLs. Each generated page is represented in the navigation hierarchy. You no longer need to author separate pages for each category in your navigation taxonomy; the framework provides a template and inheritance mechanism that creates the landing pages for each navigation link. You can associate a category page with a specific term within the term set that is used for managed navigation.

As with SharePoint 2010, you can customize navigation on WCM sites for either or both of the following:

- **Global navigation**   The top-level horizontal navigation

- **Current navigation**   The links displayed on a page's Quick Launch.

To use managed navigation on a publishing site, on the Site Settings page, in the Look And Feel section, click Navigation. Then, on the Navigation Settings page, in either the Global Navigation or Current Navigation sections, click Managed Navigation, as shown in Figure 3-12.

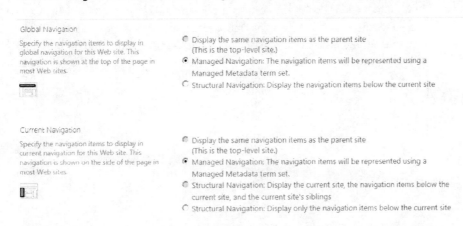

FIGURE 3-12 You can use Managed Navigation for Global Navigation and/or Current Navigation.

On the Navigation Settings page, when either of the Managed Navigation options are selected, the Managed Navigation Term Set section is dynamically displayed, in which you can select or create new term sets or open the Term Set Management Tool. You can also use this section to automatically add new pages to the navigation and create friendly URLs for those new pages, as illustrated in Figure 3-13.

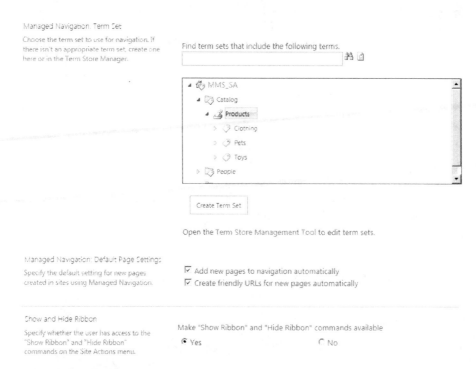

Managed Navigation: Term Set

Choose the term set to use for navigation. If there isn't an appropriate term set, create one here or in the Term Store Manager.

Find term sets that include the following terms.

- ◢ 🐾 MMS_SA
  - ◢ 📁 Catalog
    - ◢ 📁 Products
      - ▷ 📁 Clothing
      - ▷ 📁 Pets
      - ▷ 📁 Toys
  - ▷ 📁 People

Create Term Set

Open the Term Store Management Tool to edit term sets.

Managed Navigation: Default Page Settings

Specify the default setting for new pages created in sites using Managed Navigation.

☑ Add new pages to navigation automatically
☑ Create friendly URLs for new pages automatically

Show and Hide Ribbon

Specify whether the user has access to the "Show Ribbon" and "Hide Ribbon" commands on the Site Actions menu.

Make "Show Ribbon" and "Hide Ribbon" commands available

⦿ Yes   ○ No

FIGURE 3-13 Specify the default settings for new pages created in sites that use Managed Navigation.

In the Show And Hide Ribbon section, when you select Yes, a user can show or hide the ribbon, using the Show Ribbon and Hide Ribbon commands when he clicks the settings icon, as demonstrated in Figure 3-14. When No is selected, the ribbon does not display and the Show Ribbon and Hide Ribbon commands are not available on the Site Actions ribbon when the settings icon is displayed.

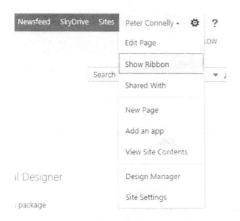

FIGURE 3-14 On the WCM site, you do not have to display the ribbon.

If you select the Managed Navigation option for both Global Navigation and Current Navigation, your page will look similar to Figure 3-15, in which Clothing, Pets, and Toys are navigation links.

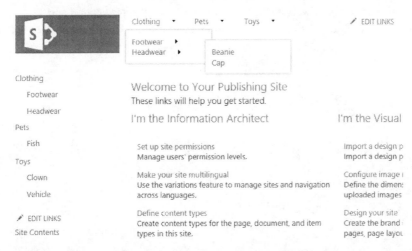

FIGURE 3-15 Global and current navigation can be created by using terms from the Term Store.

When you click one of these terms that make up the navigation, you are taken to the category page, also known as a *Term-Driven* page. However, if you selected to add new pages to the navigation automatically, you can add a new page to your navigation, and that new page will use a friendly URL, which you can see when you create the page by using the Add A Page dialog box, as shown in Figure 3-16.

FIGURE 3-16 Create a new navigation page with a friendly URL.

When you click Create, the name specified in the Give It A Name text box is added to the Term Store.

Term-Driven pages

With SharePoint 2013, using the Term Store Management Tool, you add terms to term sets to reflect the navigation that you want on your website. You can use two new tabs, Navigation and Term-Driven Pages (see Figure 3-17) to configure the navigation experience that should be rendered for the term.

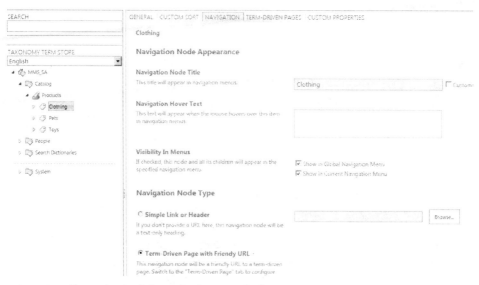

FIGURE 3-17 The navigation information for a term in the Term Store.

On the Navigation tab, you can choose between the following two Navigation Node Types:

- **Simple Link or Header** This links a term with a specific page or item.

- **Term-Driven Page with Friendly URL** Use this link to allow for friendly URLs and then click the Term-Driven Page tab to complete the configuration.

On the Term-Driven Pages tab (see Figure 3-18), you can change the friendly URL, the target page, and by clicking SEO Properties, you can set the SEO properties for the WCM page that is associated with the term.

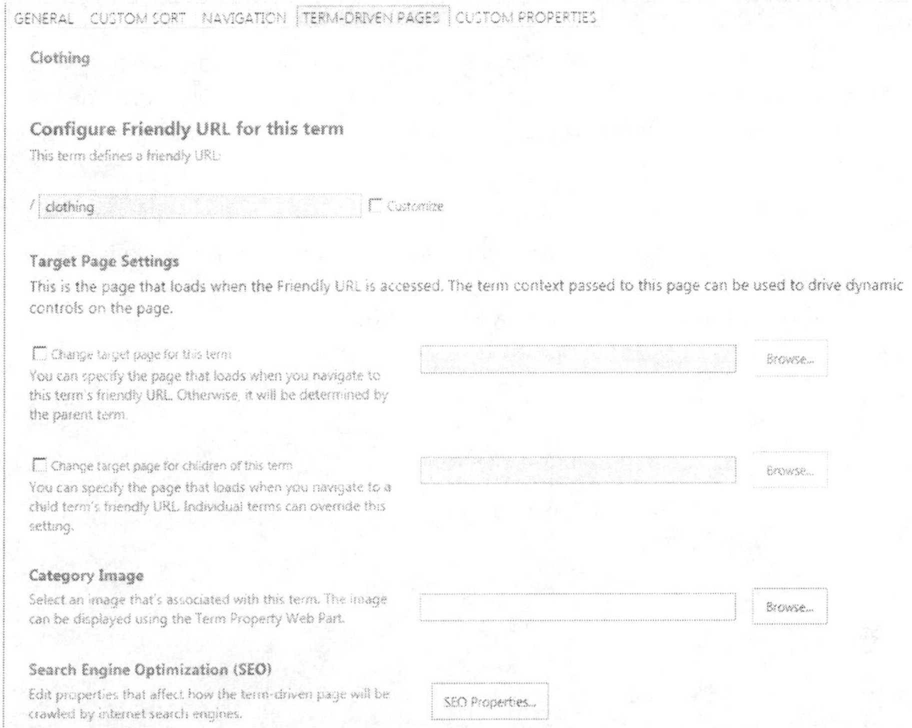
GENERAL
CUSTOM SORT
NAVIGATION
TERM-DRIVEN PAGES
CUSTOM PROPERTIES
Clothing
Configure Friendly URL for this term
This term defines a friendly URL:
/ clothing
Customize
Target Page Settings
This is the page that loads when the Friendly URL is accessed. The term context passed to this page can be used to drive dynamic controls on the page.
Change target page for this term
You can specify the page that loads when you navigate to this term's friendly URL. Otherwise, it will be determined by the parent term.
Browse...
Change target page for children of this term
You can specify the page that loads when you navigate to a child term's friendly URL. Individual terms can override this setting.
Browse...
Category Image
Select an image that's associated with this term. The image can be displayed using the Term Property Web Part.
Browse...
Search Engine Optimization (SEO)
Edit properties that affect how the term-driven page will be crawled by internet search engines.
SEO Properties...

FIGURE 3-18 Use the Term-Driven Pages tab in the Term Store Management Tool to configure what should be rendered when a user clicks the friendly URL for this term.

Variations and multilingual sites

As with SharePoint Server 2010, you can use the variations feature in SharePoint 2013 to create multilingual sites or other sites for which you need to vary the presentation of your content. The variations feature is constrained to one site collection. This means that you can create target language/locale "variants" of a source language/locale as current websites within the same SharePoint site collection.

Variations support friendly URLs, the use of the new Machine Translation Service Application to do the initial translation of pages, and have the ability to export or import content for translation by a translation agency in XML Localization Interchange File Format (XLIFF) file format. You can include labels, a page for translation and replication, and a variety of list items (for example, document libraries and navigation) in a translation package. After the translation agency has translated content, it saves it back to an XLIFF file, which is imported back into SharePoint 2013. SharePoint 2013 then places the translated content automatically in the correct variation location, where the original translation package was created, and then sets the page as a draft pending approval.

Device Channels

Device Channels are a new feature in SharePoint 2013 with which you can vary the presentation of content for mobile devices from the underlying site content and structure. Depending on the device, you can specify the master pages to use, thereby avoiding hard-coding in a master page content what needs to be localized.

To define Device Channels at a site level, on the site settings page, under Look And Feel click Device Channels. The Device Channels page is displayed and will list at least one Device Channel: Default. The Default Channel is automatically created for you. Click New Item to create a new Device Channel, enter Name, Alias, and Device Inclusion Rules, as shown in Figure 3-19, and then scroll down and select the Active check box.

Name *

Windows Phone

The name used by authors and others to identify this channel

Alias *

WindowsPhone

Pick a word to identify this channel in code, Device Channel panels, previews and other contexts. Warning: If you later change the channel alias, you will have to manually update Master Page mappings, Device Channel panels, and any custom code or markup.

Description

Windows Phone Device Channel

A quick description of the Device Channel

Device Inclusion Rules *

Mozilla/5.0 (compatible; MSIE 9.0; Windows Phone OS 8.0; Trident/5.0; IEMobile/9.0;)

Specify one or more user agent substrings (for example: Windows Phone OS), placing each substring on its own line. When the user agent string of a visiting device contains any of the specified substrings, the channel will force site pages to display using that channel's optimizations, like a different Master Page or Device Channel Panel. You can also trigger this special rendering by using query strings, cookies or custom code, in which case the substrings don't matter

FIGURE 3-19 Creating a Device Channel for mobile devices.

 Note The Device Channels page lists all the Device Channels you have created. Ensure that the Default Channel is the last channel in the list. SharePoint checks devices against the Device Channel in the order in which they appear in the list. If the Default Channel is first, any Device Channels you create will not be used.

Next, you need to develop a master page for the Device Channel you just created, and then under Look And Feel on the Site Settings page, click Master Page and select the custom master page you created. You can also specify what content is rendered in which Device Channel, by including the new Mobile Panel on your page layout. This control can be mapped to one or more Device Channels; if the device matches one or more of those Device Channels, all of the contents of the Device Channel Panel are rendered. To test the different Device Channels in your browser, append ?DeviceChannel=<*Device ChannelAlias*> to the page's URL, where <*DeviceChannelAlias*> is the alias that you assigned.

Search engine optimization

SharePoint 2013 introduces native support for SEO on WCM pages. This is particularly important on public-facing sites, on which you want your targeted visitors to be able to use web search engine sites such as Bing and Google to find content on your site, and you want your content for specific queries to appear high in the result set.

> **Note** According to Wikipedia, SEO is the process of improving the visibility of a website or a webpage in a search engine's "natural" or unpaid ("organic" or "algorithmic") search results.

SharePoint 2013 includes features such as friendly URLs, home page redirects, XML sitemaps, and custom SEO properties with which you can flexibly define the browser title and <Meta> tag descriptions and keywords, and easier-to-understand URLs for multilingual site variations.

From a search perspective, you can improve the ranking of a site's content in a number of ways. Some depend on how content is entered by content owners and some depend on SEO technology-related tactics such as XML sitemaps and meta tags.

SEO properties

With SharePoint 2010, you could extend the platform for building public-facing websites; however, it did not provide any SEO functionality out of the box. To set SEO properties, on the ribbon, on the Page tab, click the Edit Properties button, and then click Edit SEO Properties (see Figure 3-20). SharePoint 2013 allows you to set SEO properties for a WCM page, as demonstrated in Figure 3-21.

FIGURE 3-20 Use the Edit SEO Properties command to set SEO properties for a publishing page.

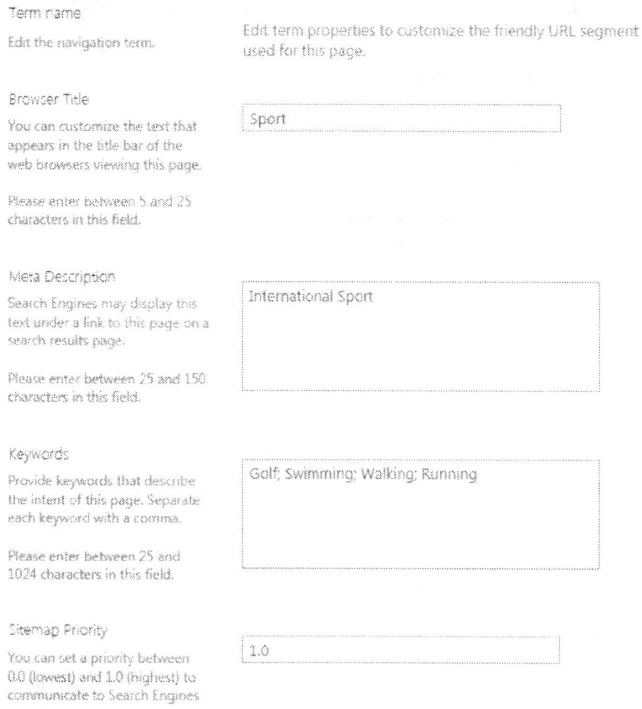

Term name

Edit the navigation term.

Edit term properties to customize the friendly URL segment used for this page.

Browser Title

You can customize the text that appears in the title bar of the web browsers viewing this page.

Please enter between 5 and 25 characters in this field.

> Sport

Meta Description

Search Engines may display this text under a link to this page on a search results page.

Please enter between 25 and 150 characters in this field.

> International Sport

Keywords

Provide keywords that describe the intent of this page. Separate each keyword with a comma.

Please enter between 25 and 1024 characters in this field.

> Golf; Swimming; Walking; Running

Sitemap Priority

You can set a priority between 0.0 (lowest) and 1.0 (highest) to communicate to Search Engines

> 1.0

FIGURE 3-21 With SharePoint 2013 you can set SEO Properties for a WCM page.

Another way that you can access the SEO Properties page is by clicking the Term-Driven Pages tab for the term in the Term Store (refer to Figure 3-18) and then clicking SEO Properties.

When a page is linked to an MMS term, the SEO properties are stored in the Term Store (Custom Local Term Properties) and as values in site columns associated with the Pages library. The SEO site columns are added to the Pages library via the Page content type. The publishing page SEO properties provided with SharePoint 2013 include the following:

- **Title Page**   The title that is used when a link to the page is displayed in any navigation interface.

- **Browser Title**   The page title displayed in the title bar of browsers. This is also used in organic search results.

- **Meta Description**   Used sometimes in organic search results.

- **Keywords**   Rarely used by web search engines.

- **Sitemap Priority**   Used when generating an XML Sitemap.

- **Sitemap Change Frequency**   Used when generating XML Sitemap.

- **Exclude from Internet Search Engines**   Sets the *noindex* value of an HTML robots meta tag and requests that automated web robots do not index the page.

You can use the SEO metadata to create views for the Pages library when using XSP or retrieve them programmatically. The ribbon command and the SEO site columns are created when the site collection feature SearchEngineOptimization is activated. This is a hidden site collection feature that is activated on publishing sites.

Site collection SEO settings

On the Site Settings page, at the top-level site of a site collection, in the Site Collection Administration section, click the link labeled Search Engine Optimization Settings to display the Search Engine Optimization Settings page, as shown in Figure 3-22.

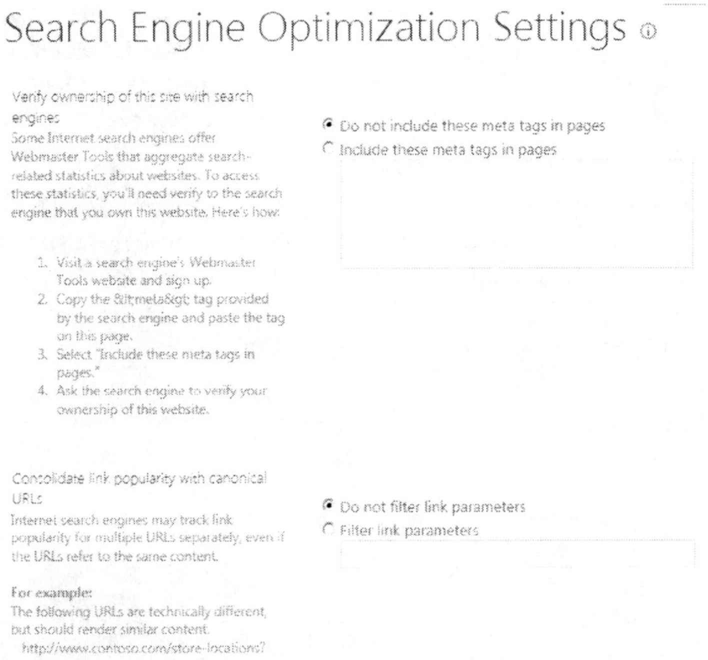

Search Engine Optimization Settings ⓘ

Verify ownership of this site with search engines
Some Internet search engines offer Webmaster Tools that aggregate search-related statistics about websites. To access these statistics, you'll need verify to the search engine that you own this website. Here's how:

1. Visit a search engine's Webmaster Tools website and sign up.
2. Copy the <meta> tag provided by the search engine and paste the tag on this page.
3. Select "Include these meta tags in pages."
4. Ask the search engine to verify your ownership of this website.

◉ Do not include these meta tags in pages
◯ Include these meta tags in pages

Consolidate link popularity with canonical URLs
Internet search engines may track link popularity for multiple URLs separately, even if the URLs refer to the same content.

For example:
The following URLs are technically different, but should render similar content.
http://www.contoso.com/store-locations?

◉ Do not filter link parameters
◯ Filter link parameters

FIGURE 3-22 Use the Search Engine Optimization Settings page to verify ownership and consolidate link popularity for all sites in a site collection.

With SharePoint 2013, you can set the following SEO settings at the site-collection level:

- Define meta tags to verify the ownership of the sites within the site collection with Web Analytics services on the Internet.

- Consolidate link popularity with canonical URLs by indicating to search engines the query string parameters that influence the meaningful rendering of content on pages in the site collection.

Note For the SEO properties to be rendered on WCM pages, the *AdditionalPageHead* Delegate control must be included on the Master Page associated with your WCM pages.

XML Sitemap

By activating the Search Engine Sitemap feature at the site-collection level, SharePoint 2013 will generate an XML Sitemap, also known as the *SEO site map*. Anonymous access must be enabled at the web application on the Default Zone to use this feature. By default, a Search Engine timer job for each web application runs daily, which generates search engine sitemaps and updates the *robots.txt* file for site collections that have activated the site collection feature.

Web design and developer enablement

With SharePoint 2013, the webpage markup has been redesigned to reduce the number of bytes-over-the-wire and the complicated CSS hierarchy. Microsoft's aim with this release of SharePoint was to make changing the look and feel of SharePoint sites easier for web designers. Designers no longer need to understand SharePoint as fully as they had to with SharePoint 2010. However, they still must understand HTML, CSS, and JavaScript.

With SharePoint 2013, web designers can continue to use the tools with which they are familiar, such as Adobe Dreamweaver and Microsoft Expression Studio. Microsoft has tried to differentiate SharePoint logic from the HTML rendering logic. SharePoint pages, the markup, ASP.NET, and SharePoint controls are exposed to generic HTML editors as HTML templates. Web Parts and Web Part zones no longer use tables, but are rendered by using HTML <div> tags.

Design Manager

SharePoint 2013 includes a new way to build master pages and page layouts, and as a result, Microsoft SharePoint Designer is no longer needed. In its place, Microsoft has created a new tool available on every WCM site called the Design Manager.

> **Note** Although you do not need to use SharePoint Designer any longer to design master pages and page layouts on WCM sites. There is no built-in design tool for a collaboration site. This would not be significant if you could still use SharePoint Designer 2013 for developing and prototyping web design solutions. However, the Design view and therefore also the Split view in SharePoint Designer 2013 has been removed. This significantly complicates the management and further development of existing SharePoint Designer customizations such as mashups and interactive solutions that made use of the Data View Web Part. This will severely impact super users or end user champions who build business solutions who are not comfortable working in code view. One workaround is to use SharePoint Designer 2010 on SharePoint 2013 sites as shown at: *http://www.wonderlaura.com/Lists/Posts/Post.aspx?ID=187*.

Figure 3-23 shows the Design Manager, which is available by clicking the Settings icon drop-down list. The Design Manager presents you with a step-by-step approach for creating design assets that you can use to brand sites.

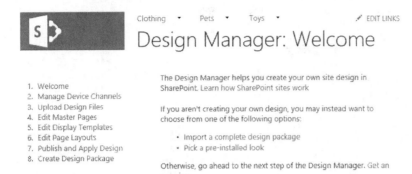

Clothing ▾   Pets ▾   Toys ▾   ✎ EDIT LINKS

Design Manager: Welcome

1. Welcome
2. Manage Device Channels
3. Upload Design Files
4. Edit Master Pages
5. Edit Display Templates
6. Edit Page Layouts
7. Publish and Apply Design
8. Create Design Package

The Design Manager helps you create your own site design in SharePoint. Learn how SharePoint sites work

If you aren't creating your own design, you may instead want to choose from one of the following options:

- Import a complete design package
- Pick a pre-installed look

Otherwise, go ahead to the next step of the Design Manager. Get an overview

FIGURE 3-23 You can use the Design Manager to create your own site designer for WCM sites in SharePoint 2013.

You can upload your design files, such as images, HTML, and CSS, and then create your master pages and page layouts.

SharePoint 2013 also includes HTML versions of several master pages and page layouts that can be used as starter templates. There is also a Master Page From Minimal Template option, which automatically creates the associated .master file.

Snippet Gallery

The Design Manager provides a Snippet Gallery (see Figure 3-24). On the ribbon, on the Design tab, you can select a component, including a Web Part, and configure its properties, update the HTML code snippets, copy the code that's generated, and paste the snippet into an HTML file. The Snippet Gallery provides you with a preview of the component, and if you copy the snippet to your HTML editor, a preview of the HTML snippet will display there, too. You add SharePoint components to your HTML files, add CSS to brand them, and then update to the HTML file. The changes are automatically synchronized to the associated master page or page layout and converted into SharePoint components.

FIGURE 3-24 The Snippet Gallery provides you with components that you can use on master pages and page layouts.

You can create an HTML snippet of ASP.NET markup and add that to your HTML master page or page layout.

Design packaging

With SharePoint 2010, when you developed design solutions with SharePoint Designer 2010 that you needed to deploy to a different site collection, you had to use Microsoft Visual Studio 2008 to create a SharePoint Solution Package (.wsp file), which you then had to upload into the Solutions Gallery and activate.

Now in SharePoint 2013, using the Design Manager, you can also create and test a design in a separate environment or site collection before deploying your changes to other site collections. With the Design Manager, you can export the package in a single .wsp file called a design package, as shown in Figure 3-25.

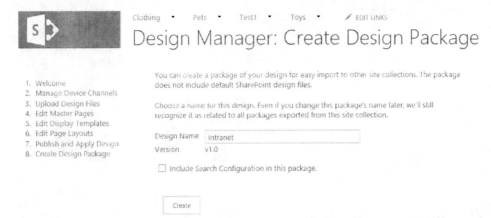

FIGURE 3-25 You can use Design Manager to create a design package.

You can export all of the contents into a design package that you have added or changed in the Master Page Gallery, Style Library, Theme Gallery, the Device Channels list, and Page content types.

 Note A design package does not include pages, navigation settings, or the Term Store.

Improvements in the text editor

SharePoint 2013 includes improvements with respect to entering static content across all page types; for example, your users will be able to use these advances on wiki pages on team sites, entering or modifying content within the Content Editor Web Part (CEWP), and on WCM pages.

Using the clipboard

When you paste content from other websites, by default, the paste command maintains the formatting from the copy or cut source. When pasting contents from other programs, such as Microsoft Word, by default, the content is unformatted, semantically correct HTML markup. This is known as Paste Clean, as depicted in Figure 3-26. This is a new option in SharePoint 2013. If the text you're copying contains links or is categorized as a heading 1, heading 2, or bold, those categories will be translated to <h1>, <h2>, and <strong> HTML tags. However, if the text is styled, such as red font, the style will not be copied to the page. To paste the unformatted text, click the down-arrow for the Paste command and then click Paste Plaintext.

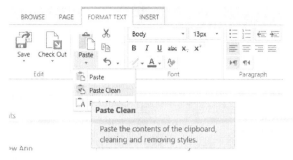

FIGURE 3-26 Paste Clean is a new option in SharePoint 2013.

Embedding and storing video in SharePoint

SharePoint 2013 includes the new content types Video, Video Rendition, and Audio that can be added to any document library or site asset library. Content owners can use these content types to manage video and audio content, add a better title, description, thumbnail, related documents, tag individuals, and so on, all side-by-side in the video player page. For an end user with a HTML5-compatible browser, SharePoint generates HTML so that the new HTML5 video player is used; otherwise, SharePoint defaults to generate code to use Silverlight. Both the video file and its metadata are crawled by search.

> **Note** SharePoint 2013 still only supports progressive download of video, not full media streaming.

SharePoint 2013 also provides the ability to embed HTML code to play audio and video that is not stored in SharePoint. On the ribbon, on the Insert tab, there are two new commands, Video And Audio and Embed Code, as shown in Figure 3-27. With these commands, you can embed external sources, such as Bing Maps, Vimeo videos, YouTube videos, and other resources directly into the HTML content on an article page. With SharePoint 2010, you had to use the HTML Form Web Part or other Web Parts.

FIGURE 3-27 Use the Video And Audio and Embed Code commands on the ribbon to embed or store video.

This new feature makes it possible for IFrames to be embedded in a page, which can be seen as a potential scripting security risk. A site collection administration can use the HTML Field Security page (see Figure 3-28) to prevent users from using these commands. To navigate to the HTML Field Security page, on the site settings page, click HTML Field Security.

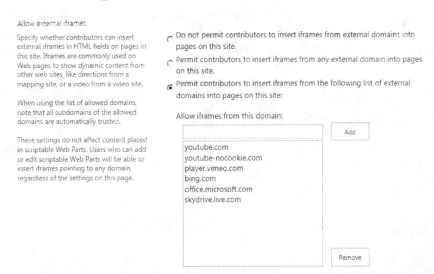

Site Settings ▸ HTML Field Security ⓘ

Allow external iframes

Specify whether contributors can insert external iframes in HTML fields on pages in this site. Iframes are commonly used on Web pages to show dynamic content from other web sites, like directions from a mapping site, or a video from a video site.

When using the list of allowed domains, note that all subdomains of the allowed domains are automatically trusted.

These settings do not affect content placed in scriptable Web Parts. Users who can add or edit scriptable Web Parts will be able to insert iframes pointing to any domain, regardless of the settings on this page.

○ Do not permit contributors to insert iframes from external domains into pages on this site.

○ Permit contributors to insert iframes from any external domain into pages on this site.

● Permit contributors to insert iframes from the following list of external domains into pages on this site:

Allow iframes from this domain:

[   ]   Add

youtube.com
youtube-nocookie.com
player.vimeo.com
bing.com
office.microsoft.com
skydrive.live.com

Remove

FIGURE 3-28 You can specify whether contributors can insert external IFrames in HTML field on pages in the site.

By default, the last option is selected. This limits what contributors can insert to only trustful web sources.

Introducing image renditions

With SharePoint 2010, many users loaded images they had taken with their camera or phone, and then reduced the size of the image on the page. This did not alter the image file, but established width and height attributes in the HTML <img> tag. The browser then uses those attributes to display the image file at a size that is different than that of the physical size of the image as stored in the image file. On WCM sites, content authors were trained to optimize images before they were uploaded into SharePoint. In many cases, they had to produce a number of different sizes for the same picture, known as renditions.

With SharePoint 2013, you can use image renditions to display uploaded images in predefined sizes, widths, and crops. You can create more than one rendition of a source image file, which means that you can set the display characteristics once and apply them to any number of images. For example, a rendition named "Article_image" displays a full-sized image in an article, whereas the rendition called "Thumbnail_small" displays a smaller version of the image. Before image renditions can be used in SharePoint 2013, the SharePoint server administrator must enable binary large object (BLOB) cache for each web application where it needs to be used.

Summary

This chapter introduced the new features with ECM. SharePoint 2013 introduces a new site collection—the Discovery Center, which serves as a portal for managing eDiscovery cases. From this single location, you can discover content in one or more SharePoint farms, in Exchange Server 2013, on file shares, and in Lync 2013 when content is archived to Exchange 2013.

WCM is another area in which Microsoft has significantly invested. There is now a new publishing model involving search-driven content with which you can see content across site collection boundaries and even web application boundaries. Using Managed Navigation, you can now define the structure of your site, and by tagging the content with the right terms, you can ensure that the content will be published at the right location in your website. Much of this is built about the new features in MMS and the new search architecture that was discussed in the Chapter 2. One of the new capabilities of SharePoint 2013 is the native support for SEO of public-facing websites.

In this context optimization with SharePoint 2013, Microsoft has not only concentrated on optimizing the code but also optimizing the site for the visitors, the content authors, and provided new tools for the web designer.

CHAPTER 4

Social computing

Social computing is a big investment area in Microsoft SharePoint Server 2013, which now functions like Facebook and Twitter. SharePoint 2013 includes a number of new social features that can assist users in your organization to share ideas. Some of the most significant include the following:

- Microblogs

- Hash tags and @mentions

- Company, site, and personal newsfeeds

- Hash tag trending and other social analytics via the new search engine

- Community sites

- Richer SharePoint user profiles populated with useful social information

- Gamification (users can now earn badges to promote engagement)

The other significant social computing event that occurred in the middle of 2013 was Microsoft's acquisition of the office social network site, Yammer, which is a tool for making companies and organizations more productive through the exchange of short frequent answers to one simple question. At the time that this chapter was written, there was no out-of-the-box integration of SharePoint Server 2013 and Yammer.

SharePoint Server 2013 Enterprise social networking

The social and collaboration features in SharePoint Server 2013 help users to connect and communicate with each other and find, track, and share important content and information. These features are exposed through the use of My Sites, Team sites, and Community sites. Community sites are created from a new site template, Community Site. My Sites and Team sites are centered on people, feeds, and following, whereas Community sites are centered on discussions and reputations; for example, What's Happening displays how many members, discussions, and replies the community has. Also community features can be activated on existing collaboration sites.

Note To investigate the important areas in Enterprise Social Networking (ESN), Microsoft hired Harris Interactive to conduct a study concerning ESN usage and adoption. The survey found that 59 percent of respondents consider it "absolutely essential" or "extremely important" for ESN software to be integrated with their companies' existing infrastructure. Regarding which types of communications ESN software should facilitate, 67 percent of respondents said instant messaging, followed by email (64 percent); video conferencing (62 percent); being able to "follow" people, documents, or sites (51 percent); audio conferencing (47 percent); activity streams (34 percent); video sharing (33 percent); being able to "like" content or people (28 percent); and microblogging (26 percent). You can find an executive summary of the report at: *download.microsoft.com/download/B/D/D/BDDDA21D-2B10-4426-BC89-944E5AC56112/Harris_Interactive-Executive_Summary.docx.*

User profiles and My Sites (also known as personal sites) have been around for a number of Share-Point Server releases. A user profile is a collection of properties that describes a single user. The User Profile service application maintains the policies and other settings associated with each property. User profiles help identify connections between users in an enterprise, such as their common managers, workgroups, group membership, and common websites. They can also contain important information about a user, such as the products a user works on, the user's interests or areas of expertise, and a user's place in the organization's structure. User Profile properties are displayed on a profile page, which is separate from a user's My Site. User profiles provide the basis for social computing in SharePoint Server 2013. Some of the ESN features that user profiles support are as follows:

- My Sites
- Profile pages
- People searching
- Organizational charts
- Expertise search
- Social tagging
- Audiences

Note Organization profiles are deprecated in SharePoint Server 2013.

Organizations can decide whether to allow users a profile page or a profile page and a My Site. If a user has a profile page but no My Site, many of the social computing features of SharePoint Server 2013 will not be available to them; however, they will be able to do the following:

- Visit and edit their profile. Users can enter any information about themselves that they want, including adding a photo.

- Follow people. Through their People page, users can see and reply to the latest Microblog posts.

- Visit the profile pages of other people.

- Have people @mention them, which results in the user receiving an email.

Users who do not have a My Site will not be able to do the following:

- Create any root microblog posts.

- View Microblog posts of people they are following in the consolidated feeds Web Part.

- Redirect from the Newsfeed page to their Profile page.

- Follow content.

- Follow tags.

- Aggregate tasks.

- Upload documents or complete any My Site activities.

- @mention somebody.

Social computing user interface improvements

SharePoint Server 2010 greatly updated the user's My Site experience. Improvements included a snapshot display of a user's presence information as well as details of what they were blogging about. Users could identify colleagues and publicize their interests and expertise. The My Site made it possible for users to organize their information, display where they were in the organization, and give other users who visited a person's profile page an opportunity to decide if the person was the right choice to contact when looking for a specific set of skills or information. SharePoint 2010 also provided the notion of tags and a note board to which users could go to post notes. Many organizations thought of the My Site experience in SharePoint Server 2010 as an outstanding phone directory that provided more information than could be found in a Microsoft Exchange global address list. With My Site, users could find people quickly. SharePoint Server 2010, therefore, provided a start of the social framework, which has now been extended in SharePoint Server 2013.

As with SharePoint Server 2010, in SharePoint 2013, the server administrator must create a User Profile service application and a location where My Sites are to be hosted. It is best to create a separate Web Application to host My Sites, where the root site collection is created using the My Site Host site template, and the user's My Sites are created as site collections under a managed path, such as, personal. Creating the User Profile server application is the same as in SharePoint Server 2010. Once provisioned, the User Profiles service application creates three databases: Profile, Social, and Sync.

Note You can find information about user profile requirements and configuration on Spence Harbar's blog post at *www.harbar.net*.

When users have the permission to create a My Site, the out-of-the-box behavior is to allow SharePoint Server to create that site when the user click Sites in the browser. Some organizations will pre-create a user's My Site. One scenario for which the pre-creation of users' My Sites might be considered is when an organization launches its first company-wide SharePoint website. Many users, all eager to try the new functionality, might click one of the links in a very short period of time, which would result in the creation of their My Site. This results in the spawning of many My Site provisioning timer jobs. This affects the ability of the SharePoint servers to respond to other user requests and therefore could detrimentally affect users' view of the team implementing SharePoint. Pre-creating users' My Sites mitigates such a scenario. Another reason of pre-creating users' My Sites is related to operational service level agreements: the IT department might not want for all My Sites to reside in one content database. The disadvantage of pre-creating My Sites is that many users in an organization might not use them or do not need them.

If a person has not created a My Site, the first time she clicks on of the social command that requires a My Site, such as the Follow on the Share menu, a Wait A Minute pop-up message box is displayed, as shown in Figure 4-1. SharePoint will then create the My Site.

FIGURE 4-1 Users who don't have a My Site will see the Wait A Minute pop-up message box when trying to use social functionality that requires a My Site.

Note SharePoint Server 2013 includes many more social features that are attributed to the individual user. These are kept within an individual user's My Site and are therefore saved within the My Site content databases.

SharePoint Server 2013 is organized into three distinct hubs:

- **Newsfeed** This is the primary landing page for social activities in SharePoint 2013; thus, it is also referred to as the *social hub*. Newsfeed is hosted on the My Site Host site collection and provides quick access to the lists of people, documents, sites, and tags that a user is following. It is in the Newsfeed hub that users can create posts or start "conversations" by using the new microblog feature.

- **SkyDrive**   The SkyDrive hub is the Documents library (My Documents) on the user's My Site. As the link to this document library is on the global navigation, users can access their personal library from anywhere.

- **Sites**   The Sites hub displays promoted sites, sites you are following, and suggested sites.

Users can find links to the three hubs on the global navigation bar, as shown in Figure 4-2. Therefore, users no longer need to specifically visit their My Site to access social features; the social features associated with My Sites are fully integrated into the SharePoint experience.

FIGURE 4-2 You can use the Newsfeed, SkyDrive, and Sites links on the global navigation bar to access social features associated with your My Site.

Below the global navigation bar, on the Sharing menu, the following links are available:

- **Share**   Use this link to quickly share a site. In SharePoint 2010 to share a site you would navigate to the Site Permissions page. You can still use this method to configure the permission settings of the site.

- **Follow**   Use this link to follow a site. You can find the sites you follow by using the Sites hub. The Follow command on the Sharing menu is only available if the Following Content site feature is activated. The Follow command can also be used to follow people, content, documents, sites, and tags. On the Newsfeed hub, you can find an aggregation of the content that you follow. Also, if you follow, for example, a document and someone else is modifying and saving that document, you will receive a notification that the user has changed the document.

- **Sync**   Use this link to create a synchronized copy of a document library in a subfolder in the SharePoint folder of your home directory (*%userprofile%\SharePoint*). The SharePoint folder is displayed under Favorites in Windows Explorer, as shown in Figure 4-3.

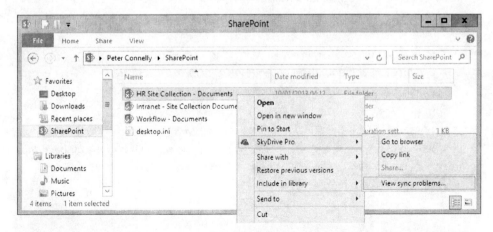

FIGURE 4-3 You can use SkyDrive Pro to take synchronized files between your computer and libraries on SharePoint sites.

The subfolder has the naming convention *<site name> - <library name>*. After you sync a library, you can access all of the files within it from Windows Explorer and Microsoft Office, even if you don't have an Internet connection. The technology used to synchronize the Share-Point library with the computer folder is SkyDrive Pro, which replaces SharePoint Workspace. SkyDrive Pro is part of Office 2013 (Standard or Professional edition) or an Office 365 sub-scription that includes Office applications.

A SkyDrive Pro icon is provided in the Windows system tray, with which you have easy access to the SkyDrive Pro menu, as shown in Figure 4-4.

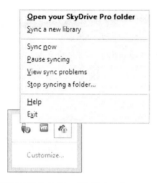

FIGURE 4-4 The SkyDrive Pro menu in the Windows system tray, which you can use to start the Sync Library Wizard.

The Newsfeed hub

Figure 4-5 shows the Newsfeed hub. It consists of four Web Part zones which you can see when the page is in edit mode. The Web Part zones are named Top Zone, Middle Left Zone, Middle Right Zone, and Bottom Zone. The Newsfeed Web Part and two hidden Web Parts—MySite Personal Site Upgrade On Navigation and MySite First Run Experience—are placed in the Middle Left Zone, and the Followed Counts and Trending Hashtags Web Parts are placed in the Middle Right Zone.

> **Note** You can find a SharePoint Newsfeed app for Windows Phone at *office.microsoft.com/en-us/office365-sharepoint-online-enterprise-help/try-the-sharepoint-newsfeed-preview-app-HA103683516.aspx*.

The MySite Personal Site Upgrade On Navigation Web Part creates or upgrades a user's personal site when the user navigates to My Site, such as, when he clicks Sites in the global navigation bar or when he clicks the down-arrow to the right of his name and then clicks About Me.

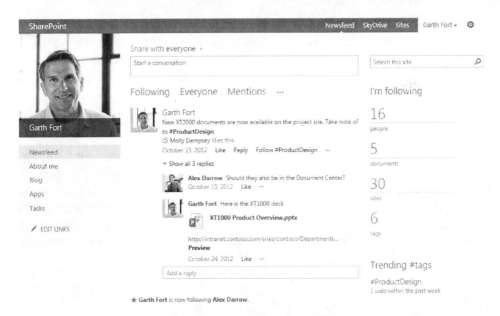

FIGURE 4-5 The Newsfeed hub, also known as the social hub of SharePoint Server 2013.

As the My Site is created, the MySite First Run Experience Web Part displays the We're Almost Ready page and the Let's Get Social dialog box, also known as the My Site privacy notification dialog box, as shown in Figure 4-6.

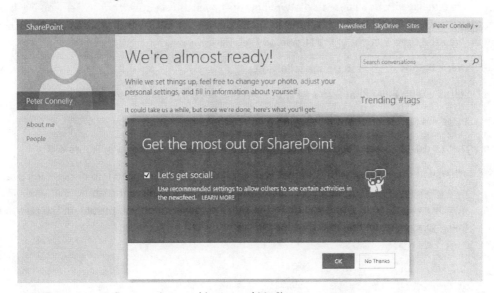

FIGURE 4-6 A user's first experience to his personal My Site.

The Followed Counts Web Part displays the counts of followed users, content, and tags for the current user. The Trending Hashtags Web Parts, also known as *AnalyticsHashTagWebPart*, is a client-side Web Part that helps the user find new social content. Together with the Newsfeed Web Part, the user can take advantage of these two Web Parts to narrow down all the information that is scattered throughout the enterprise and ensure that they can tag and follow tags.

The Newsfeed Web Part

The Newsfeed Web Part, also known as *MicroFeedWebPart*, consists of two parts: the microblogging text box (labeled Share With Everyone), and a unified overview of content that you can filter by the content that you're following, content available to everyone in your organization, content where you are mentioned, content that you like, and social activities that you have completed (such as following or microblogging and replies). The last two filters might not be immediately visible within the Newsfeed Web Part. To display the Additional Options menu, click the ellipsis to the right of Mentions, as shown in Figure 4-7.

FIGURE 4-7 Select the Additional Options menu to display Tasks assigned to you (Activities) or content that you like (Likes).

If you're familiar with popular social networking sites, such as Facebook and Twitter, you will know how to use the new microblogging features in SharePoint Server 2013, which you can use to participate in threaded conversations in the Newsfeed Web Part.

With microblogging, you can do the following:

- Start a conversation that is shared with everyone in your organization.

- Share entire conversations by copying a link to the conversation.

- Share a post to a newsfeed on a site that you are following, as shown in Figure 4-8.

    When you share a post with sites that you're following, the Newsfeed hub displays the post with site name to the right of your name. The site name is a link to the site so that you can quickly navigate to it. When you go to the site, the conversation you posted on the Newsfeed hub also appears on the newsfeed for the site.

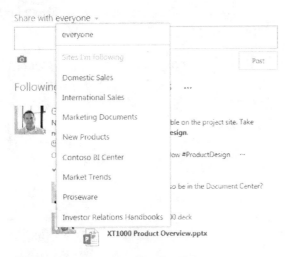

FIGURE 4-8 With the microblogging Share menu, you can post conversations to everyone in your organization or to a select group of people.

- "Like" posts in your newsfeed. People following you see posts you found interesting in their newsfeeds. You can view your "likes" later and find these posts again.

- Include pictures, videos, links to documents, and web URLs in your posts. You can modify web URLs to display as text.

- Refer to other people in your posts by entering the "@" character followed by sufficient characters to suggest the person in the autocomplete box, as shown in Figure 4-9. Initially the autocomplete box displays people who you are following, but as you type more characters and less people are found as a result, the search is expanded to Everyone. People are notified when they are mentioned in a post.

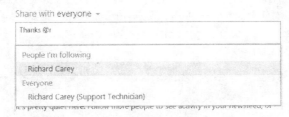

FIGURE 4-9 As you type a person's name, the autocomplete provides suggestions.

- Include tags in newsfeed posts, which are dynamically pulled from or added to the Managed Metadata Service (MMS). Similar to @mentions, an autocomplete box displays MMS tags. You can quickly view all conversations that reference that tag by clicking the tag to display the About #tag page. Also while on this page, you can add a description, edit the tag, and add related tags. When you place the cursor over a post a hover card is displayed that contains more information about the conversation, as shown in Figure 4-10.

FIGURE 4-10 You can use the About #tag page to view all conversations that reference a tag.

Site feeds

Newsfeeds are available by default on a number of sites other than My Sites, such as team sites, project sites and community sites; however, they are not available on publishing sites. The Newsfeed functionality is enabled by activating the Site Feed site feature, which creates the Microfeed app (list) and makes it possible for you to add the Site Feed Web Part to pages. It is the Site Feed Web Part that displays the microblogging text box and the aggregation newsfeeds posted to the site. By default, when the Site Feed site feature is activated on a site, the Site Feed Web Part is added to the site's home page, identified by the title Newsfeed.

Site feeds will appear on the Sites hub only when both the Site Feeds and Following Content site features are activated.

> **Note** If the Site Feed Web Part is removed from the home page so that users can quickly navigate to the site's Newsfeed, consider adding a link to the Newsfeed page. The link to a site's newsfeed follows the format http://<*sitename*>/newsfeed.aspx.

The Sites hub

Figure 4-11 shows that when a user clicks Sites on the global navigation bar, the Sites view (*sites.aspx*) of the Social app (list) on the user's My Site displays.

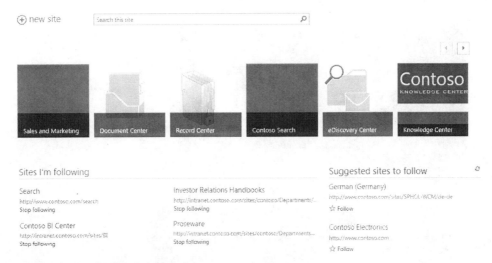

FIGURE 4-11 Use the Sites hub to find sites.

If Self-Service Site Creation is enabled on the Web Application that is hosting the My Sites, and the Start A Site Link is configured not to be hidden from users, the page contains a link to create a new site collection. The page also contains the following three Web Parts:

- The PromotedSitesWebPart displays a set of thumbnails with links to sites that are registered as promoted sites in the User Profile service application. When there are no promoted sites, the Web Part does not display anything, and users will only see the other two Web Parts. You can use Audiences if you want a link to a site that you want to display for a specific set of users.

- The Sites I'm Following Web Part, which is an XsltListViewWebPart that displays the contents of the Social app (list) that have been created by using the Followed Item content type.

- The Suggested Sites To Follow Web Part, known as ProjectSearchBrowseWebPart, suggests links to sites which are calculated by using search results based on what your colleagues are following.

Note Two new site templates included with SharePoint Server 2013 are the Community Site and Community Portal. The Community Site is designed to bring together large groups of people around a shared topic or interest, whereas the Community Portal is used at the root of a site collection to provide a directory of Community Sites. If your organization uses communities, a link is provided from the Sites hub to the Community Portal. You can only have one Community Portal per SharePoint farm. For more information on communities, go to *technet.microsoft.com/en-us/library/jj219805.aspx*.

The SkyDrive hub

When you click SkyDrive in the global navigation bar, the All view of the My Sites document library titled My Documents displays, as shown in Figure 4-12. This document library is where users can store, share, and sync their personal files.

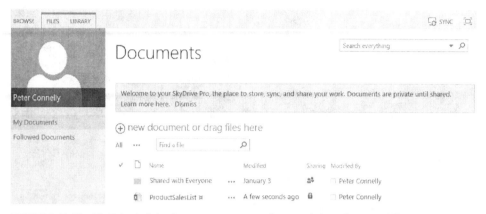

FIGURE 4-12 The SkyDrive hub is where you can store private and shared personal files.

By default any files uploaded to the SkyDrive hub are private, which is denoted by a padlock icon in the Sharing column. A folder named, Shared With Everyone, is provided in the Documents library, which can be seen by everyone. If you want to change the share permissions, click the people icon in the Sharing column to display the Shared With dialog box, as shown in Figure 4-13.

FIGURE 4-13 Use the Shared With dialog box to invite people, send everyone an email, or to change the permissions of people with whom you already share your files.

The other link on the SkyDrive hub Quick Launch is Followed Documents. When you click Followed Documents, the Followed Contents view (*FollowedContent.aspx*) page of the Social list on the user's My Site displays, as shown in Figure 4-14.

FIGURE 4-14 In the Followed Documents view of the Social list, you can find documents that you are following and suggested documents to follow.

The Followed Documents page contains two Web Parts that the Sites view of the Social list contains: an XsltListViewWebPart of the Social app (list) that displays Followed Document content type items, and ProjectSearchBrowseWebPart.

My Sites

You can visit your My Site by clicking Newsfeed or by clicking the down-arrow to the right of your name in the global navigation and then clicking About Me to display the About Me page (*person. aspx*), as shown in Figure 4-15. If you click SkyDrive or Sites, you can click the photo or name in the Quick Launch to display the About Me page.

FIGURE 4-15 Use the About Me page to edit your profile and see your most recent conversations and social activities.

The About Me page, contains the following Web Parts:

- **AskMeAboutWebPart**   This shows a list of keywords that others can ask questions on.

- **PublishedFeedWebPart**   This Web Part displays a user's most recent conversations and activities.

- **MySitePersonalSiteUpgradeOnNavigationWebPart**   This Web Part was also included on the *Newsfeed.aspx* page described earlier in this chapter.

- **ProfileInfoWebPart**   This shows basic profile information for the user.

- **MySharedContext**   This Web Part shows what is in common between the visitor to the About Me page and the user.

- **ProfileManages**   This shows the organization and reporting hierarchy of the user.

After you are on your My Site, you can use the links on the Quick Launch to create or navigate to your blog subsite and track your tasks by using the My Tasks page.

> **Note** The three Newsfeeds Web Parts, MicroFeedWebPart, PublishedWebPart, and SiteFeedWebPart, replace the functionality provided by the SharePoint 2010 Recent Activities Web Part. These three Web Parts support multithreaded conversations and dynamic feed retrieval. When they execute, they produce HTML that is used by JavaScript to retrieve information asynchronously.

The My Tasks page

The My Tasks page includes your personal tasks as well as tasks assigned to you in SharePoint, Exchange, and Project Server. All Tasks displayed in My Tasks can be connected to Microsoft Outlook, as you can with a SharePoint Tasks app. However, this does have performance implications; thus, the use of the Outlook connector with My Tasks should be closely monitored. To set up the task management feature as well as the Search and User Profile service applications, there must be a Work Management service application. To aggregate tasks from Exchange and Project servers, additional tasks must be completed as described on the Microsoft TechNet site at *technet.microsoft.com/en-us/library/jj554516(office.15).aspx*.

The My Tasks functionality is in fact a number of pages stored in the root of your My Site. You can view each page by clicking the links in the My Tasks section. The link names and their respective page names are as follows:

- **Important And Upcoming**   *Highlights.aspx*, as shown in Figure 4-16.

- **Active**   *AllTasks.aspx*.

- **Completed**   *CompleteTasks.aspx*.

- **Recently Added**   *RecentlyAssigned.aspx*. You can choose this link from the Additional Options menu.

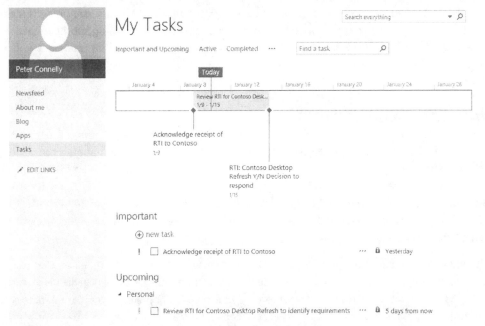

FIGURE 4-16 On the My Tasks page, you can view your personal tasks.

Apps

When you click Apps on the Quick Launch, the Site Contents page is displayed, which makes it possible for the user to create other apps and subsites. Users can also use the Site Contents page to navigate to the following three apps:

- Microsoft Feed, which is used to display some of the content on the Newsfeed hub.

- Social, which contains the two views used on the Sites hub and SkyDrive hub.

- Documents, which is the SkyDrive hub.

There are also a number of hidden lists.

My Site storage

The About Me page is stored in the My Site Host site collection content database. The Profile pictures and any pictures posted in a user's microblog are stored in the User Photos library on the My Site Host site; therefore, if a quota is placed on the My Site Host site collection that is insufficient for the number of users in your organization, users will not be able create My Sites, add profile pictures, or include pictures on their newsfeed. When a user modifies their profile properties, they are stored in the Profile database.

The quota applied by default to each personal site collection is 100 MB. If a user uploads many files into his Documents folder (SkyDrive hub), microblog, or posts to their blog subsite excessively and reaches that quota, they will not be able to post or complete any tasks that result in a write to the content database. In Office 365, each user receives a quota of 7 GB for personal sites.

Planning for social computing

As with any ESN technology, the success of social computing within an organization is not dependent on the installation of one or more products. You should not install SharePoint Server 2013, enable all the social computing features, and expect them to be adopted by users. "Technology is only a smaller portion of the answer," said by many consultants, "Sometimes as little as 10 percent." For any ESN project, you will need to spend more time and effort on people and the way they work than the products that they use.

Nearly every company and every person in a company will have a different idea of what to expect out of social computing. When you begin to deploy social computing in your organization, start with a vision. Take your time as to discover what exactly your organization wants to accomplish: to what business process are you attempting to add social capabilities, and try to figure out where you will get the most value. This will drive your strategy, which will usually entail some measurable goals so that you can prove to the business that it has achieved some return on its investment.

Enterprise social computing is different from consumer social computing—you should not try to replicate exactly the Twitter or Facebook experience in the organization. The aim of enterprise social computing is to find a way of giving users more information in the areas where they need it and more tools to make their jobs easier. It's really about providing the means for users to be more productive.

Installation lifecycle

Another aspect to take into consideration when you plan your implementation is that at the Share-Point Conference 2012, Microsoft announced the move away from major releases of SharePoint every two and a half to three years. The idea is to have a more agile approach and to push out functional changes more quickly on a recurring basis. Over the past two releases SharePoint has incorporated infrastructure changes that support such a model; therefore, any new functionally will not need a major upgrade as the core infrastructure will remain unchanged. However, there will be times when key components will be switched out; for example, in SharePoint 2013, search is an example of a component that has been drastically re-engineered. With the acquisition of Yammer, social computing might be the next component that will have a major step change.

Many organizations expect a new installation on new hardware every three years and plan their deployments and finances around a three-year release model. Now, with this agile approach to releasing new functionality in SharePoint, you might need to change your approach to implementing SharePoint projects to ensure that you build a durable solution that can accommodate rolling releases. This increases the importance of appropriate planning and governance.

If you are migrating from SharePoint Server 2010 to SharePoint Server 2013, you might consider a module approach to your SharePoint implementation, where multiple connected SharePoint farms are deployed, where each farm hosts specific functionally. The emphasis is away from one SharePoint farm, which you must ensure is of the right size, to the subsequent monitoring of performance and capacity of that farm as well as completing other daily operational tasks to ensure it continues to meet your needs. In a connected model, one or more of the farms could be managed by a third party, thereby making it possible for your organization to concentrate on taking advantage of the features and building solutions to meet business needs.

Social computing might be the trigger to consider going to a connected model, whereas previously, you only installed one farm. One farm could host your organization's My Sites and collaboration sites on SharePoint 2013; the rest of the farms could still be using SharePoint Server 2010. The farm that hosted your My Sites could be SharePoint Online, which is often referred to as a hybrid model. The advantage of using SharePoint Online as compared to other third-party hosting companies is the Active Directory synchronization capabilities of Office 365 with on-premise Active Directory domains.

Related SharePoint components

To take advantage of the full social computing functionality, you must deploy the following:

- Search is a major dependency for social computing within SharePoint Server 2013. It is used for security trimming, for returning social activities, and for improving the ranking. Before deploying any other components you must install Search and verify that it is working correctly.

- MMS, because this is used for #Tags and interests.

- You will need a number of Web Applications. The number you need can be reduced with the preference to use Host Named Site Collections (HNSC), which were discussed in Chapter 1, "Architectural Enhancements"; however, it is still best to separate My Sites site collections (and the My Site Host site collection) in their own Web Application from the Web Application(s) for other site collections.

- A User Profile service application. In SharePoint Server 2013 the User Profile process is still based on a User Profile service application, and because the service application infrastructure has not changed in SharePoint 2013, creating a User Profile service application has not changed.

Optional services could include the Business Connectivity Services (BCS) as well as the supporting infrastructure to incorporate properties from the authoritative identity management source.

 Note You can find planning worksheets to assist in the planning of user profiles or the planning and configuring of profile synchronization at *www.microsoft.com/en-us/download/search.aspx?q=sharepoint+2013+profile+worksheets.*

Identity management

Undoubtedly, any social computing project will entail internal politics, especially as nearly all the social computing features within SharePoint Server take advantage of User Profiles in some way. Therefore, your organization's strategy to Identity Management (IdM) is important, and it will become more important as the breadth of social features in SharePoint Server grows.

Business decisions must be made as to what makes up a individual's persona, where the profile properties are to be obtained, which properties are to be exposed, and who will be able to see them, as well as taking into consideration privacy policies, regional regulations, and so on.

Although Active Directory (AD) plays a major role in your SharePoint installation, it might not be the authoritative source for identity and you will need to discover or get agreement as to where the authoritative source is. All the identity information might not reside in one location. Wherever you are going to get the properties, they need to be up to date and fresh, and there needs to be a business process backup by technology that keeps them in that state. Properties in AD can be augmented with properties from other systems by using the BCS.

The User Profile synchronization process

When SharePoint 2010 was first released, there were problems starting the User Profile synchronization process. Now, the results of a monumental effort—implemented in stages through cumulative updates to SharePoint 2010—form the basis for the synchronization process in SharePoint 2013. The User Profile service application in SharePoint Server 2013 uses the same build of Microsoft Forefront Identity Manager (FIM) and Microsoft Identity Manager Synchronization Service (FIMSS), 4.0.2450.47 (see Figure 4-17) that first appeared in the SharePoint Server 2010 February 2012 cumulative update (CU). The locations of the files for these two services are:

- FIM (*Microsoft.ResourceManagement.Service.exe*):

  %ProgramFiles%\Microsoft Office Servers\15.0\Service

- FIMSS (*miiserver.exe*):

  %ProgramFiles%\Microsoft Office Servers\15.0\Synchronization Service\Bin

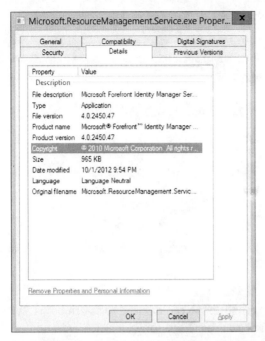

FIGURE 4-17 The details of the FIM Windows service.

In SharePoint Server 2013, you can see several optimizations that were already added in Share-Point 2010, such as the following:

- The addition of indexes to certain user properties that eliminate full table scans

- Importing data from the BDC in batches

- Removing unused provisioning steps

- Cleaning up unused historical data

- Moving resolution of some objects out of SharePoint and into the sync system

Profile synchronization options

As in SharePoint Server 2010, SharePoint Server 2013 has a two-way (read and write) AD synchronization process implemented via FIM; however, new with SharePoint Server 2013 is the introduction of an AD Import capability, also known as *AD Direct Mode*, as shown in Figure 4-18. Even with the optimization improvements to FIM, AD Import is faster.

Synchronization Options

To use the full-featured SharePoint Profile Synchronization option, select 'Use SharePoint Profile Synchronization'.

To use the light-weight Active Directory Import option (with some limitations - see documentation), select 'Use SharePoint Active Directory Import'.

To use an external identity manager for Profile Synchronization, select 'Enable External Identity Manager'.

Note: Enabling external identity manager will disable all Profile Synchronization options and status display in SharePoint.

◉ Use SharePoint Profile Synchronization
○ Use SharePoint Active Directory Import
○ Enable External Identity Manager

FIGURE 4-18 To use AD Import, select Use SharePoint Active Directory Import in the Synchronization Options section on the Configure Synchronization Settings page.

Note The Configuration Synchronization Settings page can be used to switch between AD Import and FIM; however, the configurations (such as filters) for your synchronization connections will not be migrated.

This is similar to the AD import functionality of Microsoft Office SharePoint Server 2007. However, in SharePoint Server 2013, it is a new implementation of this functionality. AD import is a one-way (read-only) synchronization process by which SharePoint can import AD properties but cannot update those properties. The account used to read the properties from AD still needs the Replicating Directory Permissions on the domain from which you want to read the properties.

The AD Import runs as part of the User Profile Service instance; therefore, the User Profile Synchronization Service instance does not need to be started, and although the Sync database is created when the User Profile service application is created, it will not be used.

Note You must configure synchronization settings and select AD Import before creating a synchronization connection. You can find an overview of directory synchronization at *technet.microsoft.com/en-us/library/gg188041.aspx*.

On the Add New Synchronization Connection page (see Figure 4-19), you can define one synchronization connection per AD domain; that is, if you have a forest with multiple domains, you need to create one synchronization connection for each domain in the forest.

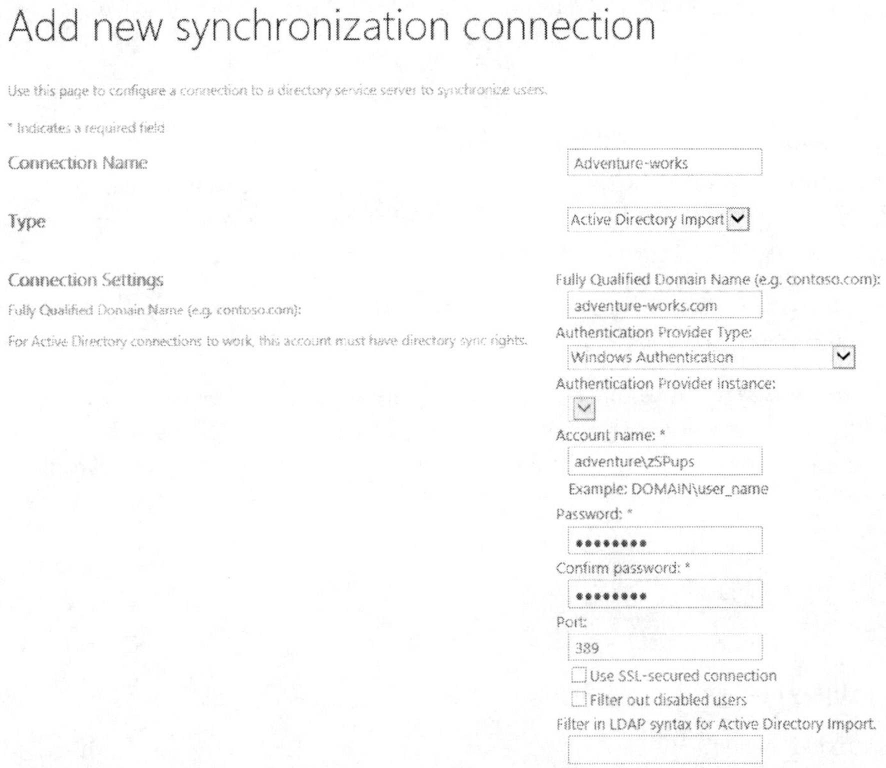

Add new synchronization connection

Use this page to configure a connection to a directory service server to synchronize users.

* Indicates a required field

Connection Name

Adventure-works

Type

Active Directory Import

Connection Settings

Fully Qualified Domain Name (e.g. contoso.com):

For Active Directory connections to work, this account must have directory sync rights.

Fully Qualified Domain Name (e.g. contoso.com):

adventure-works.com

Authentication Provider Type:

Windows Authentication

Authentication Provider Instance:

Account name: *

adventure\zSPups

Example: DOMAIN\user_name

Password: *

••••••••

Confirm password: *

••••••••

Port:

389

☐ Use SSL-secured connection

☐ Filter out disabled users

Filter in LDAP syntax for Active Directory Import:

FIGURE 4-19 You use the Add New Synchronization Connection page to enter the AD domain name and account that has Replicating Directory Permissions on the domain.

On the Add New Synchronization Connection page, you can select the Organizational Units (OUs) that contain the users and groups, and you can also specify a Lightweight Directory Access Protocol (LDAP) filter. After a full import is started, you will notice that a timer job is configured by default to complete incremental imports every five minutes. When you configure Profile Synchronization, the timer job is configured by default to complete an incremental import daily.

The AD Import functionality is constrained by the following limitations:

- You are tied to a single forest.

- Links across forests via the AD contact object are not processed.

- Mapping multivalue user profile properties to single-value profile properties, or vice versa, is not supported.

- Mapping to system SharePoint properties, that is, those that begin with SPS-, is not supported.

- Mapping two different AD attributes to the same SharePoint property is not supported.

- You cannot import additional user properties by using BCS.

Timer jobs and the role of distributed cache

Although the service application architecture has not changed, there are some aspects of the supporting platform architecture that have changed because of the new social computing features. Social computing in SharePoint 2013 consists of a number of activities that can be divided into two types:

- **User generated**   For example, microblogging activities, such as when a user creates, includes @mentions, likes, or replies to a post.

- **System generated**   These are activities that are mostly triggered by information stored in the Profile or personal site databases. For example, an activity is generated when it's a user's birthday or a user changes his job title. System-generated activities do not display on Site feeds. The User Profile Service Application - Activity Feed Job creates system-generated posts for the following events:

  - Following a tag

  - Tagging an item

  - Birthday celebration

  - Job title change

  - Workplace anniversary

  - Updates to Ask Me About

  - Posting on a note board

  After you configure My Sites, check that the User Profile Service Application - Activity Feed Job is enabled. By default, this time job is schedule to run every 10 minutes. There are a number of User Profile Service-related timer jobs, as shown in Figure 4-20.

Job Definitions

Timer Links		Service: User Profile Service ▾	View: Service ▾
Timer Job Status			
Scheduled Jobs	Title	Web Application	Schedule Type
Running Jobs	Health Analysis Job (Daily, User Profile Service, Any Server)		Daily
Job History	Health Analysis Job (Hourly, User Profile Service, Any Server)		Hourly
Job Definitions	Health Analysis Job (Monthly, User Profile Service, Any Server)		Monthly
	Health Analysis Job (Weekly, User Profile Service, Any Server)		Weekly
Central Administration	User Profile Service Application - Activity Feed Cleanup Job		Daily
Application Management	User Profile Service Application - Activity Feed Job		Minutes
System Settings	User Profile Service Application - Audience Compilation Job		Weekly
Monitoring	User Profile Service Application - My Site Suggestions Email Job		Monthly
Backup and Restore	User Profile Service Application - Social Data Maintenance Job		Hourly
Security	User Profile Service Application - System Job to Manage User Profile Synchronization		Minutes
Upgrade and Migration	User Profile Service Application - User Profile ActiveDirectory Import Job		Minutes
General Application Settings	User Profile Service Application - User Profile Change Cleanup Job		Daily
	User Profile Service Application - User Profile Change Job		Hourly
Apps	User Profile Service Application - User Profile Incremental Synchronization		Disabled
Configuration Wizards	User Profile Service Application - User Profile Language Synchronization Job		Hourly

FIGURE 4-20 User Profile Service-related timer jobs.

Both the user and system-generated activities are reported by a number of feeds such as the Web Parts on the Newsfeed and Sites hubs, which were described earlier in this chapter. The information for these feeds is stored and retrieved from the following:

- Content databases

- Distributed Cache, which was described in Chapter 1. Information is written to the Distributed Cache quickly and retrieved almost in real time. The Distributed Cache is divided into several caches, the two that are related to social computing are as follows:

  - **Feeds Cache (DistributedActivityFeedCache)** The Feeds Cache is where all the activity information is captured and displayed by Web Parts. This includes activities from personal sites and other sites; for example, where newsfeeds are used, such as on team sites, project sites, and community sites.

  - **Last Modified Time Cache (DistributedActivityFeedLMTCache)** The Last Modified Time Cache is used to keep track of when something was written to the My Sites content databases and to the content database of other types of sites.

This is completely different from SharePoint Server 2010, wherein all the social tagging information was stored in the Social database. Multiple User Profile service applications in a farm can cause delays in notifications. This is especially true because you can only have one Social database per User Profile service application and it is recommended that you only have one User Profile Application service application in your farm. Now, in SharePoint Server 2013, whereas much of the social tagging is stored in content databases, social computing can scale much better.

It is also best if site feeds and communities are in the same farm as the web application that hosts the My Site Host and personal site collections; otherwise, notifications in the Newsfeed and Sites hubs will not occur. This might change with future updates. Also the My Site web application and the web application that contains the collaboration sites that use newsfeeds should use the same application pool account.

Privacy settings

Privacy settings can be configured at the User Profile service application level and by users on their My Site. So, when you are planning your social computing deployment, you need to decide whether everything is to be available to all users within your organization or whether to prevent others from seeing a user's information. Remember, many of the social features available in the latest versions of SharePoint depend on open privacy settings so that others in the organization to see profile information.

Note Users can overwrite the privacy settings at the User Profile service application level regarding activities and following people privacy settings.

User Profile Service Application settings   You can modify the Privacy settings by using the SharePoint Central Administration website or by using Windows PowerShell. To display the Manage Policies page (see Figure 4-21), in the browser, on the Manage Profile Service page, in the People section, click Manage Policies.

The new settings in the Privacy Settings section are as follows:

- Following A Document Or Site On My Site

- Tagging An Item On My Site

- Workplace Anniversary On My Site

- Following A Tag On My Site

- Updating "Ask Me About" On My Site

- Liking Or Rating Something

- Participation In Communities

- Following A Person On My Site

- Posting On A Note Board On My Site

- Job Title Change On My Site

- Posting A New Blog Post

- Birthday Celebration On My Site

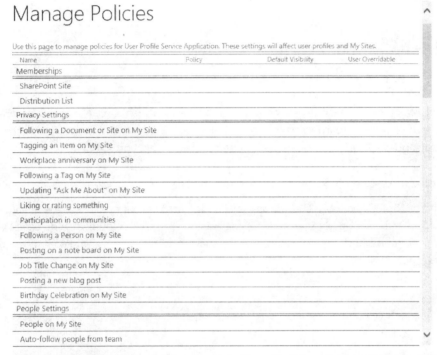

FIGURE 4-21 Use the Manage Policies page to configure the Privacy Settings at the User Profile Service Application level.

The following are the new settings in the People Settings section:

- People On My Site

- Auto-Follow People From Team

- People Recommendations

On the Manage Policies page, by hovering over a policy, a down-arrow appears that you can click to display a menu with which you can edit the policy by displaying the Edit Policy page, as shown in Figure 4-22.

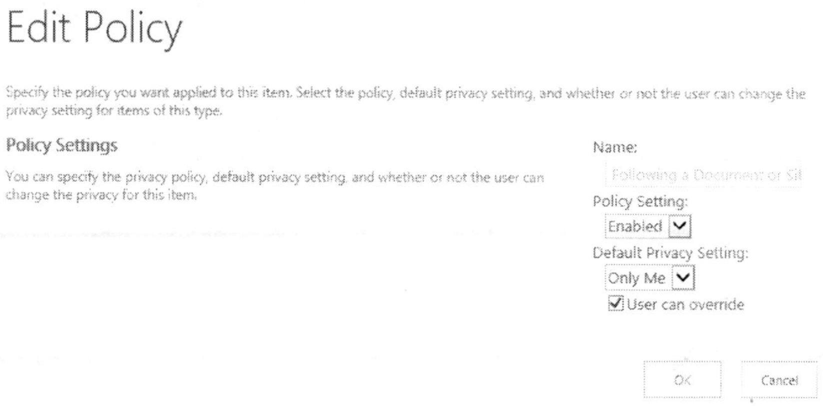

Edit Policy

Specify the policy you want applied to this item. Select the policy, default privacy setting, and whether or not the user can change the privacy setting for items of this type.

Policy Settings

You can specify the privacy policy, default privacy setting, and whether or not the user can change the privacy for this item.

Name:

Following a Document or Sit

Policy Setting:

Enabled ▾

Default Privacy Setting:

Only Me ▾

☑ User can override

OK   Cancel

FIGURE 4-22 On the Edit Policy page, you can specify the privacy policy settings and whether or not the user can change the policy.

> **Note** The Default Privacy Settings for policies contain two settings: Only Me and Everyone. The three settings that were available in SharePoint Server 2010—My Manager, My Team, and My Colleagues—have been removed. By selecting Only Me, you are deactivating feed events.

The default setting for all the My Sites privacy settings is Only Me; that is, My Sites are private by default. However, on the Set Up My Sites page for the User Profile server application, you can select the Make My Sites Public checkbox (see Figure 4-23) to make public the people who are following information and activities.

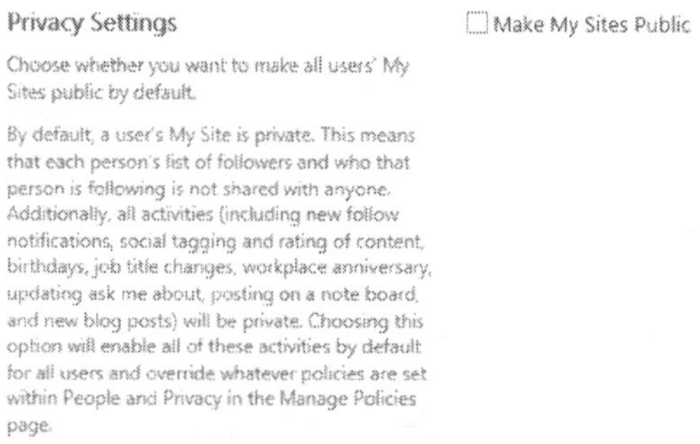

Privacy Settings

Choose whether you want to make all users' My Sites public by default.

By default, a user's My Site is private. This means that each person's list of followers and who that person is following is not shared with anyone. Additionally, all activities (including new follow notifications, social tagging and rating of content, birthdays, job title changes, workplace anniversary, updating ask me about, posting on a note board, and new blog posts) will be private. Choosing this option will enable all of these activities by default for all users and override whatever policies are set within People and Privacy in the Manage Policies page.

☐ Make My Sites Public

FIGURE 4-23 On the Set Up My Sites page, you can choose to make all user's My Sites public by default.

When the Make My Sites Public check box is selected, this has precedence over the privacy settings on the Manage Policies page; that is, the user's list of followers, the user's list of people they are following, and all activities—including new follow notifications, social tagging and rating of content, birthdays, job title changes, workplace anniversary, updating Ask Me About, posting on a note board, and new blog posts—will be public. For those privacy settings that cannot be managed by using the Manage Policies page, a message on that page informs you that "People on My Site" policy and all policies under "Privacy Settings" are ignored, as shown in Figure 4-24.

Manage Policies

Use this page to manage policies for User Profile Service Application. These settings will affect user profiles and My Sites.
The 'Make My Sites Public' feature is enabled. The 'People on My Site' policy and all policies under 'Privacy Settings' are being ignored.

Name	Policy	Default Visibility	User Overridable
Memberships			

FIGURE 4-24 A message on the Manage Policies pages displays when the Make My Sites Public option is enabled.

My Site privacy settings   When a user first visits her My Site a privacy notification displays (see Figure 4-6, earlier in this chapter). If a user clicks Learn More, a new browser window opens and displays a SharePoint Help page that explains how she can update her privacy settings.

On the privacy notification, by accepting the default, Let's Get Social, the privacy settings are automatically updated to let others see and respond to site activities. To leave the privacy settings as set at the User Profile service application level, clear the check box before clicking OK.

For users to update their privacy settings, they should complete the following steps:

1. If they are on their My Site, on the Quick Launch, click About Me. Or, at the top of a Share-Point Site, under their name, click About Me.

   The user's profile page opens.

2. To display the Edit Details page, click Edit Your Profile.

3. To the right of Details, click the ellipsis to display additional options and then click Newsfeed Settings, as shown in Figure 4-25.

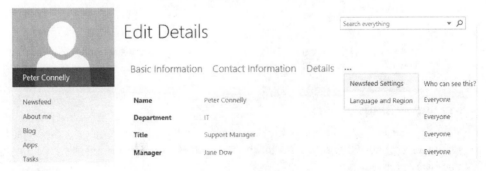

FIGURE 4-25 Users can click Newsfeed Setting to modify their privacy settings.

The Newsfeed Settings are displayed, as shown in Figure 4-26. On this page users can do the following:

- Pick what email notifications they want to receive.

- Allow others to see the people a user is following and the people following the user when they view the user's profile.

- Pick the activities that the user wants to make public.

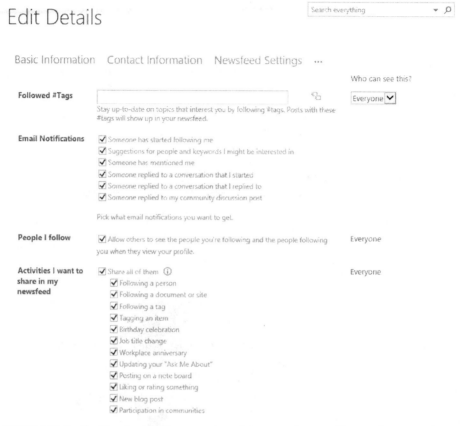

FIGURE 4-26 Use the Newsfeed Settings page to update your privacy settings to allow co-workers to see your activities in their newsfeeds.

My Site settings

Make My Sites Public is just one of the new settings on the My Site Settings page in the User Profile service application. Other settings with which you should familiarize yourself with during the planning stage are as follows:

- **Security Trimming Options** When the Check All Links For Permission option is selected, users do not see links to activity feeds, ratings, social tags, and notes if they do not have permissions to see them. Site feeds and newsfeeds posted on sites will use the permission settings on that site. Search is used for security trimming; therefore, the frequency of your incremental crawls will affect the freshness of the social activity links. This can delay the links from appearing on the My Site pages, such as the About Me page and the Newsfeed and Sites hubs. The other options in this section are: Check Only Specific Links For Permissions, and Show All Links Regardless Of Permission (see Figure 4-27). However, remember that if you decide to microblog to everyone, which is the default on the Newsfeed hub, the options in this section are irrelevant.

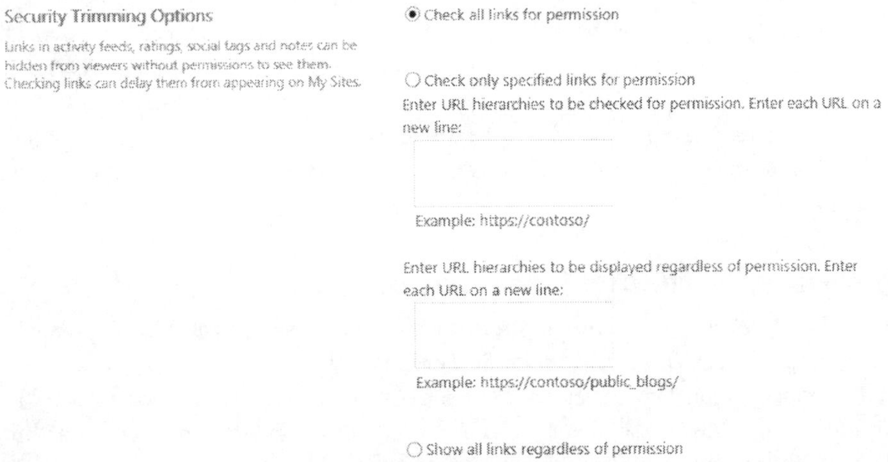

FIGURE 4-27 You can use the options in the Security Trimming Options section to decide whether to hide social activity from users who do not have permissions to see them.

- **Newsfeed** This section on the My Site Settings page contains two options, as shown in Figure 4-28. You can enable or disable activities on My Sites newsfeeds. Also, although SharePoint Server 2010 newsfeeds are deprecated, if you migrated from SharePoint Server 2010 and used newsfeeds in SharePoint Server 2010, you can incorporate those newsfeeds by selecting the Enable SharePoint 2010 Activity Migration check box. However, if you choose to incorporate them, the newsfeeds are not migrated and remain as they were in SharePoint 2010.

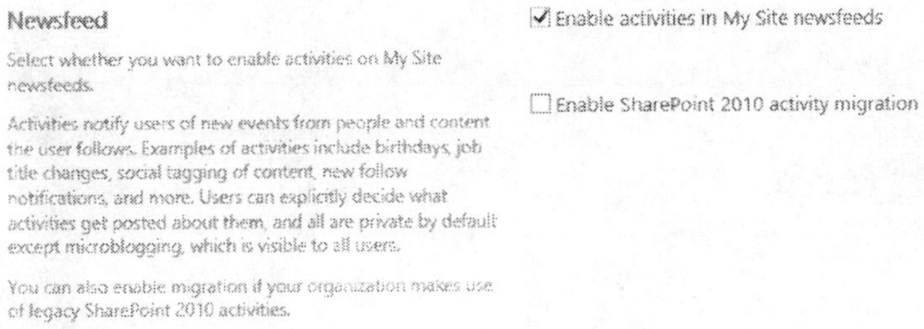

FIGURE 4-28 Use the Newsfeed section to enable SharePoint 2013 and SharePoint 2010 newsfeeds.

- **Email Notifications**   In this section, you can provide an email address that will be used as the sender's email when certain email notifications are sent. Such an email notification could be if someone mentions you in their microblog. The sender's email does not have to be a monitored email address. Also in this section, you can select whether you want users to receive emails for newsfeed activities, such as replies to conversations in which they've participated and conversations in which they have been mentioned. For these email notifications to be sent, the outgoing email settings for the farm must be configured.

- **My Site Cleanup**   In this section, you can decide when to enable access delegation and provide a secondary owner. When a user's profile has been deleted, that user's My Site is flagged for deletion after fourteen days. To prevent inadvertent data loss, if access delegation is enabled, access is granted to the user's manager so he can retrieve content from the former user's My Site before it is deleted. If the user has no manager or the user's manager cannot be determined, the name provided as the secondary owner is granted access to the former user's My Site.

Permissions for the User Profile Service Application

Using the SharePoint Central Administration website, you can control who can create My Sites and use other features provided by the User Profile Service Application, by clicking Manage User Permission, in the People section. On the Permissions For User Profile Service Application dialog box shown in Figure 4-29, in the Permissions For list, as in SharePoint Server 2010, there are three options; however, the text for each option explains clearly and reflects the new social computing features in SharePoint Server 2013.

FIGURE 4-29 The Permissions for User Profile Service Application dialog box.

Yammer integration

Yammer's strength has traditionally been in stand-alone, cloud-based, social networking. Now, with its acquisition by Microsoft, Yammer can be used for stand-alone social computing as well as an aggregator of all social communications a user might have in an organization, such as integrating feeds of external cloud-based activity along with information from existing business application (for example, ERP and CRM).

Currently, there is a kind of a convergence of social computing between SharePoint 2013 and Yammer. However, full integration of the two products is not there at the moment. Therefore, there are similar social offerings within both products. For example, both SharePoint Server 2013 and Yammer have microblogging, and both allow you to follow objects, such as documents.

You can integrate Yammer with SharePoint's enterprise collaboration capabilities by using Yammer Web Parts. With these Web Parts, users can add a Yammer feed to a SharePoint page, view and move between Yammer feeds, and post messages and links.

In the future, you should expect to see deep integration of Yammer into SharePoint, Microsoft Dynamics, and other Microsoft products such as Office 365 and Skype; especially as Yammer announced at the SharePoint Conference 2012 that it is adopting the open graph protocol that was used in Facebook. Using this protocol, developers can create relationships between objects that the new Yammer Web Parts use. Notifications of activities that occur in SharePoint, such as uploading a document, will be able to be sent into Yammer. Similarly, links to files attached to Yammer posts will be provided as a link in SharePoint; however, much of the movement of data between Yammer and SharePoint is manual at the moment.

Going forward, it appears that both Yammer and SharePoint are going to be separate products; Yammer will still be cloud-based and aimed at organizations, where each organization has its own home Yammer network using its own email address. There is also now the ability to join organization network with external networks. At the same time, Yammer has been putting a special effort on simplifying the way its software can be made into components and meshed with third-party business applications.

The Yammer's Business edition is to be eliminated and the price for the Enterprise edition will be reduced from $15 to $3 per user, per month. In addition, Microsoft will bundle Yammer Enterprise with SharePoint Online, the cloud-hosted version of the product, which can be bought on a stand-alone basis or as part of the broader Office 365 suite.

 Note You can find information about the new Yammer SKU plan and pricing at *sharepoint. microsoft.com/blog/Pages/BlogPost.aspx?pID=1049.*

Summary

Social computing is a big investment area in SharePoint Server 2013, which now offers Facebook-like and Twitter-like functionality. This chapter described the new social functionality, such as microblogging, the use of #Tags, and @mentions, with which users can mention other people. Users can follow people, content, documents, sites and tags.

We also explored the three hubs, Newsfeed, SkyDrive, and Sites, where social activities can be viewed in groups, such as following, likes, mentions, and activities. These hubs are accessed from the global navigation bar. Thus, social computing is available from any site, even though the hubs are hosted either in the My Site Host site or a user's personal site. However, site feeds can be added to collaboration sites and the new community sites.

Planning is critical to any social computing project, regardless of the technologies that will be used. The organization's strategy with regard to IdM is important, and it will become more important as the breadth of social features in SharePoint Server grows.

The chapter then finished by briefly looking at the integration of Yammer with SharePoint.

CHAPTER 5

Building composite solutions

Microsoft SharePoint 2013 is often seen as a repository of data; a set of collaboration features and a basis for creating websites. However, it is a rich tool, designed to be used by information workers, business analysts, project managers, administrators, and developers—in fact, just about anyone who needs to design, develop, or prototype solutions to meet the needs of specific business processes or sets of tasks in your organization. The data and components that are needed for such solutions might not be stored in or be part of SharePoint or Microsoft Office; however, with Share-Point, you can rapidly create solutions by assembling, connecting, and configuring the components. Such solutions are known as composite solutions or *mashups*.

Many of the most successful SharePoint composites are built by the people who use them; the users of the site become the designers and the developers of solutions. These users are known as *citizen developers* or *consumer developers*. Such solutions built for the individual or a team can grow into solutions for the department or the organization.

> **Note** Gartner, Inc. reports that citizen developers will build at least 25 percent of new business applications by 2014 (see *www.gartner.com/it/page.jsp?id=1744514*). It further warns that IT departments that fail to capitalize on the opportunities that citizen development presents will find themselves unable to respond to rapidly changing market forces and customer preferences.

Many SharePoint composites are created using nothing more than the browser; others are enhanced with the use of SharePoint Designer and the Microsoft Office client products such as, Microsoft Excel, Microsoft Access, Microsoft Visio, and Microsoft InfoPath or their service application equivalents, as well as other service applications such as Business Connectivity Services (BCS).

SharePoint and Office are particularly noteworthy because of how easy they make it for you to complete tasks and produce solutions—without the need for code—that traditionally required highly skilled technical users. SharePoint 2013 and Office 2013 have continued with this self-service ethos, also referred to as "do-it-yourself."

This chapter will detail the improvements in SharePoint 2013 and related tools for the IT Professional and for someone who builds or advises users who build composite solutions. This will not include the Business Intelligence (BI) tools provided by SharePoint Server 2013, because they are detailed in the next chapter.

More Info To learn more about SharePoint 2013 composites, read the updated SharePoint Composites Handbook, which is available on Microsoft's download site.

Business Connectivity Services

In SharePoint 2013, BCS is still implemented as a Business Data Connectivity (BDC) service application. There is no difference between SharePoint 2013 and SharePoint 2010 with respect to creating the service application topology. BCS continues to centrally store the definition of the external content—its location, the type of data it is, and the behavior of the data when it is integrated into SharePoint and Office client applications—in the BDC metadata store, which is a SQL Server database. The definition of the external content, known as the External Content Type (ECT), together with the definition of the location of the external system are referred to as the *BDC Model*. Once an ECT is defined, by using the browser or SharePoint Designer, you can manipulate the data from the external system by using an external list, similar to other SharePoint objects such as lists and Web Parts.

Note Similar to SharePoint 2010, in SharePoint 2013, the out-of-the-box business Web Parts, external lists, external columns and SharePoint Designer 2013 will only use the BDC service application that is configured as the default. If you associate a web application with multiple BDC service applications, you can only use the non-default BDC service application with custom code.

The new and enhanced capabilities of BCS in SharePoint 2013 Products include the following:

- Enhancements to external lists

- Support for SharePoint Apps and Office Apps

- An event listener, which makes it possible for SharePoint to receive events from external systems

- Support for Open Data (OData) BDC connection

- Representational State Transfer (REST) and SharePoint Client Object Model (CSOM) enhancements against both external lists and ECTs

As with SharePoint 2010 and Office 2010, you can use external data with Office client applications, such as Word, Access, and Outlook. New in Microsoft Visio 2013, you can now link data from an external list to a diagram and its shapes.

When using Office 2013 Office client applications, those applications must be installed on Windows 7 or later operating system, in addition to the following three software components:

- SQL Server Compact 4.0

- .NET Framework 4

- WCF Data Services 5.0 for OData V3

If a user tries to connect to data within an Office application via BCS and these three components are not installed, he will be prompted to download and install them. In addition, the Office client applications must be installed with the Business Connectivity Services Office Shared Feature, as shown in Figure 5-1.

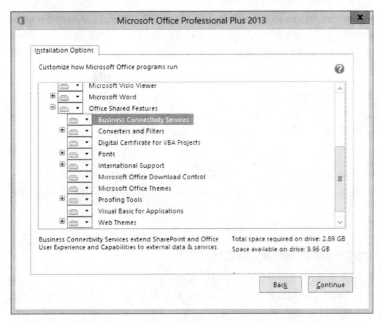

FIGURE 5-1 The Business Connectivity Services installation option.

External list enhancements

SharePoint 2013 introduces many enhancements to bring external lists into parity with internal SharePoint lists, including the following:

- **Performance improvement** BCS now limits the data returned from the external system by processing the data source filters on the external system as well as sending sort requests to the external system when a user sorts the data in an external list. This reduces the load on the SQL servers that are hosting the SharePoint databases.

- **Export data to Excel**   When data is displayed in a view of an external list, you now have the option to export that data to Excel. In the Excel workbook the data is linked to the external list. Therefore, when you choose to refresh the Excel workbook, the data is retrieved from the external system. As with internal SharePoint lists, this is a one-way synchronization process; that is, when you modify or delete data in the Excel workbook, the data is not changed in the external system. Thus, when you synchronize the workbook with the external system, all modifications in the Excel workbook are lost.

Support for SharePoint apps and Office apps

In SharePoint 2010, BDC Models are stored within the BDC service application database and therefore can only be scoped at the service-application level or at the tenant level when the BDC service application was created in partition mode. In SharePoint 2013, the BDC Model can also be saved in a SharePoint App, known as an App-scoped BDC Model. This makes it possible for SharePoint Apps to connect to external data. You can also include a BDC Model in an Office App.

> **Note** If the App-scoped BDC model is not using anonymous access, when a SharePoint App is installed that contains the App scoped BDC model, the administrator will be asked to specify a separately defined OData BDC connection supplying the authentication details.

In a SharePoint App, only the automatically generated forms and views for external lists are supported. You cannot, for example, create InfoPath Forms for the external list; nor are the BDC Web Parts supported.

Using the event receiver infrastructure

In SharePoint 2013, BCS has the ability to listen for events that occur in an external system. A developer can use remote event receivers attached to external lists and BDC entities to write code that is triggered when data in the external system has changed.

You can now create alerts on external lists similar to creating alerts on internal lists or libraries. In addition, you can now initiate workflows on external data; for example, an email message could be sent to the sales staff when a product's price is reduced.

However, such scenarios are not available out of the box. A number of components need to be installed and configured on the SharePoint servers and the external system.

The BDC Model must use BDC connectors, such as OData, SQL, or WCF, and contain EventSubscriber and EventUnsubscriber stereotypes. A developer must create the necessary event receivers. The External Systems Events site feature (feature ID: 60c8481d-4b54-4853-ab9f-ed7e1c21d7e4) must be activated on the site where the BDC Model and event receivers are to be used. This can be done programmatically or by using the Site Features page in the browser, as shown in Figure 5-2.

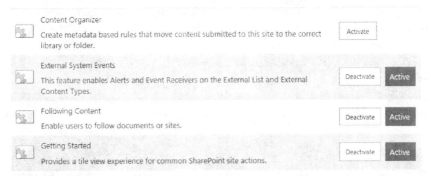

FIGURE 5-2 To activate the External System Events site feature, navigate to the Site Features page from the Site Settings page.

The external system must be configured to do the following:

- Determine when its data changes

- Implement a subscriptions store so that it can record who should receive change notifications

- Send a notification about the data change event as an OData payload from the external system OData endpoint to a SharePoint REST endpoint, where the SharePoint event receiver is listening

SharePoint 2013 includes three new Windows PowerShell cmdlets that you can use to manage the notification site that can receive and forward external system notifications. The three cmdlets are: *Get-SPBusinessDataCatalogEntityNoticationWeb*, *Clear-SPBusinessDataCatalogEntityNotificationWeb*, and *Set-SPBusinessDataCatalogEntityNotificationWeb*.

More Info You can read more about all of the BCS Windows PowerShell cmdlets at *technet. microsoft.com/en-us/library/ff793361.aspx*.

Introducing OData support

SharePoint 2013 now supports the OData connection protocol. OData is an industry standard web protocol by which systems—in this case, SharePoint 2013—can access external data and support anonymous, basic, and Windows authentication when used with the secure store service (SSS). You can achieve even more fine-grained permission control by using OAuth 2.0 with OData connections.

More Info To read an introduction to OData, go to Microsoft's MSDN site at *msdn.microsoft. com/en-us/data/hh237663*. This should be considered required reading for anyone who wants to learn about or work with OData.

There are OData producers and consumers. OData producers expose their applications and data, which OData consumers make use of in their applications. OData producers include, SharePoint, SQL Server Reporting Services, Windows Azure Table Storage, Azure Data Marketplace, Facebook, Netflix, and others, such as those built by using Open Government Data Initiative (OGDI) as well as the .NET Framework. In fact, Windows Server 2012 includes a new feature with which you can expose Windows PowerShell commands and scripts as OData web service entities. Data is return from the OData producers as JavaScript Object Notation (JSON), Atom, or plain XML data.

 Note You can find more OData providers as well as consumers at *www.odata.org/ ecosystem*. One OData provider mentioned on the Ecosystem page is Duet Enterprise for Microsoft SharePoint and SAP Server, which is a jointly developed product from SAP and Microsoft with which you can establish interoperability between SAP applications and SharePoint via BCS. With the release of SharePoint 2013, a new version was released, Duet 2.0, which pulls data from SAP by using an OData custom BDC connector.

When using OData to return list data with SharePoint 2010, you would use the *ListData.svc* endpoint, such as *http://intranet/sites/it/workflow/_vti_bin/LisdtData.svc/Tasks*. This endpoint still works in SharePoint 2013; however, you are no longer limited to retrieving data from only lists. In SharePoint 2013 the REST/OData access point can be used for all client-side object model (CSOM) application programming interfaces (APIs) that can be accessed as either *http://intranet/sites/it/workflow/_vti_bin/ client.svc* or by using the shorter URL *http://intranet/sites/it/workflow/_api*. There are five _api services: site, web, userProfiles, search, and publishing. For example, to retrieve the title of all list items in the Task list, with all the fields returned, on the workflow subsite you would use the URL *http://intranet/ workflow/_api/web/lists/getByTitle('Tasks')/Items*.

OData can be likened to a set of REST endpoints that you can use to access data together with its schema, built on HTTP verbs, such as GET, POST, PUT, and DELETE, which then can be easily mapped to BDC Model operations, as demonstrated in Table 5-1.

TABLE 5-1 OData operations mapped to BDC (ECT) operations

BDC Model Operation (used in Visual Studio)	ECT Operation (used in SharePoint Designer)	HTTP operation	Sample SharePoint OData endpoints
Finder	Read List	GET	http://intranet/_api/web/lists/getByTitle('Tasks')/Items
Specific Finder	Read Item	GET	http://intranet/_api/web/lists/getByTitle('Tasks')/Items(1)
Creator	Create	POST	http://intranet/_api/web/lists/getByTitle('Tasks')/items
Updater	Update	PUT	http://intranet/_api/web/lists/getByTitle('Tasks')/items(2)
Deleter	Delete	DELETE	http://intranet/_api/web/lists/getByTitle('Tasks')/items(2)
Association Navigator	Association	GET	http://intranet/_vti_bin/LisdtData.svc/Customers('Contoso')/ Invoices

To support the OData BDC connector, additional enhancements include the following:

- **Automatic generation of BDC models for OData data sources**   The tooling to create a BDC Model for OData has been included within Visual Studio 2012 and not SharePoint Designer. The BCS tooling within SharePoint Designer 2013 remains as it was in SharePoint Designer 2010. By including the new tooling within Visual Studio 2012, the BDC Model can either be included in a SharePoint or Office App, or imported into a BDC metadata store using the SharePoint Central Administration web site, Windows PowerShell or in a tenant environment, such as Office 365, using the tenant admin site.

- **Six new Windows PowerShell cmdlets**   You can use these cmdlets to create and delete OData BDC connections as well as view and modify OData BDC connection objects and metadata properties.

Microsoft Visual Studio BCS tooling

Visual Studio 2012 includes additional tooling for BCS—the SharePoint Customization Wizard—that was not included in Visual Studio 2010. You can use this wizard to create an OData BDC Model and the BDC Model operations that match the external system operations that are exposed via the OData endpoints. The Visual Studio wizard creates ECTs with fewer clicks than it would take you to create them in SharePoint Designer. Unfortunately, you cannot create or modify an OData ECT with SharePoint Designer. To create a BDC Model based on an OData producer by using Visual Studio, complete the following steps:

1. In the Solutions Explorer (see Figure 5-3), right-click the project name. In the shortcut menu that appears, select Add, and then in the submenu that opens, click Content Types for an External Data Source to display the SharePoint Customization Wizard page.

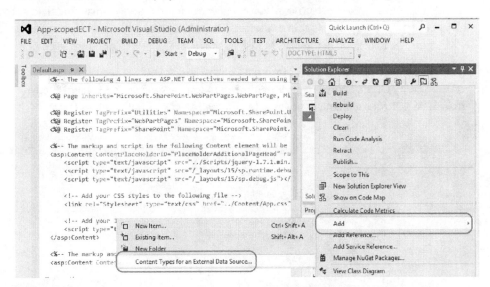

FIGURE 5-3 Use the shortcut menu to add OData content types to your Visual Studio project.

2. On the Specify OData Source page of the SharePoint Customization Wizard, type the OData Service URL and the Data Source Name, as shown in Figure 5-4.

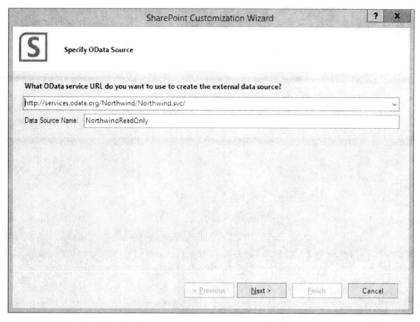

FIGURE 5-4 Use the Specify OData Source page to enter the OData service URL for the external data source that you want to use.

3. Click Next.

Visual Studio connects to the $metadata endpoint and then displays the data entities available from the OData provider in the Select The Data Entities page. Use this page to select those entities to include in the BDC Model, as shown in Figure 5-5, and then click Finish.

In the Solutions Explorer, under External Content Types, you will see the data source you entered on the Specify OData Source page. When the data source is expanded, as illustrated in Figure 5-6, there is an ECT for each data entity selected on the Select The Data Entities page.

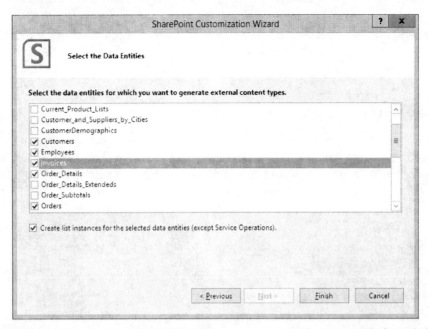

FIGURE 5-5 Use the Select The Data Entities page to automatically create an ECT for each data entity selected.

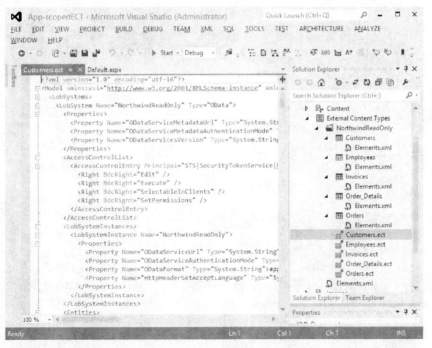

FIGURE 5-6 Use the Solution Explorer to display the ECT files and the external list definitions.

Note Visual Studio automatically generates the OData ECTs to use HTTPS. If your OData provider endpoints use HTTP, you will need to modify the ECTs.

When the Create List Instances For The Selected Data Entities check box is selected on the Select The Data Entities page, in the Solution Explorer, an external list definition *Elements.xml* file is created.

The ECT files can be opened to display their contents as XML, or if you double-click an ECT file, it will open in Designer view (see Figure 5-7). You can use the Designer view to easily configure the columns for the ECT and to add filters that you can use to limit the data that is returned from the data source. A filter named Limit is automatically generated. The filter has a default value of 100.

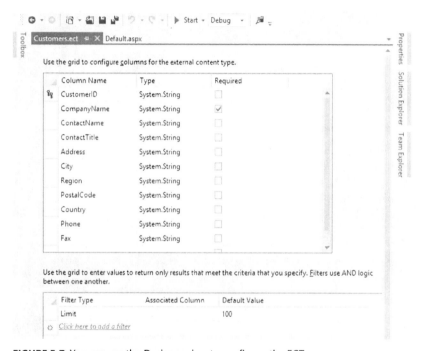

FIGURE 5-7 You can use the Designer view to configure the ECT.

OData Windows PowerShell cmdlets

There are six OData Windows PowerShell cmdlets: *Get-SPODataConnectionSetting* and *Set-SPO DataConnectionSetting*, *New_SPODataConnectionSetting* and *Remove_SPODataConnectionSetting*, and Get-SPODataConnectionSettingMetadata and *Set-SPODataConnectionSettingMetadata*. You can find information about the cmdlets on TechNet or by using the *Get-Help* command.

SharePoint BCS hybrid solutions

In SharePoint 2010, you could use BCS to connect SharePoint on-premises to external systems that were also on-premises. Also if you were using SharePoint Online, BCS could be used to connect to online data. Initially, SharePoint Online could only connect to external data systems by using Windows Communication Foundation (WCF). Now, however, WCF, OData, and SQL Azure are supported. Search using BCS data does not work with SharePoint Online; that is, you cannot configure search to use a BDC Model.

New to SharePoint 2013, you can create hybrid solutions that use BCS. This means that you can now create on-premises BCS solutions that connect to data that is held in SharePoint Online, and similarly, you can create SharePoint Online BCS solutions that connect to data that is held within SharePoint on-premises. In either scenario, only the OData connection is supported. In either case, configuration is needed around connectivity and security.

Whether your BCS solution is a hybrid solution or just a SharePoint Online BCS solution, without the help of Microsoft support, you can retrieve tenant level logs to investigate errors or exceptions that occur when SharePoint Online BCS is connected to external systems. Use the new Windows PowerShell cmdlet, *Get-SPOTenantLogEntry* with the parameters *UserID*, *CorrelationID*, *TimeRange*, and *MaxRows* to filter the logs returned.

 More Info You can find information about hybrid solutions at *www.microsoft.com/en-us/download/details.aspx?id=35593*.

SharePoint composite tools

SharePoint composites can be built by using SharePoint Designer 2013, Access 2013, Visio 2013, InfoPath 2013, and Visual Studio 2012. With most of these tools, you can build no-code solutions for which the instructions generated are either declarative or client-side code; that is, the code generated is human readable and needs to be parsed either on the server by SharePoint or on the client computer by the browser.

Most composites require the generation of a number of pages, sometimes called forms or dashboards. These forms/dashboards aggregate the information and are designed to allow the user to dynamically interact with the data. Most composite tools provide the creator of these pages with a WYSIWYG environment so that the creator can visually amend the content without learning the different declarative or coding languages.

For code-based solutions, Visual Studio 2012 is still the tool to create, debug, and package custom solutions; although as SharePoint 2013 and Office 2013 are more web-standard based than previous versions, several other tools can be used, including TypeScript, jQuery libraries, and "Napa" Office 365 Development tools.

SharePoint Designer

You can use SharePoint Designer to edit and build solutions with SharePoint Foundation and Share-Point Server sites. After you are connected to a SharePoint site, you can use SharePoint Designer for administration, to create workflows, and to customize pages. As with the previous release, SharePoint Designer 2013 is free and available from Microsoft's download site at *www.microsoft.com/download/ details.aspx?id=35491.*

Note As with SharePoint Designer 2010, SharePoint Designer 2013 comes in two versions: a 32-bit version and a 64-bit version. If you have the 32-bit version of SharePoint Designer 2010 already installed so that you can customize earlier versions of SharePoint, you must download the 32-bit version of SharePoint Designer 2013. Be aware, however, that 64-bit Office applications will not run with the 32-bit versions of SharePoint Designer installed. Also note, that unlike SharePoint 2010, which does not support the Edit In Datasheet view functionality, if the 64-bit Office client is installed, the Edit in Datasheet view in SharePoint 2013 does not require a client-side control. Therefore, if you have the 64-bit version of Office 2010 or Office 2013 installed, Edit In Datasheet will work correctly on SharePoint 2013 sites.

You can still use SharePoint Designer 2013 to create data-driven solutions by doing the following:

- Use a Data View, also known as the Data Form Web Part (DFWP).

- Manipulate eXtensible Markup Language (XML) and eXtensible Stylesheet Language Transfor-mations (XSLT) code and client-side code.

- Connect to external data sources, including the creation of External Content Types (ECTs).

- Use Web Part connections to pass data from a Web Part on one page to one or more Web Parts on another page.

The major change with SharePoint Designer 2013 is in the area of workflows, which is detailed in the next section; however, there is another change which will affect you and citizen developers. Unlike SharePoint Designer 2010 and earlier versions, SharePoint Designer 2013 does not render the pages so that you can visually modify the content in a WYSIWYG environment. SharePoint Designer 2010 provides three views for editing HTML and ASPX pages: Code view, Design view, and Split view. Design view and Split view have been removed from SharePoint Designer 2013. Thus, if you want to edit pages in SharePoint Designer 2013, you must use Code view. This means that to achieve many of the same results with SharePoint Designer 2013 that you created by using SharePoint Designer 2010, you will need to learn code. Another option would be to use SharePoint Designer 2010 on a

SharePoint 2013 site. Or, users who previously displayed data in a tabular format by using the DFWP or XSLT List View (XLV) Web Part could investigate the visualization options in Visio Services or Excel Service or a third-party tool.

> **Note** If you want to design or brand an internet-facing website for which the publishing feature is activated, you can use any professional HTML editor such as Microsoft Expression Web or Adobe Dreamweaver. This means that professional web developers can connect their tool of choice to SharePoint 2013. Then, they can import their HTML files into a publishing site by using the new Design Manager.

SharePoint workflow

Microsoft SharePoint 2010 introduced a considerable array of new functionality concerning the creation, maintainability, reusability, and deployment of workflows. However, this new functionality was difficult to scale in organizations that make heavy use of workflows (if their SharePoint farm was not properly designed). The workflows could have a negative effect on the ability of the SharePoint servers to respond to a user's requests for SharePoint webpages. Fortunately, SharePoint Server 2013 introduces new capabilities to help mitigate these challenges.

Chapter 1, "Architectural Enhancements," details that in Microsoft SharePoint Server 2013, you have an option of no longer running a workflow within a SharePoint process. SharePoint Server 2013 introduces a new, highly scalable workflow framework: the Workflow Manager. This is not installed automatically; therefore, a default installation of SharePoint Server 2013 can only use the same workflows as those used in SharePoint 2010. Workflow Manager is not designed to work with Microsoft SharePoint Foundation 2013. Accordingly, with SharePoint Foundation you can only use and create SharePoint 2010 workflows.

The basic usage and manageability of workflows has not changed, whether they are SharePoint 2010 or SharePoint 2013 workflows. You interact with workflows by using the browser or Office applications. You use the browser to add workflow templates to lists, libraries, content types, and sites. However, it's likely that adding workflow templates to lists or libraries will still be the most popular type of SharePoint workflow.

You can use SharePoint Designer to create reusable workflows that can be associated with multiple lists or libraries, and you can then save the reusable workflow as a workflow template in the form of a Windows SharePoint solution file (.wsp). This workflow template can then be imported to another site to be used to create the same workflow on the new site or imported into Visual Studio 2012 where it can be further enhanced.

SharePoint Server does not contain any SharePoint 2013 workflow templates only SharePoint 2010 workflow templates. As a result, even though you might have installed the Workflow Manager, you will still only be able to use SharePoint 2010 workflows until SharePoint 2013 workflows and/or SharePoint 2013 workflow templates are created.

Tip You can create SharePoint 2013 workflows or SharePoint 2010 workflows by using SharePoint Designer 2013 or by using Visual Studio 2012. SharePoint 2013 also contains new Windows PowerShell cmdlets with which you can manage workflows.

SharePoint 2010 workflows in SharePoint 2013 remain unchanged: you have the same actions and conditions as in SharePoint 2010, and they are built on Microsoft .NET Framework 3.5. If you are upgrading from SharePoint 2010 to SharePoint 2013, all of your workflows that were built by using SharePoint 2010 will continue to work in SharePoint 2013. You can modify SharePoint 2010 workflows in SharePoint 2013 by using either SharePoint Designer 2010 or SharePoint Designer 2013.

However, SharePoint 2010 workflows are categorized as deprecated in SharePoint 2013, which means that in future versions they might not be available. To future-proof your SharePoint 2013 installation, wherever possible you should use SharePoint 2013 workflows. This can be difficult to achieve as some actions and conditions are not available out of the box with SharePoint 2013 workflows.

Note If you have upgraded from Windows SharePoint Services 3.0 or Microsoft Office SharePoint Server 2007 to SharePoint 2010 and subsequently to SharePoint 2013 and you attached SharePoint 2007 workflows to lists or libraries in your Windows SharePoint Services 3.0 or Microsoft Office SharePoint Server 2007 environment, and they are still attached to those lists and libraries in your SharePoint 2013 installations, they will continue to work.

Using Visio diagrams to gather requirements

The ability for a Business Analyst to communicate effectively with developers is greatly improved by using Visio process diagrams. This capability was first introduced in SharePoint 2010 when used with Visio 2010 Premium, and you can use this same method in SharePoint 2013. Visio Premium no longer exists, but all of the features it offered are now rolled into Visio Professional. You can create your SharePoint process diagram in Visio 2013 Professional by using either the Microsoft SharePoint 2013 Workflow template or the Microsoft SharePoint 2010 Workflow template, as shown in Figure 5-8.

SharePoint Designer 2013 does provide a new way of creating Visio diagrams. When you have Workflow Manager installed and you want to create a SharePoint 2013 workflow, you can create Visio diagrams by using SharePoint Designer's built-in Visual Designer, a Visio ActiveX control. Custom Actions are now supported in Visio, and you can also copy and paste SharePoint workflow shapes from one diagram to another.

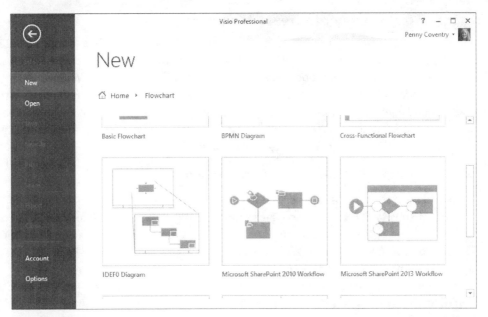

FIGURE 5-8 In the Backstage view, on the New tab, you can select either the Microsoft SharePoint 2013 or 2010 workflow template.

Note If you create a Visio workflow diagram but find that you cannot configure the conditions and actions within Visio, you will need to complete the configuration within SharePoint Designer.

To save your workflow diagram so that you can import it into SharePoint Designer, you need to complete one of the following tasks:

- If you are creating a SharePoint 2013 workflow, select the File tab, and then on the Backstage view, click the Save As tab. In the Computer section on the Save As page, click Browse to open the Save As dialog box. Navigate to where you want to save the .vsdx file, which is a new file format for Visio 2013.

- If you are creating a SharePoint 2010 workflow, on the Process tab, in the SharePoint Workflow group, click Export. The Export Workflow dialog box opens so that you can navigate to where you want to save the *.vwi* file.

Using SharePoint Designer to create workflows

To create workflows by using SharePoint Designer, you must have either .NET Framework 3.5 installed on your computer to create SharePoint 2010 workflows or .NET Framework 4.5 to create SharePoint 2013 workflows. Typically, the client operating system is Windows 8, Windows 7, Windows Vista, or Windows XP. Windows 7 includes the .Net Framework 3.5; however, if you are using Windows Vista or Windows XP, you might need to install the .NET Framework 3.5 before you can work with workflows in SharePoint Designer. Both versions of the .NET Framework are available from the Microsoft Download Center at *www.microsoft.com/download/details.aspx?id=21*.

SharePoint Designer 2013 provides the following new features:

■ A Visual Designer that uses a Visio 2013 ActiveX control. This makes it possible for you to author SharePoint 2013 workflows visually, similar to the experience in Visio. Visio 2013 Professional must be installed on your computer. The Visual Designer will not work on SharePoint 2010 sites, because SharePoint 2013 workflows cannot be created on SharePoint 2010 sites. With SharePoint 2010 workflows, you can only use the Text-Based Designer which is the method used in SharePoint Designer 2010 to edit workflows. With SharePoint 2013 workflows you can choose between using the Text-Based Designer or the Visual Designer.

■ New workflow building blocks, such as the following:

- **Stage** All actions in a SharePoint 2013 workflow must be placed in a stage, and each stage has a Transition To Stage that defines how the workflow exits the stage.

- **Loop** SharePoint 2013 workflow in SharePoint Designer includes two types of loops: Loop N Times and Loop With Condition. Both are very useful when using the new variable type called Dictionary. With a Dictionary variable, you can store multiple data points in a single variable.

- **App Step** Declarative workflows can be incorporated into SharePoint Apps. Use the App step when you do not want the workflow logic to run under the workflow initiator, but instead under only the Workflow App permission, which is Read/Write to all SharePoint App site lists. This is similar to the SharePoint 2010 Impersonation step. The Impersonation step is not available in SharePoint 2013 workflows.

■ New actions, such as the following:

- Dictionary related actions: Build Dictionary, Count Items In A Dictionary, and Get An Item From A Dictionary.

- Call HTTP Web Service action that enables no-code web service calls from within a workflow. Generally, you will use a Dictionary variable to store the results of this action and then use the looping abilities of SharePoint 2013 workflows to process each value returned from the web service.

- New coordination actions with which you can start a workflow built on the SharePoint 2010 Workflow platform from a workflow built on the SharePoint 2013 Workflow platform. With SharePoint 2013 workflows, only those activities built on .NET Framework 4.5 and Windows Workflow Foundation 4 runtime can be used. If you need to use any Windows Workflow Foundation 3.5 artifacts, you need to create a SharePoint 2010 workflow that you start from a SharePoint 2013 workflow; control is passed to the SharePoint 2010 workflow host in SharePoint 2013 to process the SharePoint 2010 workflow conditions and actions. When the SharePoint Windows Workflow Foundation 3 process completes the SharePoint 2010 workflow, control returns back to Workflow Manager, whereupon SharePoint 2013 continues to the next condition or action.

- Start A Task Process action, which is similar to the SharePoint 2010 workflow, Start Approval Process, Start Custom Task Process and Start Feedback Process actions.

More Info To read more about SharePoint 2013 workflow actions, go to *msdn.microsoft. com/en-us/library/jj163867.aspx*.

- Ability to copy and paste within the Text-Based Designer. You can use the command in the Clipboard group on the ribbon as well as using keyboard combinations, such as Ctrl+C to copy, Ctrl+V to paste, or Ctrl+X to cut. There is no undo or redo. You can also use the context menu of any selected item, as shown in Figure 5-9.

FIGURE 5-9 Use the context menu on actions and conditions to copy and paste.

You can copy Stages, Steps, or individual actions or condition blocks as well as selecting multiple lines of actions, steps, condition blocks, or multiple stages. Selected items are highlighted in a sky-blue color.

- In SharePoint 2010, you could only package and deploy reusable workflows. Now, in SharePoint 2013 you can deploy list, site, and reusable SharePoint 2013 workflows. SharePoint 2010 workflows can only be packaged if they are reusable workflows.

- Initiation, association, and task forms for SharePoint 2013 workflows are created as *.aspx* pages and not as InfoPath forms. SharePoint 2010 workflows still use InfoPath forms.

- Workflow Visualization of SharePoint 2013 workflows is not available; however, you can still use it for SharePoint 2010 workflows if Visio Services is installed.

Authoring SharePoint 2013 workflows by using the Visual Designer The Visual Designer is available when you have created a SharePoint 2013 workflow in SharePoint Designer by completing one of the following tasks:

- Import a *.vsdx* file of a SharePoint 2013 workflow that you created in Visio.

- Create a SharePoint 2013 workflow within SharePoint Designer.

To switch to use the Visual Designer, on the Workflow tab, in the Manage group, click the View split button, as demonstrated in Figure 5-10.

FIGURE 5-10 Click the Views split button to switch between the three views for a SharePoint 2013 workflow.

You can use the content area of the workspace and Workflow tab as you would within Visio. In the content area, you have a Shapes pane, a drawing area, and when you click Check For Errors in the Save group on the Workflow tab, an Issues pane is displayed below the Shapes pane.

In the Shapes pane, when you hover or select the action, a workflow settings type icon appears at the lower-left corner of the shape. When the icon is clicked the Action Tags menu is displayed, as illustrated in Figure 5-11.

The Action Tag is a context-sensitive drop-down list which displays the attributes for that action or condition in the workflow as well as a Properties link. When you click Properties, a dialog box opens in which you can modify parameter values for that action.

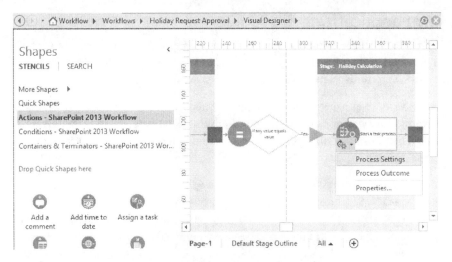

FIGURE 5-11 Shapes displayed in the Visual Designer have Action Tags.

Displaying the workflow as a Stage Outline diagram   The Visual Designer displays can also generate a stage-level diagram. When you are in the Visual Designer view, on the Workflow tab, in the Manage group, click Generate Stage Outline to display a high-level view of your SharePoint 2013 workflow, as shown in Figure 5-12. It shows the stages within your workflow, not the individual conditions and actions.

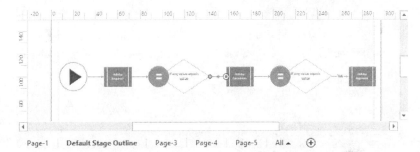

FIGURE 5-12 You can see the Stage View to display the stages and how they are connected.

To use the Stage Outline within SharePoint Designer, the workflow must be displayed in the Visual Designer. You can toggle between the original diagram and the Stage Outline by using the Generate Workflow Outline and Generate Stage Outline commands in the Manage group on the Workflow tab. To view the workflow in the Text-Based Designer, the workflow must be displayed as a Workflow Outline diagram.

Access form applications

As detailed in Chapter 1, SharePoint 2013 provides two Access service applications, the Access service application as provided in SharePoint 2010, and Access 2013 service application. To use either of these service applications, Enterprise client access licenses (CALs) are required.

Using the Access service application, you can quickly build no-code, web-based form applications, known as *web apps*. These web apps are SharePoint Apps that can be deployed to SharePoint App stores. With SharePoint Designer 2013 being de-emphasized as a no-code forms tool, Access web apps is a welcome addition.

Data and Access objects for each Access web app is saved in its own SQL Server 2012 database, not in SharePoint lists. This SQL-integrated approach improves the performance, manageability, and scalability of the web app. Also, makes it possible for SQL server developers to extend the solution by directly connecting to the tables in the database, including building reports with Desktop Access Reports, Excel, and Power View. However, as the data is not stored in SharePoint, some functionality is lost when compared to creating a forms-based application by using InfoPath. For example, you cannot create or initiate a SharePoint workflow on data in Access form applications.

The servers that run SQL Server 2012 where the Access web apps databases are to be created does not have to be the same SQL Server instance that SharePoint uses. In fact, it is recommended that the databases for the Access web apps use a different SQL Server instance than the one used for the SharePoint databases, it must be a SQL Server 2012 server, though, because you cannot use SQL Server 2008 to host Access Services databases. If you are using SharePoint Online, the SQL Server instance could be hosted on SQL Azure servers.

Whenever a user visits the app, enters data, or modifies the design of the app by using the browser or Access 2013, she will be interacting with the database; however, the user interface will give no indication of this.

SQL Server configuration

Before creating the Access services application, complete the following tasks on the SQL Server:

1. Configure the SQL Server to be in mixed security mode; that is, SQL Server authentication and Windows authentication.

2. During the SQL Server installation on the Feature Selection page, in the Database Engine Services section, select Full-Text and Semantic Extractions For Search. If you are using a previously installed SQL Server 2012, you can install the feature by selecting the SQL Server Installation Center from the Start menu.

3. After installation, right-click the SQL Server instance and click Properties to display the Server Properties dialog box (see Figure 5-13). In the Select A Page section, click Advanced, and then in the right pane, perform the following:

a. In the Containment section, set Enable Contained Databases to True. This ensures that each Access web app database is isolated from one another; that is, isolated permissions-wise because each database is able to have logins "contained" within them directly and not at the SQL Server level, making the databases truly isolatable and importantly portable. Also, each web app database can have its own collation and sort orders.

b. In the Miscellaneous section, set Allow Triggers To Fire Others to True. This makes it possible for Access web apps to use macros.

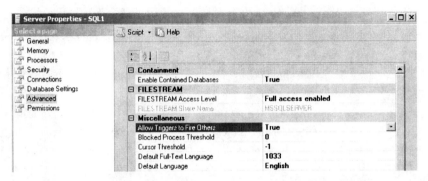

FIGURE 5-13 At the SQL Server level, set two advance options to True.

4. The service account for the application pool that Access service application uses should have the server roles, dbcreator and security admin.

5. Use the SQL Server Configuration Manger to enable both TCP/IP and Named Pipes protocols for MSSQLSERVER.

Note Despite SQL Server aliases being recommended for SharePoint generally, they do not work for Access Services databases. For more information on installing Access Services for an on-premises installation, go to *www.microsoft.com/en-us/download/details. aspx?id=30445*.

SharePoint Server configuration

On your SharePoint servers, complete the following tasks:

1. Install the following five components, if they are not already installed. These components are available in the Microsoft SQL Server 2012 Feature Pack, which can be downloaded from the Microsoft download site.

- Microsoft SQL Server 2012 Data-Tier Application Framework (*DACFramework.msi*)

- Microsoft SQL Server 2012 Transact-SQL ScriptDom (*sqldom.msi*)

- Microsoft SQL Server CLR Types for Microsoft SQL Server 2012 (*SQLSysClrTypes.msi*)

- Microsoft SQL Server 2012 Local DB (*SQLLocalDB.msi*)

- Microsoft SQL Server 2012 Native Client (*sqlncli.msi*)

 Note The first three components are not specific to Access web apps. They are actually needed for all SharePoint Apps.

2. Configure your SharePoint 2013 for SharePoint Apps as described in Chapter 1.

3. Start the Access service and then create the Access service application. You will need to type the name of the SQL server on which the Access web app databases are to be created; you can then decide whether to create a new service application pool or select an existing service application pool.

4. Using the Internet Information Services (IIS) Manager, select the application pool used by the Access service application. In the Actions pane, click Advanced Settings. In the Advanced Settings dialog box, in the Process Model section, set Load User Profile to True, as illustrated in Figure 5-14. This creates isolation between service accounts and creates a writeable app data folder, which is needed for the Access web app to create queries and data sets for linked SharePoint lists and libraries.

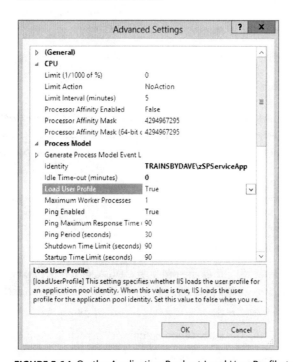

FIGURE 5-14 On the Application Pool set Load User Profile to True.

5. If you used the Configuration Wizard to create the Access service application, the SQL Server that will be used for Access web app databases is the same SQL server as that on which the SharePoint config database resides. If you want to change the SQL server on which the Access web app databases are created, navigate to the Manage Service Applications page; click the Access service application to display the Manage Access Services page. At the bottom of the page, click New Application Database Server and type the name of the SQL Server, as shown in Figure 5-15.

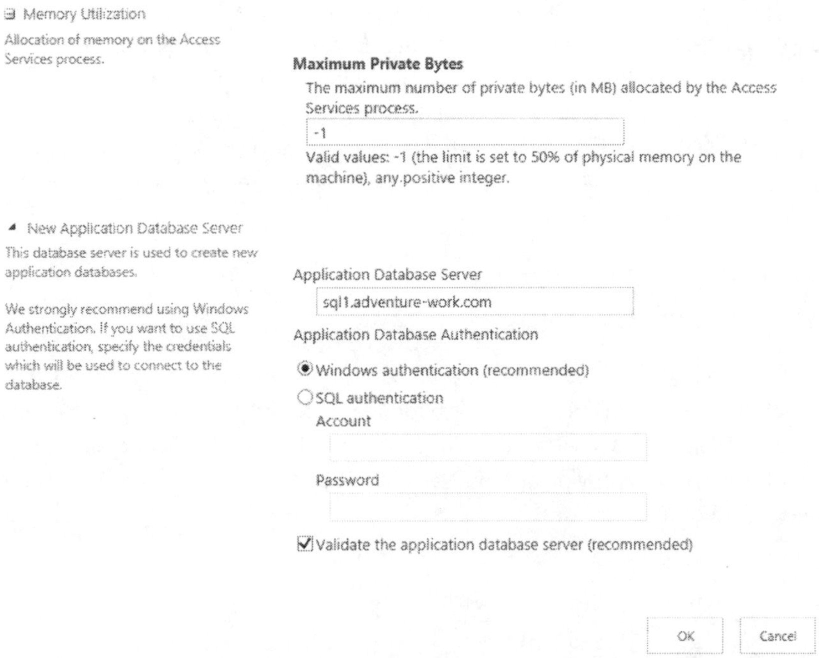

⊟ Memory Utilization

Allocation of memory on the Access Services process.

Maximum Private Bytes

The maximum number of private bytes (in MB) allocated by the Access Services process.

| -1 |

Valid values: -1 (the limit is set to 50% of physical memory on the machine), any positive integer.

◢ New Application Database Server

This database server is used to create new application databases.

We strongly recommend using Windows Authentication. If you want to use SQL authentication, specify the credentials which will be used to connect to the database.

Application Database Server

| sql1.adventure-work.com |

Application Database Authentication

◉ Windows authentication (recommended)
○ SQL authentication
   Account
   | |
   Password
   | |

☑ Validate the application database server (recommended)

[OK] [Cancel]

FIGURE 5-15 Use the Manage Access Services page to set the database server on which the new Access web app databases are to be created.

6. Access web apps are created as subsites. As a result, there must be at least one site collection in the web application(s) associated with the Access service application where users can create the Access web apps. You can access, manage, or uninstall (delete) Access web apps by using the Site Contents page of the parent site for the subsite.

7. As Access web apps are created, databases named db_<GUID> are created, where <GUID> is a generated number. Because Access web apps use separate databases from SharePoint databases, you need to ensure that these databases are included in your data recovery and high-availability plans. Also, when users search for information within an Access web app, they will be using the full-text search capabilities of SQL Server 2012 and not the results from the SharePoint search indexes; therefore you should also consider creating content sources to crawl, process, and add Access web app content to the SharePoint search index.

There are 14 Access Services Windows PowerShell cmdlets and three Access 2010 Service Windows PowerShell cmdlets. You can find information about the cmdlets by using the command *Get-Help*, or on TechNet at *technet.microsoft.com/en-us/library/ee906548.aspx and http://technet.microsoft.com/en-us/library/fp161268.aspx.*

 Note For each db_<*GUID*> database created, two SQL userids are created. Those userids are db_<GUID>_custom and db_<GUID>_db, which are mapped to the database users: AccessExternalReader and DatabaseProvider. It is these two SQL userids that the Access web app uses to connect to its database. The Access service application uses the Access services application pool ID to create the Access web app database. Therefore, the application pool ID is set as the dbo for the database. Because SQL Server does not support claims, when a user accesses the Access web app, their SharePoint security settings of the parent site are used to map to the Access web app security roles. Therefore, all users will share one of the two the SQL userids to access the database. To find the SQL Server login in credentials in Access, display the Backstage view, click the Info tab, and then click the Manage button in the Connections section.

Creating an Access web app

Access 2013 includes a set of templates that can be used to jump start the creation of these apps. Any template that does not contain the word "desktop" can be used to create an Access web app. They include: Custom Web App, Asset Tracking, Contacts, Issue Tracking, Project Management, and Task Management. You need to provide an App Name and the parent site, where the subsite is to be created, as shown in Figure 5-16.

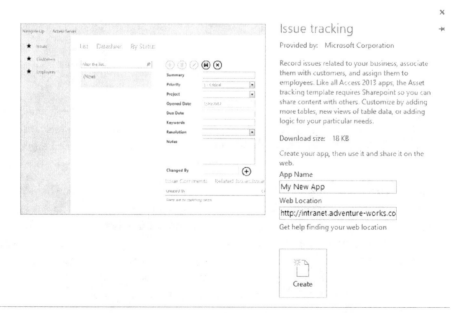

FIGURE 5-16 Enter the App Name and Web Location once a web app template is selected.

To determine the SQL server name, the SQL database name, and where the Access web app was created, display the Access 2013 Backstage view and then click the Info tab, as demonstrated in Figure 5-17.

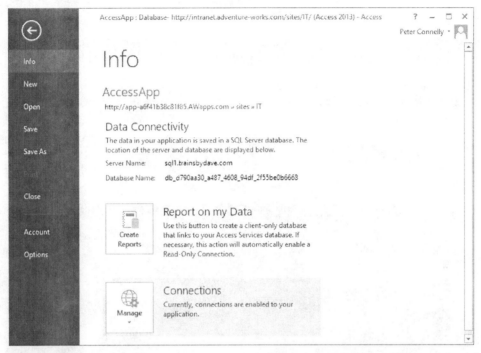

FIGURE 5-17 The Info tab in the Backstage view contains SQL server and SharePoint location information.

The Access web app inherits the site permissions and branding from its parent's site. Your Access web app can contain:

- **Tables**   Each Access table is created as a SQL Server table, which has the same name that it was given in Access. Access provides you with a number of table templates (nouns), which you can use as a basis for new tables. You can also create linked tables, for example you can connect to and display real-time data from SharePoint lists, including external lists.

 Note   Currently, Access 2013 only supports read-only connections to SharePoint lists. Also, to set up a connection to a list, the user who creates the linked table must have Change Permissions rights to the list, because he will be giving the Access web app the rights to read the data.

- **Views**   For each table, two views are automatically generated: List and Datasheet. You can think of each as the views on SharePoint internal lists and libraries. These are the pages in the browser that users see when they navigate to the Access web app and will use to interact with the data. The pages are not stored as SQL Server objects; rather, they are stored as text because they contain HTML and JavaScript. Users can create additional views to display the data. There are four types of views: List Details, Datasheet, Summary, and Blank.

Note Views are known as *forms* in Access desktop databases; hence, the reason why Access web apps are also known as Access Form Applications.

Each view has an Action Bar (see Figure 5-18). This is the same for each view. With the Action Bar, users can add, delete, edit, save, and cancel changes. You can customize the Action Bar by replacing the five default commands with custom commands. You can even hide the Action Bar, if you prefer.

FIGURE 5-18 An Access web app as viewed in the browser.

- **Queries**   Queries in the Access web app are created as SQL Server views or a table-valued function (TVF), if the query has parameters.

- **Data macros**   There are two types of macros:

- User Interface macros, which perform actions, such as navigating to another view, show, or hide controls. They can be attached to command buttons or combo boxes.

- **Data macros** You create these by selecting Data Macros from the Advanced split button in the Create group on the Home ribbon tab. These macros are used to implement business rules at the data level and therefore can be used to create, edit, and delete records.

Generally, the browser is used to add, edit, view, and delete data, and Access 2013 is used to design the web app. This means that Access 2013 is used to create and customize views, tables, queries, and macros.

Note Access web databases cannot be created using Access 2013. You can still view and edit a web database that was previously created by using Access 2010 and SharePoint Server 2010, and you can republish it to SharePoint Server 2013. You cannot automatically convert a web database to an Access web app; however, you can manually convert a web database to an Access web app to by importing the data from the web database into a new Access web app and then re-create the user interface and business logic. You can find more information about how to configure Access Services 2010 for web databases in SharePoint Server 2013 at *technet.microsoft.com/en-us/library/ee748653.aspx*.

Visio Services and Visio

The infrastructure for Visio Services has not changed. However, both Visio Services and the Visio client application contain improvements that introduce compelling new options for composites. With SharePoint Designer being de-emphasized as a no-code page editor, you might turn to using Visio diagrams to fill this gap. This will be particularly true when you want to move away from the tabular representation of data to a visual display, using shapes and diagrams. This section details changes in Visio Services and the client application Office Visio 2013.

Note You can find a Visio Services Mashup Starter project template for Visual Studio 2012 at *blogs.msdn.com/b/chhopkin/archive/2012/08/17/updated-mashup-project-template-for-visual-studio-2010-2012.aspx*.

Visio 2013

Visio 2013 contains new XML-based file formats, based on the Open Packaging Conventions (OPC) standard (ISO 29500, Part 2). This makes it possible for Visio to provide new functionality and improve interoperability with other applications. Office 2007 introduced new XML file formats for Word (.docx), Excel (.xlsx), and PowerPoint (.pptx). Just as those file formats were a combination of a ZIP archive package and XML content, so too are the new file formats for Visio. The benefits offered by this new functionality include:

- Smaller file sizes due to the new compressed format, which can be up to 75 percent smaller than the comparable binary document.

- Greater security. This the result of data being stored in a standard structure, with a separate file extension for files with executable macro code. The macro-free file extensions are: *.vsdx* for Visio drawings, *.vstx* for Visio templates, and *.vssx* for Visio stencils. The equivalent macro-enabled file extensions are *.vsdm*, *.vstm*, and *.vssm*.

- Improved data recovery via segmenting and separating different components within the file.

> **Note** Visio 2013 provides several compatibility features to help organizations move to the new file format. You can find more information in the Office IT Pro blog post, "What IT Pros need to know about the new VSDX file format in Visio 2013," at *blogs.technet.com/b/office_resource_kit/archive/2012/10/26/what-it-pros-need-to-know-about-the-new-vsdx-file-format-in-visio-2013.aspx*.

- The ability to view diagrams natively in the browser by using Visio Services, both with on-premises installations of SharePoint 2013 and Office 365.

- Updated diagram templates with a more Windows 8-centric look, with improved containers and callouts.

- Support for co-authoring when a Visio Drawings are saved to SkyDrive, SharePoint, or Share-Point Online in Office 365.

When more than one user is editing a Visio file, the Visio client application displays an icon on the status bar that indicates the number of users editing the file. When the icon is clicked, the list of authors is displayed, as shown in Figure 5-19. By hovering over the author names, you can display contact information along with the options to call, send an instant message, or an email to a contact. You can see similar information in the Backstage view, on the Info tab.

FIGURE 5-19 The Visio status bar displays the number of authors editing the file.

When a user is editing a shape, the shape is not locked against editing; instead, a person icon is added to the upper-right corner of the shape (see Figure 5-20) to inform you that someone else is editing the shape. When you hover over the icon, a ScreenTip is displayed. When you click the icon, the name of the person is displayed. You can then contact that individual by clicking the name. Visio does not prevent either user from editing the shape; therefore, a more correct name for this feature would be collaborative authoring. Shapes that have been deleted by someone else display an exclamation mark in a square box along with a small red cross in the lower-right corner of the box.

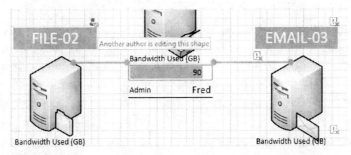

FIGURE 5-20 You can use the editing and delete icons to see what is being changed by other users.

- When the diagram is saved in SharePoint and viewed in the browser by using Visio Services, users who do not have the Visio client application can add comments to a shape or at the page level which are indicated by a cloud icon, as shown in Figure 5-21.

FIGURE 5-21 You can attach comments to a page or to shapes.

You can view all comments in the Comments pane. You can add, edit, and delete comments within the Visio client application. To display the Comments pane in Visio, on the Review tab, in the Comments group, click Comments Pane.

- You can configure your data-connected diagrams directly from Visio. When the diagrams are saved in SharePoint, Visio Services can refresh the data from those data sources.

- New themes, each offering four unique variants that you can use to fine-tune your diagrams. A set of Quick Styles, which is a style and color pairing, is provided for each theme. You can use these to format at the page, shape, or selection level. You can also customize the default themes. You can apply themes by using the Quick Styles split button, which is on the Home tab, in the Shape Styles group.

- The ability to change one shape with another by using the Change Shape split button in the Editing group on the Home tab. The new shapes can retain the position, connections, formatting, shape text, and/or shape data of the originals. If another shape in the drawing references the original shape in a formula, Visio restores this reference after the operation and updates the reference to point toward the resulting shape. Hyperlinks, connections, callout associations, shape comments, container membership, and list membership are likewise restored.

Note 2-D shapes can only be replaced by other 2-D shapes, and single-dimension shapes by other single-dimension shapes. For example, a connector cannot be replaced with a rectangle.

- Additions to the shape sheet, including a range of visual effects such as 3-D Rotation that gives height to a two-dimensional shape and the sketch effect that gives a diagram a more "penciled-in" look. Other effects include reflection, glow, and gradients.

Visio Services

Visio Services is still implemented as a service application, and because the service application architecture has not changed in SharePoint 2013, you install Visio Services as you would in SharePoint Server 2010. It is still an Enterprise feature. Therefore, you will need to purchase an Enterprise CAL for each user who will use it. Changes within Visio Services include the following:

- Support for the new Visio 2013 file format. A *.vsdx* or *.vsdm* file can be saved within a SharePoint library and displayed by using Visio Services in the browser without the need to publish the file as a Visio Web Drawing, *.vdw*. The Visio files, *.vsdx* and *.vsdm*, are displayed in raster format as a *.png* on Visio Services, whereas *.vdw* files can still be displayed using Silverlight. The default to display Visio diagrams is no longer Silverlight. The aim is to provide a mechanism to render any Visio diagram on any of multiple different devices.

  The Visio ServicesECMAScript (JavaScript, JScript) object model contains a new API to support the new file format, which can be used to determine whether the file displayed in the Visio Web Access Web Part is a Visio drawing or a Visio Web Drawing.

- Visio 2013 diagrams can connect to external lists that are created from ECTs. You can refresh the Visio diagrams, which forces the BDC runtime to retrieve data from the external data source to update the diagram.

Note In Office 365, Visio Services do not support SQL, SQL Azure, OLEDC, ODBC, or custom data providers.

- Programmatic support for the new commenting framework. Visio Services includes JavaScript APIs to retrieve the comments associated with a shape or a page.

- The Visio Process Repository site template is available in SharePoint Server 2013; however, it will be removed in the next major release of SharePoint.

- Visio Services can recalculate formulas in the ShapeSheet. In addition to refreshing Data Graphics, Visio Services can refresh all shapes with data and visuals that depend upon data, including SmartShapes. Most ShapeSheet functions are supported for recalculation.

- Greater extensibility via the JavaScript API and Web Part Connections. You can now create a page that displays a library which contains the new formatted Visio diagram files in one Web Part and connects to a Visio Access Web Part, as shown in Figure 5-22.

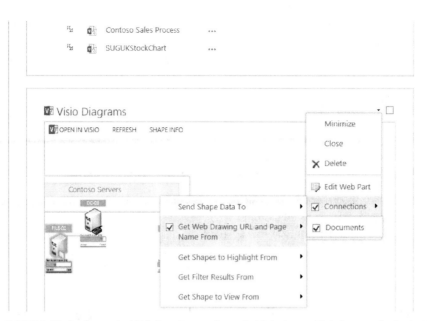

FIGURE 5-22 Configure the Web Part Connections of a Visio Access Web Part to obtain the Web Drawing URL from files saved in a library.

When you click a file in the library Web Part, the diagram is displayed in the Visio Web Access Web Part. If the Visio diagram is connected to external data, you can configure the Visio Web Part to periodically retrieve the latest data.

- A new Visio parameter Maximum Cache Size has been added to the Central Administration Visio Graphics Service Application Global Settings page. A value between 100 and 1024000 MB can be entered; the default value is 5120 MB. A larger size limit can lead to more disk resources used by the service, whereas a smaller unit can impact performance. The addition of the new service application parameter is reflected in the following two components:

  - **Health Analyzer rules**   New corresponding Health Analyzer rules have been added to reflect the new Maximum Cache Size parameter.

  - **Updated PowerShell** *Set-SPVisioPerformance* **cmdlet**   This cmdlet has been updated to include the new Maximum Cache Size parameter.

InfoPath

InfoPath 2013 has not changed much from InfoPath 2010, and that is also the same for InfoPath Form Services in SharePoint 2013. InfoPath 2013 has the new look as do other Office 2013 client applications, and in the top right corner it includes the ability to sign on using a different userid. The Microsoft Visual Studio Tools for Applications integrated development environment is removed from InfoPath Designer 2013. The developing environment is now Visual Studio 2012 with the Microsoft Visual Studio Tools For Applications 2012 add-on installed. However, no new functionality or scenarios have been introduced.

Summary

Using SharePoint, you can rapidly create solutions by assembling, connecting, and configuring the components. Such solutions are known as composite solutions or mashups. Many SharePoint composites are created with nothing more complex than the browser; others are enhanced with the use of SharePoint Designer and the Microsoft Office client products, such as Excel, Access, Visio, and InfoPath, or their service application equivalents as well as other service applications such as BCS

This chapter explained the improvements in SharePoint 2013 and related tools with which you can build composite solutions. Improvements include:

- BCS support for OData data sources. BDC Models for OData are created by using Visual Studio 2012 only. BDC Models can be included in SharePoint Apps. Event listeners for external data have been introduced. This makes it possible for both you and custom code to receive notifications of events that occur in the external systems. External lists can be exported to Excel.

- SharePoint 2013 provides two workflow platforms: the SharePoint 2010 workflow platform and the SharePoint 2013 workflow platform hosted on the server running the Workflow Manager. SharePoint Designer 2013 includes a visual workflow development environment that uses a Visio 2013 add-in.

- SharePoint 2013 introduced a new Access Services service application that host Access web apps, which are SharePoint Apps for which the data is stored in SQL Server 2012 databases, not in SharePoint lists. You create Access web apps by using Access 2013, and you use the browser to enter data.

- Visio Services includes support for the new Visio 2013 file format, co-authoring, and commenting features and supports BCS data sources.

- With SharePoint Designer 2013 being de-emphasized as a no-code forms tool, you should look at Access web apps, Visio Services, and BI tools to build no-code interactive pages. BI tool are detailed in the next chapter.

CHAPTER 6

Business Intelligence

Microsoft SharePoint Server 2013 provides a comprehensive set of Business Intelligence (BI) tools that integrate across Microsoft Office applications and other Microsoft technologies. Microsoft's BI toolset is extensive. Its aim is to give everyone within an organization access to BI solutions so that they can make better, faster, and more relevant business decisions. The BI toolset can be divided according to the users who build the solution and the intended audience for the solution:

- **Personal BI** Users in this group build BI solutions for their own consumption. This is known as *self-service BI*. The tool most often used to build solutions in this category is Microsoft Excel. Each Excel workbook contains a number of worksheets that contain data. The collection of workbooks that contain data and their relationship is known as a *Data Model*. When the data is stored in databases, the term Data Model can also refer to a number of tables and their relationship.

  Users build a worksheet that collates information from the Data Model. They often present the data visually as charts and graphs so that viewers can monitor it at a glance. Such worksheets are known as *dashboards*. These dashboards are not created by the IT department; they are created by the user who will use and consume the data. As the data changes in the Data Model, the visualizations on the dashboard update automatically. No intervention by the user is required.

  Typically, the dashboard is set up so that the user can interact with the data by providing functionality such as filtering and drill-downs. No internet connectivity is needed, although data need not necessarily be stored in Excel worksheets. Even though users find Excel intuitive, there is a learning curve to creating dashboards and gaining insight into the data; thus, this category relies on the users being technically savvy such as data analysts and researchers.

- **Team BI** This group of users builds BI solutions that they want to share within their team or to a group of users. For this category, the Enterprise edition of SharePoint Server is the backbone of sharing. The tools most often used in this scenario are Excel Services, Power-Pivot, Power View, Visio Services and Access Services. Many of these SharePoint services are now being made available in Office 365. As such, users who have a cloud-based installation of SharePoint can now build BI solutions. The dashboards in this scenario are webpages, which again are built by business users, not by the IT department. To build solutions using these tools requires additional skills and training beyond personal BI solutions. Such users are also knowledge workers, information managers, citizen developers, or consumer developers.

- **Corporate BI**   The BI solutions in this category require more planning and enterprise data strategies, such as data modeling. The dashboards built for these solutions are also webpages; however, the data is usually retrieved from several dissimilar data sources. These solutions are often known as *mashups*. The BI toolset used by this group of users are Performance Point Services and SQL Reporting Services. As of this writing, these tools are not available in Office 365; therefore, such solutions are usually built with an on-premises installation of SharePoint Server and SQL Server.

Personal and team BI solutions, also known as *decentralized solutions*, are created by users, individual departments, workgroups, or teams that have the knowledge and skills to deploy and manage their own BI solutions. The data used in personal and team BI solutions tend to be tabular, for which the data is contained in one or more worksheets or tables in a database. Corporate BI solutions are managed centrally. They contain a large amount of data, which is usually complex and analyzed by the multidimensional engine or tabular engine.

SharePoint Server 2013 together with Office 2013 include improvements in all three BI solution scenarios; however, most of the improvements are in self-service BI, which is the purview of the personal and team BI areas, and in which, near parity has been achieved for solutions with Excel and Excel Services in SharePoint.

Personal Business Intelligence

The biggest enhancement in Excel 2013 is that all of the popular BI features are embedded within the core application. This means that it is no longer necessary to download any add-ins to use Power-Pivot, Power View, or the new features in Excel 2013 such as Inquire. Now, all Excel 2013 users have their own built-in set of BI tools. They can analyze and visually explore data of any size, and integrate and show interactive solutions without needing to connect to a SharePoint server or an SQL Server database.

In Excel 2013, much of that functionality, including the infrastructure that supports it, is built directly into the Data Model in Excel. Improvements in Excel 2013 include:

- **In-Memory BI Engine (IMBI)**   IMBI, also known as the xVelocity engine, is fully integrated in the Excel client and makes it possible for you to perform nearly instant analysis of millions of rows. First introduced in Microsoft Excel 2010 as an in-memory engine as an add-in (then known as Vertipaq), xVelocity engine highly compresses the data, which results in manageable-sized files in which the data is stored in the Excel workbook, thus making it portable. xVelocity quickly analyses large datasets. The only limitation to the amount of data that can be analyzed is the amount of memory on your computer. With IMBI, you can now do the following:

  - Import millions of rows from multiple data sources by using a new internal Data Model. A workbook can only contain one internal Data Model.

- Create relationships between data from different sources and between multiple tables in a PivotTable.

- Create implicit calculated fields (previously named *measures*). These are calculations that are created automatically when they add a numeric field to the Values drop zone of the Field List.

- Manage data connections

- Build Data Models that can be used as a basis for PivotTables, PivotCharts and Power View reports.

- **Power View**   Power View (previously named *Crescent* in its early project phase) was previously only available with Reporting Services and only if you had an Analysis Services SQL Server running as a tabular engine. Power View is now embedded into Excel 2013 and makes it possible for users to visualize and interact with modeled data by using highly interactive visualizations, animations, and smart querying. Clicking one chart filters/affects other charts on the page. You can liken Power View to a combination of Microsoft PowerPoint and Excel, where you can use, present, and transform data. You can present and share your solutions with other users by creating a Power View connected to Data Models and displaying the results on dashboards, also known as *storyboard presentations*. Power View improvements include the following:

  - A single Excel workbook can contain multiple Power View sheets, and each of the sheets can be based on a different Data Model, one internal Data Model and many external data sources.

  - Each Power View sheet has its own charts, tables, and other visualizations. You can copy and paste a chart or other visualization from one sheet to another, but only if both worksheets are based on the same Data Model.

  - You can make some changes to the Data Model while viewing the Power View sheet, such as creating relationships and creating key performance indicators (KPI)s.

  - Power View sheets created in Excel can be viewed and interacted with on-premises in Excel Services as well as in Office 365. You can only edit Power View sheets in Excel 2013 on your computer.

  - New presentation features, such as pie charts, maps, KPIs, hierarchies, drill-up and drill-down, and format reports with styles, themes, and text resizing. You can also change the background of each view.

 More Info   You can read more about what's new in Power View in Excel 2013 and in SharePoint Server at *office.microsoft.com/en-001/excel-help/whats-new-in-power-view-in-excel-2013-and-in-sharepoint-server-HA102901475.aspx*.

- **PowerPivot**   As with Power View, there is no separate add-in. Using Power Pivot, you can do the following:

  - Filter data when importing. Data can be imported into both worksheets and a PowerPivot, but when importing data into a PowerPivot, unnecessary data can be filtered out, making it possible for you to import just a subset.

  - Rename tables and columns as data is imported into PowerPivot.

  - Manage the Data Model and create relationships by using drag-and-drop in the Diagram View.

  - Apply formatting in Power View and PivotTable reports.

  - Define calculated fields that can be used throughout a workbook.

  - Define KPIs to use in PivotTables.

  - Create user-defined hierarchies to use throughout a workbook.

  - Define perspectives.

  - Author calculations by writing advanced formulas that use the Data Analysis Expressions (DAX) expression language.

  - Use other more advanced data and modeling operations.

Note If your organization used PowerPivot in the past, a few features available in earlier releases are not available in PowerPivot in Microsoft Excel 2013. You can find more information at *office.microsoft.com/en-001/excel-help/whats-new-in-powerpivot-in-excel-2013-HA102893837.aspx.*

- **Decoupled PivotChart and PivotTable reports**   Users can now create PivotChart reports without having to include a PivotTable report on the same sheet.

To use PowerPivot and Power View, you need at least Office Professional Plus.

Note While the SQL Server 2008 R2 and SQL Server 2012 versions of PowerPivot for Excel 2010 are not compatible with Excel 2013, you still can install PowerPivot for Excel 2010 on your computer if you want to run Excel 2010 side-by-side with Excel 2013. In other words, the two versions of Excel can coexist and so can the corresponding PowerPivot add-ins.

Using PowerPivot and Power View

Both PowerPivot and Power View use the new xVelocity in-memory analytics engine and the new Data Model, which can be likened to a small in-memory tabular database. Traditional Input/Output (IO) bottlenecks are gone, and there is no need to create indexes. However, although PowerPivot and Power View are included in Excel 2013, they are not enabled by default.

Enabling PowerPivot and Power View

To enable PowerPivot and Power View, perform the following steps:

1. Open your Excel workbook (if you do not have one, open a blank workbook). Click the File tab to display the Backstage view.

2. Click the Options tab to open the Excel Options dialog box.

3. In the column on the left, click Add-Ins to display the Microsoft Office add-ins.

4. At the bottom of the page, in the Manage list box, select COM Add-Ins from the Manage list, as shown in Figure 6-1, and then click Go to open the COM Add-Ins dialog box.

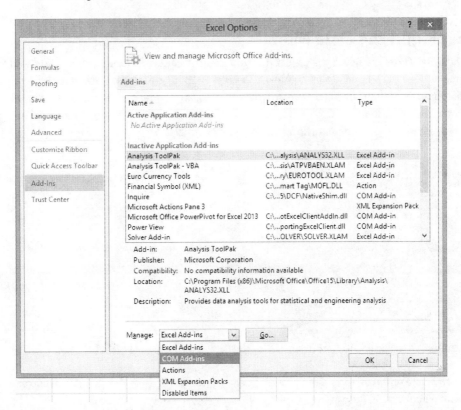

FIGURE 6-1 The Microsoft Office Add-Ins page in the Excel Options dialog box. At the bottom of the page, select COM Add-Ins from the Manage list box.

5. In the Add-Ins Available section, select Microsoft Office PowerPivot For Excel 2013 and Power View, and then click OK. You could also select Inquire at the same time (see Figure 6-2).

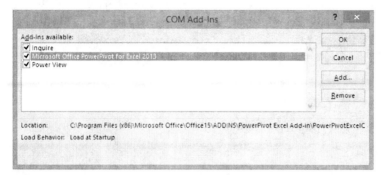

FIGURE 6-2 Use the COM Add-Ins dialog box to enable Inquire, Power Pivot, and Power View.

Note Because PowerPivot, Power View, and Inquire are enabled by using COM Add-Ins, they are not available in Office on a Windows RT-based device.

Exploring the Data Model

The Data Model is a new Excel object that you use to create PivotTables, PivotCharts, and Power View reports. There is no one global command in Excel 2013 for creating a Data Model. There are various dialogs in Excel with which you can add data to the Data Model depending what your users need to do. You can add to the Data Model by using the Import Data dialog box, as shown in Figure 6-3, which is displayed when importing data from an external source.

FIGURE 6-3 Use the Import Data dialog box to add data to the Excel Data Model.

To create and manage a Data Model, on the PowerPivot tab, in the Data Model group, click the Manage button, as illustrated in Figure 6-4.

FIGURE 6-4 Click the Manage button on the PowerPivot tab to create and manage PowerPivots.

> **Note** The PowerPivot tab is not displayed if the PowerPivot COM Add-In has not been enabled or if Excel determines that the add-in is destabilizing Excel. This might occur if Excel closes unexpectedly while the PowerPivot window is open. To restore the PowerPivot tab, disable and re-enable the COM Add-In. If that fails, use *regedit.exe* to delete the following two keys:
>
> *HKCU/Software/Microsoft/Office/15.0/User Settings/PowerPivotExcelAddin*
> *HKCU/Software/Microsoft/Office/Excel/Addins/PowerPivotClientAddIn.NativeEntry.1*

The Manage command opens the PowerPivot window (see Figure 6-5). Each dataset is displayed as a tab at the bottom of the PowerPivot window. Together, all tabs are known as the PowerPivot model, wherein each dataset is referred to as a table. Use the PowerPivot window to filter data as you add it to the workbook, create relationships between tables, and create calculations. You can display a relationship diagram by clicking the Diagram icon, in the lower-right corner.

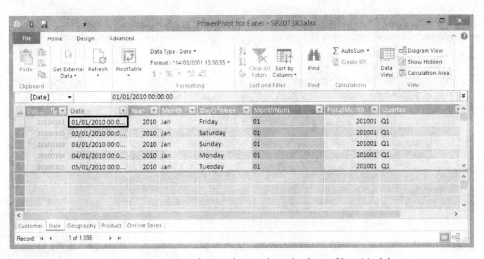

FIGURE 6-5 You can use the PowerPivot for Excel to explore the PowerPivot Model.

Team BI

Many team solutions are first built for personal use and then later shared, deploying it to an Excel Services service application in SharePoint or Office 365. Excel Services is the SharePoint component that does the workbook calculations on the server and renders the workbooks in the browser.

Excel Services

Using Excel Services, you can view and interact with Excel workbooks that have been published to SharePoint sites. Now, with SharePoint 2013 you can explore data and conduct analysis in a browser window just as you would by using the Excel 2013 client, including PowerPivot and Power View. New features supported by Excel Services in SharePoint 2013 include the following:

- **Data exploration improvements**   You can more easily explore data and conduct analysis in Excel Services reports that use SQL Server Analysis Services (SSAS) data or PowerPivot data models. For example, you can point to a value in a PivotChart or PivotTable report and see suggested ways to view additional information. You can also use commands such as Drill Down to conduct analysis. The Drill Down command can be applied with a single mouse click.

- **Field list and field well support**   Through Excel Services, you can view and change which items are displayed in rows, columns, values, and filters in PivotChart reports and PivotTable reports that have been published to Excel Services.

- **Calculated measures and members**   Excel Services supports calculated measures and calculated members that are created in Excel.

- **Enhanced timeline controls**   Excel Services supports timeline controls that render and behave as they do in the Excel client.

- **Application BI Servers**   Administrators can specify SSAS servers to support more advanced analytic capabilities in Excel Services.

- **Business Intelligence Center update**   The Business Intelligence Center site template has been streamlined. In addition to sporting a new look (see Figure 6-6), it is easier to use.

FIGURE 6-6 The Business Intelligence Center site template is used to create sites to host Dashboards, Data Connections, and PerformancePoint Content.

> **Note** Excel workbooks saved to SharePoint or Office 365 are subject to a maximum file size. For example, by default the maximum file size for rendering a workbook in Excel Services is 10 MB, and yet the default maximum file size that can be saved to a document library is 50 MB. These are the same limits as in Excel Services with the Enterprise Edition of SharePoint 2010. To see more information on Data Model specifications and limits, go to *office.microsoft.com/en-us/excel-help/data-model-specification-and-limits-HA102837464.aspx*.

From the perspective of an IT Professional, the underlying architecture of SharePoint service applications has not changed from SharePoint 2010 to SharePoint 2013. From a licensing perspective, there is no such thing as an Enterprise edition of SharePoint Server 2013; however, to use Excel Services or other BI-related functionality, your organization needs to purchase SharePoint Server licenses for each server in the farm and Enterprise Client Access Licenses (CALs) for each user who wants to use BI features.

If you want the full PowerPivot and Power View functionality that is experienced in Excel 2013, such as clicking slicers and doing analysis, Excel Services must be connected to an instance of SQL Server Analysis Services running in SharePoint Integrated Mode, which is a special instance of SSAS with a tabular engine. This new component works with SharePoint 2013 and is available with SQL Server 2012 SP1. SQL Server 2012 SP1 was specifically released to accompany the release of Office 2013 and SharePoint 2013. The licenses for SQL Server are not included in the licenses that you purchase for SharePoint.

When you first upload an Excel workbook in a SharePoint library, Excel Services automatically creates a Data Model (database) in the Analysis Services SharePoint Mode instance. When you update that workbook, Excel Services creates a new Data Model; that is, it creates a new database and deletes the old one.

In SharePoint Server 2010, there was a SQL Server 2008 R2 and SQL Server 2012 product called PowerPivot for SharePoint, which included a special instance of Analysis Services and ran the tabular mode engine (xVelocity). The Excel Services service application works with the new tabular engine to manage the automatic refresh of the data in the stored workbooks. A PowerPivot gallery was also deployed to site collections.

In SharePoint Server 2013, there is now, Analysis Services SharePoint Mode, which does not need to be installed on a SharePoint server. It can be installed on one or more stand-alone servers. It has no dependencies on SharePoint and is also referred to as the *backend service*. This has implications from a licensing and scaling perspective. You can separate the calculations needed for PowerPivots from servers that are responding to web requests and other SharePoint-related tasks.

Note You no longer need to install PowerPivot for SharePoint. However, if you don't, you will not get the automatic refresh of workbook data.

Excel and SharePoint PowerPivot compatibility

Office 2013 contains the third major release of PowerPivot. Correspondingly, there have been three versions of the xVelocity engine. Not all companies will migrate to Office 2013 immediately, and therefore the question of compatibility across Excel, SQL Server, and SharePoint might be an important one to you. To use PowerPivot for Excel and PowerPivot for SharePoint together, the versions must match.

As the core xVelocity engine is relatively unchanged, models created with any versions of Excel PowerPivot add-in should work with Excel Services 2013 and Analysis Services SharePoint Mode. However, although PowerPivot is backward compatible, it is not forward compatible. You can upload an Excel 2010 PowerPivot workbook to SharePoint 2013, open it in Excel Services and base a Power View report on it. Conversely, if you upload an Excel 2013 workbook with a Data Model to SharePoint 2010, it might not work properly in Excel Services; for example, if you base a Power View report on it, you get an error if you click a slicer, change a filter, or drag a new field onto the PivotTable. Table 6-1 summarizes PowerPivot compatibility.

TABLE 6-1 xVelocity compatibility matrix

Cient Software	PowerPivot for SharePoint (SQL Server 2008 R2)	PowerPivot for SharePoint (SQL Server 2012)	Analysis Services SharePoint Mode (SQL Server 2012 SP1)
Excel 2010 with PowerPivot (2008R2)	Yes	Yes[1]	Yes[1]
Excel 2010 with PowerPivot (2012)	Yes	Yes	Yes[3]
Excel 2010 with PowerPivot (2012 SP1)	No	Yes[2]	Yes[2]
Excel 2013 with or without PowerPivot	No	No	Yes

1. Can only refresh slicers

2. Cannot use SQL Server 2012 SP1 features with Power View

3. Limited to pre SQL Server 2012 SP1 PowerPivot feature set

More Info To read more about upgrading a PowerPivot Data Model to Excel 2013, go to *office.microsoft.com/en-001/excel-help/upgrade-powerpivot-data-models-to-excel-2013-HA103356104.aspx.*

Corporate BI

Corporate BI solutions make use of Analysis Services SharePoint Mode, PowerPivot, and Power View. Such solutions also use SSAS, SQL Server Reporting Services (SSRS) and SQL Server Integration Services (SSIS), for which the data models can be multidimensional or tabular. In addition to PerformancePoint Services—with which you can build dashboards for which data could come from multiple data sources—Reporting Services can be installed as a shared services in a SharePoint farm and a SSRS add-in makes it possible for you to use PowerPivot in your reports. Reporting Services can also be used to report on data that is stored within SharePoint lists and libraries as well as external data sources. However, corporations usually store large amounts of data in a data warehouse, and this might mean that you export the data from SharePoint by using SSIS.

PerformancePoint Services

You can use the PerformancePoint Services (PPS) service application to create interactive dashboards that display KPIs and data visualizations in the form of scorecards, reports, and filters. It has a number of assets that you will not find elsewhere in SharePoint, such as Analytic Charts and Analytic Grids. If your users need to uses those assets, they will need to be connected to an instance of SSAS in either tabular or Multidimensional and Data Mining Mode.

In SharePoint Server 2013, PerformancePoint Services includes the following new features to support Business Intelligence applications:

- **Dashboard Migration**   You can copy entire dashboards and dependencies, including the *.aspx* file, to other users, servers, or site collections. With this feature, you can also migrate single items to other environments and migrate content by using Windows PowerShell commands. This is a considerable improvement and one that has been requested by many organizations over the years.

- **Filter Enhancements & Filter Search**   The user interface (UI) has been enhanced so that you can view and manage filters including giving users the ability to search for items within filters without having to navigate through the tree.

- **BI Center Update**   The new BI Center is cleaner and easier to use, with folders and libraries configured for easy use.

- **Support for Analysis Services Effective User**   This new feature eliminates the need for Kerberos delegation when per-user authentication is used for Analysis Services data sources. By supporting Analysis Services Effective User feature, authorization checks are based on the user specified by the *EffectiveUserName* property instead of using the currently authenticated user.

- **PerformancePoint Support on iPad**   You can view and interact with PerformancePoint dashboards on iPad devices via the Safari web browser.

- **Themes**   PerformancePoint now supports SharePoint's new theming capabilities.

- **Custom Target Applications from Secure Store**   You can specify any secure store target application when defining a data source in the dashboard designer.

- **Dashboard Designer in Ribbon**   The dashboard designer not only appears on the home page of a site created from the BI site template, it also appears in any libraries where the "Web Part Page" content type is added as well as in lists where any of the PerformancePoint content types have been added.

Reporting Services

There are two components that integrate SSRS with SharePoint: Reporting Services SharePoint Mode, which installs as a SharePoint service application, and a Reporting Services add-in.

Note As of this writing, there is no integrated SSRS functionality within Office 365. There is Reporting Services for Azure, to which you can connect from Office 365.

Reporting Services SharePoint Mode

Reporting Services SharePoint Mode—also known as Reporting Service Integrated Mode—is based on a completely new architecture, which is why you will see it in the SharePoint Central Administration website as a service application with a SharePoint Shared Service Application Pool. It supports claims-based authentication and SharePoint cross-farm support for view reports. You configure it by using the SharePoint Central Administration website or via Windows PowerShell cmdlets. You no longer use the Reporting Services Configuration Manager.

As with the previous version of SharePoint, the SSRS report server must be configured for Share-Point Mode, not Standalone Mode. You can install it with SharePoint Foundation, although it has a licensing requirement from a SQL Server perspective. You can use SQL Server 2012 Standard edition or higher. However, if your users want to take advantage of advanced features offered by SSRS, such as data alerting on a report, you will need to install either the BI or Enterprise editions of SQL Server 2012.

Note SSRS within SQL Server 2012 Express (the free version) can only be installed in stand-alone mode and therefore cannot be used to install Reporting Services SharePoint Mode.

You need to install the Reporting Services SharePoint Mode on each computer where the Reporting Services service application is to run. If your users would like to use Power View, they will need to connect to an instance of SSAS running a tabular engine. This is a different SSAS instance than the instance that is running SSAS in SharePoint Mode.

Another new feature for Reporting Services SharePoint Mode is Data Alerts. When set up, emails can be sent to users to inform them of changes in report data that might interest them. You can create and manage Data Alerts by using Data Alert Designer, Data Alert Manager For Users, and Data Alert Manager For Alerting Administrators.

After the Reporting Services service application is installed and configured, you can publish Reporting Services content to a SharePoint library and then view and manage those documents directly from a SharePoint site.

Note In SQL Server 2012, the Business Intelligence Developer Studio (BIDS) is replaced by a Visual Studio add-in, SQL Server Data Tools (SSDT) which you can use to create report server projects. SSDT is very similar to BIDS.

To browse to the report server, type **http://<sitename>/_vti_bin/reportserver** into the browser.

Reporting Services add-in

The Reporting Services add-in for SharePoint provides features to integrate a SSRS report server with a deployment of SharePoint product. The add-in also includes Power View (SSRS) reports, which are RDLX file format. Power View does not replace Report Builder. Instead, it addresses the need for web-based, ad hoc reporting.

For SharePoint 2013 you must use the SQL Server 2012 SP1 version; otherwise, there are no real differences with how to install the Reporting Services add-in when compared to installing the SQL Server 2010 Reporting Service add-in on a SharePoint Server 2010 farm; nothing needs to be installed on a server that already has SharePoint installed. You should install this add-in on all SharePoint servers that are responding to web requests. It does not need to be installed on SharePoint application server.

> **Note** Although you can install the Reporting Services add-in on a server prior to including the server in a SharePoint farm or prior to creating a SharePoint farm, this is not recommended. If you do, you will need to run Windows PowerShell cmdlets to register the Reporting Services service application.

Building a BI ecosystem

If you build personal BI dashboards using the BI tools mentioned earlier in this chapter, you will find that it is relatively easy. However, it is not possible to build team or corporate BI solutions unless the BI components are installed into the SharePoint infrastructure. Also as the number of users that consume BI solutions increases, so will there be a need to scale the infrastructure.

BI functionality assets such as Excel Services and PerformancePoint Services are built into Share-Point Server; therefore, after a SharePoint farm is created, you can enable these assets by using the SharePoint Central Administration website or Windows PowerShell.

The BI assets, such as Analysis Services and Reporting Services SharePoint Mode and the add-ins are SQL Server assets. To install these assets, you need a copy of SQL Server 2012 SP1, or to use the add-ins, you need to download the appropriate SQL Server 2012 SP add-in from the Microsoft download site. Some of these assets will need to be installed on servers that are running SharePoint. This does not mean you should install SharePoint on the server that is hosting your SharePoint databases. Typically, you install the SQL Server BI assets that integrate with SharePoint on the servers that are a part of the SharePoint farm. It is recommended that you do not add SharePoint to a server that is running the instance of SQL Server that is hosting your SharePoint databases. This does mean that although the instances of SSRS and SSAS in SharePoint Mode and the add-ins have to be SQL Server 2012 SP1, the instance of SQL Server that is hosting your SharePoint databases does not have to be SQL Server 2012 SP1; it could be SQL Server 2012 or SQL Server 2008 R2 SP1, which ever version matches your service level and operational requirements for SharePoint. Table 6-2 summaries the relationship between the BI assets and SharePoint.

TABLE 6-2 BI features available in SharePoint

	Features	Install or Configure
SharePoint only	Native application services such as Excel Services Features and PerformancePoint Services	Excel Services and other service applications with SharePoint Server 2013
SharePoint with Analysis Services in SharePoint Mode	Basic BI features	Install Analysis Services in SharePoint Mode Register Analysis Services server in Excel Services
SharePoint With Reporting Services in SharePoint Mode	Use of Power View in reports Administration pages in SharePoint Administration website Reporting Services Data Alerts pages Subscription and data alert processing	Install Reporting Services in SharePoint Mode Install Reporting Services add-in for SharePoint
All PowerPivot features	Schedule data refresh PowerPivot Gallery Management Dashboard BI Sematic Model link file content type	Deploy PowerPivot for SharePoint 2013 Add-In

Analysis Services SharePoint Mode, PowerPivot add-in for SharePoint, Reporting Services SharePoint Mode, and Reporting Services add-in for SharePoint can be installed from the SQL Server 2012 SP1 installation medium. However, the SQL Server Installation Wizard needs to be used twice because the Setup Role page does not allow you to select all options to install the four components. To install the SQL Server 2012 SP1 BI features on a single server, complete the following steps (more details of the steps are provided in subsequent sections in this chapter):

1. Install SharePoint Server 2013 and create an Excel Services service application, modifying default settings to suit your business needs, such as, changing the default maximum file size for rendering a workbook.

2. Install an instance of Analysis Services in SharePoint Mode.

3. Configure Excel Services in SharePoint Server to use the Analysis Services.

4. Install Reporting Services in SharePoint mode and the Reporting Services add-in for SharePoint Products.

5. Start a Reporting Services SharePoint service on the server and create at least one Reporting Services service application.

Installing Analysis Services SharePoint Mode

An instance of the Analysis Service SharePoint Mode does not need to be installed on a server where SharePoint is installed; however, the server must be joined to a domain in the same Active Directory forest as the SharePoint farm that contains the Excel Services service application where you will register the Analysis Service instance.

To install Analysis Services SharePoint Mode, you need at least SQL Server BI or Enterprise. When installed on a server by itself, the minimum system requirements for Analysis Service SharePoint Mode are based on SQL Server 2012 rather than SharePoint Server requirements. If you install Analysis Services SharePoint Mode on a SharePoint server, you need to be aware that PowerPivot is data intensive, and thus, only use the standard SharePoint 2013 hard and software recommendations when the workload is small, for example, less than 100 users or workbooks. Larger PowerPivot deployments require more computing power.

 More Info To read more about hardware and software requirements for Analysis Service SharePoint Mode, go to *msdn.microsoft.com/en-us/library/fb86ca0a-518c-4c61-ae78-7680c57fae1f.*

To install Analysis Services SharePoint Mode, on the SQL Server 2012 Setup page, select SQL Server PowerPivot For SharePoint, as demonstrated in Figure 6-7. Notice that the setup page does not mention Analysis Services SharePoint Mode. Instead, when you select SQL Server PowerPivot for SharePoint you are choosing to install Analysis Services SharePoint Mode. This can be confusing.

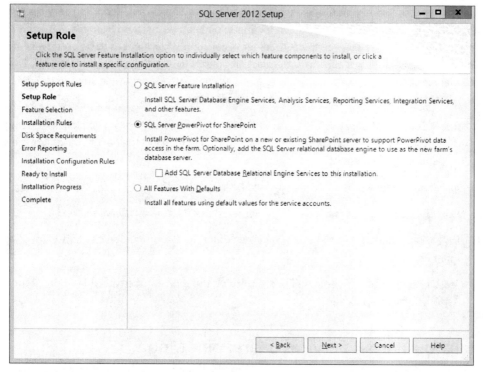

FIGURE 6-7 Select SQL Server PowerPivot for SharePoint to install Analysis Services SharePoint Mode.

When you install Analysis Services SharePoint Mode on a server that does not have SharePoint installed, only Analysis Services SharePoint Mode is installed; when you install Analysis Services SharePoint Mode on a server where SharePoint is installed, PowerPivot for SharePoint add-in is also installed.

Note If you only want to install the PowerPivot for SharePoint add-in on a SharePoint server, do not use the SQL Server 2012 SP1 image. Instead, download the add-in from the Microsoft download site and use that program to install the add-in.

Click Next on the setup page to display the Feature Selection page (see Figure 6-8). This page clearly demonstrates that you are installing the SharePoint Integrated Analysis Services, as does the Installation Rules page, as shown in Figure 6-9, when the installation is complete.

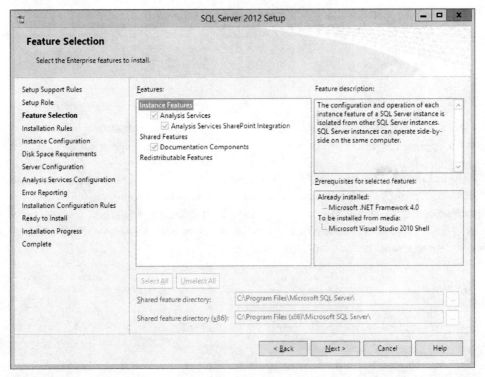

FIGURE 6-8 The Feature Selection page specifies that you are installing Analysis Services SharePoint Integration.

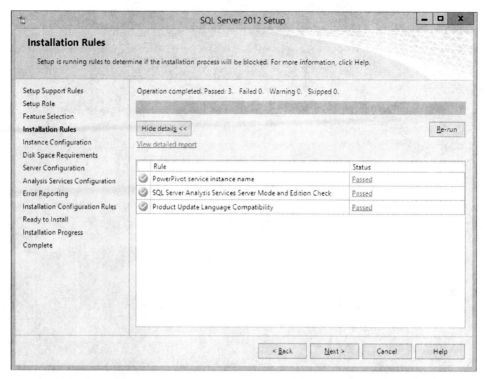

FIGURE 6-9 On the Installation Rules page, click Show Details to verify the components installed.

On the Instance Configuration page of the wizard (see Figure 6-10), a read-only instance name of "POWERPIVOT" is displayed for informational purposes. This instance name is required, and it cannot be modified; therefore, an existing PowerPivot-named instance cannot exist on the computer where Analysis Services SharePoint Mode is being installed. However, you can enter a unique Instance ID to specify a directory name and registry keys.

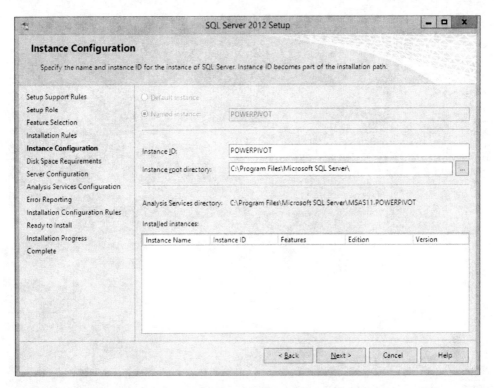

FIGURE 6-10 Use the Instance Configuration page in the wizard to change the Instance ID.

On the Server Configuration page (see Figure 6-11), you need to specify an Active Directory or Network Service account that the instance of Analysis Services can use. The ability to use a Network Service account is new for SharePoint 2013 and as this account has limited access, it helps safeguard your system if individual services or processes are compromised. You will not be able to use a local account; therefore, you cannot use Analysis Services SharePoint Mode with a stand-alone SharePoint installation. This account is used for PowerPivot queries and data refresh jobs in the SharePoint farm. When installing multiple Analysis Services server instances in a farm, all of the instances must run under the same domain user account.

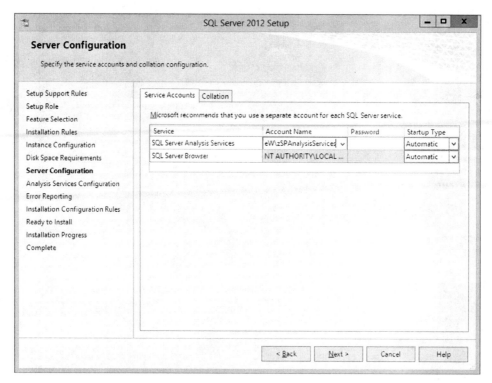

FIGURE 6-11 On the Server Configuration page, you specify an account name that the instance of Analysis Services SharePoint Mode can use.

When the Analysis Services Configuration page is displayed, ensure that you add the accounts that need to administer Analysis Services, such as the SharePoint farm account, the Excel Services application pool service account, the PowerPivot Service application pool service account, and any user accounts that need to administer Analysis Services.

SQL Server 2012 PowerPivot for SharePoint 2013

SQL Server 2012 PowerPivot for SharePoint 2013 includes enhancements to the PowerPivot experiences in SharePoint, including PowerPivot gallery, schedule data refresh, management dashboard, and data providers. PowerPivot for SharePoint does not have any additional license requirements beyond that of Analysis Services.

If you are not installing PowerPivot for SharePoint as part of the Analysis Services SharePoint Mode installation, you can find it at *www.microsoft.com/en-us/download/details.aspx?id=35577*. This is a Microsoft Windows Installer package (*SpPowerPivot.msi*) that supports both a graphical user interface and a command-line installation which require you run the .msi with administrator privileges. For a command-line installation, open a command prompt with elevated permissions and then run the *SpPowerPivot.msi*, as shown here:

```
Msiexec.exe /i SpPowerPivot.msi.
```

 Note In an Office 365 environment, you can interact with both Power Views and PowerPivots in the browser because Excel Services and an Analysis Services SharePoint Mode farm have been built into the cloud. However, as of this writing, Office 365 did not include PowerPivot for SharePoint 2013; therefore, in Office 365, you cannot schedule unattended data refresh or other features that PowerPivot for SharePoint 2013 installs.

PowerPivot for SharePoint deploys Analysis Services client libraries and copies PowerPivot for SharePoint 2013 installation files to the computer; it does not deploy or configure features in Share-Point. The following features are installed by default:

- PowerPivot for SharePoint 2013

  This feature includes the PowerPivot Web Service that provides the interface from SharePoint front-end servers to the PowerPivot System Service on SharePoint application servers.

- Microsoft OLE DB Provider for Analysis Services (MSOLAP)

- ADOMD.NET data provider

- SQL Server 2012 Analysis Management Objects

PowerPivot for SharePoint copies three SharePoint solution files to the *C:\Program Files\Microsoft SQL Server\110\Tools\PowerPivotTools\SPAddinConfiguration\Resources* folder.

The solution file, *PowerPivotFarmSolution.wsp*, is scoped at the farm level, whereas the files, *Power-PivotFarm14Solution.wsp* and *PowerPivotWebApplicationSolution.wsp* are scoped at the site-collection level.

After PowerPivot for SharePoint is installed, run the PowerPivot for SharePoint 2013 Configuration Tool to configure and deploy the solutions in the SharePoint farm, create the PowerPivot service application, and then add the Analysis Services instance in the Excel Services. You can find the configuration tool for Windows Server 2008 by clicking Start, All Programs, Microsoft SQL Server 2012, Configuration Tools, and then clicking PowerPivot For SharePoint 2013 Configuration. For a Windows Server 2012, you can find it on the Start screen, as shown in Figure 6-12.

FIGURE 6-12 On Windows Server 2012 Start screen, click PowerPivot for SharePoint 2013 to start the configuration tool.

Note The SQL Server 2012 SP1 Installation Wizard installs two different configuration tools: PowerPivot Configuration and PowerPivot For SharePoint 2013 Configuration. Ensure that you select PowerPivot For SharePoint 2013 Configuration. You will need to provide values for a number of parameters and you can optionally remove actions that you do not want the configuration tool to process. In the Default Account UserName text box, ensure that you specify the SharePoint installation account. This is not the SharePoint farm account, but the account that you used to install SharePoint. For more information on the configuration tool, see PowerPivot for SharePoint 2013 Configuration tool at *go.microsoft.com/ fwlink/p/?LinkId=248415*.

After the configuration tool is done, a SQL Service Pivot System service and a PowerPivot service application, together with the PowerPivot Service Application Proxy, are installed and started on the server. If you did not specify a name in the configuration tool, for the service application, it will be Default PowerPivot Service Application. Similarly, the name of its database will be DefaultPowerPivot-ServiceApplicationDB-*<GUID>*, where *<GUID>* is a generated number.

You can also use the configuration tool to specify a site collection where the feature PowerPivot Feature Integration For Site Collections will be activated. If you previously created a site collection with a top-level site based on the BI site template, such a site collection would be a good choice. You can activate this feature on any site collection after the add-in is installed.

Registering Excel Services to use Analysis Services

The Excel Services service application connects directly to an instance of Analysis Services SharePoint Mode when it needs to. If you used the downloaded *spPowerPivot.msi* file or you ran the SQL Server Installation Wizard on a server where SharePoint is not installed, you will need to add the Analysis Services instance in the Excel Services, using the Data Model Settings link on the Manage Excel Services Application—this is new in SharePoint 2013.

If you have installed Analysis Services SharePoint Mode on multiple servers, it is Excel Services service application that load balances across those servers and not an internal component of SharePoint.

To verify that Analysis Services SharePoint Mode and the PowerPivot add-in have been successfully installed, you should upload a new workbook that contains a PowerPivot. Each workbook that contains a PowerPivot, Excel Services creates a database in an Analysis Services instance. When you view the PowerPivot within the browser, the PowerPivot database is first cached to hard disk before it is loaded into memory.

Integrating Reporting Services with SharePoint

The SQL Server Installation Wizard does not make it obvious how to install Reporting Services SharePoint Mode and a Reporting Services add-in. On the SQL Server 2012 Setup page, select SQL Server Feature Installation, and then on the Installation Type page, select Perform A New Installation Of SQL Server 2012. On the Feature Selection page, select Report Services – SharePoint and Reporting Services Add-In For SharePoint Products, as shown in Figure 6-13.

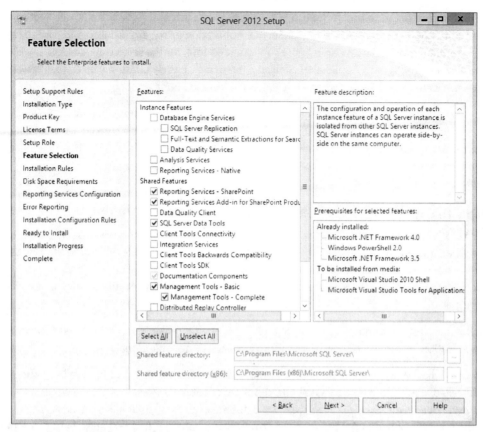

FIGURE 6-13 In the SQL Server 2012 Setup Wizard, in the Shared Features section of the Feature Selection page, select the check boxes for the two Reporting Services.

The Reporting Services Configuration page (see Figure 6-14) confirms that you are installing Reporting Services SharePoint Integration Mode.

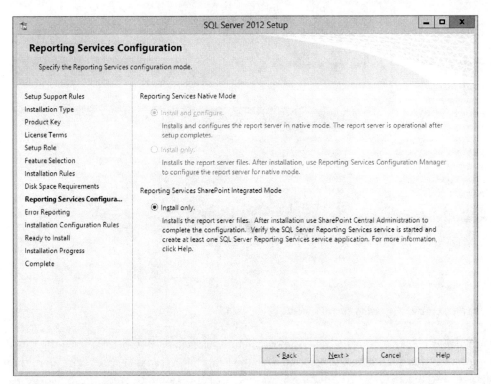

FIGURE 6-14 The Reporting Services Configuration page confirms that the Reporting Services configuration mode is to be installed.

After the SQL Server Installation Wizard completes, a SQL Server Reporting Services service is installed and started on the server. Check that this service is started by using either Windows PowerShell or the SharePoint Central Administration website. You can then use the SharePoint Central Administration website to create the Reporting Services service application by clicking New on the Manage Service Applications page, as illustrated in Figure 6-15.

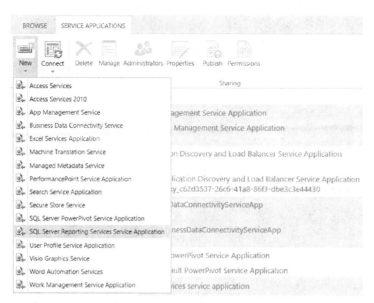

FIGURE 6-15 Create a Reporting Services service application.

At the bottom of the Create SQL Server Reporting Services Service Application page, ensure that you select the web applications to associate with the Reporting Services service application. Three databases are created for each Reporting Services service application created: *<Reporting Services>* (where *Reporting Services* is the name of the database provided on the create service application page), *<Reporting Services>*_Alerting, and *<Reporting Services>*TempDB.

> **Note** Reporting Services SharePoint Mode can be installed by using the command line. You can find more information at *msdn.microsoft.com/en-us/library/gg492275.aspx*. You can configure Reporting Services SharePoint Mode by using the SharePoint Central Administration website or Windows PowerShell. You cannot use the Reporting Services Configuration Manager, *rskeymgmt.exe* or *rsconfig.exe*, nor can you use WMI interfaces.

Installing other SQL Server 2012 SP1 components

SQL Server 2012 Service Pack 1 (SP1) provides a number of data-related, stand-alone utilities and add-ins for Microsoft Office that your BI users might also find useful. These do not integrate with SharePoint 2013, but they do require Microsoft .NET Framework 4.0 on the user's machines. Such BI utilities and add-ins include the following:

- Report Builder

- Master Data Services (MDS) Add-In for Excel

- Data Mining Add-In for Microsoft Office

Report Builder

Using this stand-alone utility which provides a report-authoring environment, IT professionals and power users can create reports and shared datasets. Use Report Builder to create reports that incorporate data visualizations, including charts, maps, sparklines, and data bars. You can find the Report Builder at *www.microsoft.com/en-us/download/details.aspx?id=35576*.

Master Data Services add-in

The MDS add-in for Excel is a data management tool with which users can publish data to the MDS database with the click of a button. Administrators can use the add-in to create new model objects and load data without ever launching any administrative tools, helping to speed deployment. With the MDS add-in for Excel, all master data remains centrally managed in MDS, whereas the ability to read or update the data is distributed to those who need it. You can download the MDS add-in for Excel from *www.microsoft.com/en-us/download/details.aspx?id=35581*.

Data Mining add-ins

SQL Server 2012 SP1 Data Mining add-ins can help your users to take advantage of SQL Server predictive analytics in Excel and Visio. These add-ins are supported on Office 2010 and Office 2013. You can find the download at *www.microsoft.com/en-us/download/details.aspx?id=35578*, which includes the following components:

- **Table Analysis Tools for Excel**   This add-in provides easy-to-use tasks that take advantage of SQL Server 2012 data-mining models within Excel by using either your spreadsheet data or external data, accessible through your SQL Server 2012 Analysis Services instance.

- **Data Mining Client for Excel**   By using this add-in, you can create, test, explore, and manage data-mining models within Excel by using either your spreadsheet data or external data accessible through your SQL Server 2012 Analysis Services instance.

- **Data Mining Templates for Visio**   Use this add-in to render and share your mining models as annotatable Visio drawings.

If you choose, you can install each of these components separately.

Summary

Excel 2013 and SharePoint Server 2013 include enhanced support for BI. New BI features in the client application Excel, such as calculated measures and timeline controls, are supported by Excel Services.

Excel 2013 also includes an in-memory tabular engine called the xVelocity engine. Excel Data Models can be used as a basis for PowerPivots, PivotTables, PivotCharts and Power View reports. When you save workbooks that contain these PowerPivots, PivotTables, PivotCharts and Power View reports to SharePoint, you can display them in webpages, because the same in-memory engine can be used in SharePoint 2013. If you want the full PowerPivot and Power View functionality that users experience in Excel, such as clicking slicers and doing analysis, Excel Services must be connected to an instance of Analysis Services SharePoint Mode. To use features, such as scheduling data refresh, PowerPivot for SharePoint needs to be installed.

There are two components that integrate SQL Server Reporting Services with SharePoint: Reporting Services SharePoint Mode and a Reporting Services add-in. These two components, together with Analysis Services SharePoint Mode and the PowerPivot add-in for SharePoint, can be installed from the SQL Server 2012 SP1 installation medium. Although these four components must be SQL Server 2012 SP1 components, the instance of SQL Server that is hosting your SharePoint databases does not need to be SQL Server 2012 SP1; it could be SQL Server 2012 or SQL Server 2008 R2 SP1.

Reporting Services SharePoint Mode and Analysis Service SharePoint Mode are installed as service applications and are managed by using the SharePoint Central Administration website or Windows PowerShell.

Index

X

Y

About the Author

 PENELOPE COVENTRY, MCITP, MCDST, MCTS, MCSA, MCSE, is a Microsoft MVP for SharePoint Server and an independent consultant based in the UK. She has more than 30 years of industry experience and has authored and coauthored several books on SharePoint, including *Microsoft SharePoint Designer 2010 Step by Step, Microsoft SharePoint 2010 Inside Out,* and *Microsoft SharePoint 2010: Business Connectivity Services.* Penny has worked with SharePoint since 2001, and when she's not writing, she works on large SharePoint deployments.

What do you think of this book?

We want to hear from you!
To participate in a brief online survey, please visit:

microsoft.com/learning/booksurvey

Tell us how well this book meets your needs—what works effectively, and what we can do better. Your feedback will help us continually improve our books and learning resources for you.

Thank you in advance for your input!

CPSIA information can be obtained at www.ICGtesting.com
Printed in the USA
BVOW06s0742291013

334919BV00013B/305/P

9 780735 675520

The Springer Ghost Book

© 2003 by Paul Pierce

ISBN 0-9741819-0-0

Printed by Communicorp
Edited by Scooter MacMillan

Acknowledgements

The author wishes to thank Dona Pierce,
Lori Edwards, the Columbus Ledger-Enquirer
newspaper, the board of directors of the
Springer Opera House and all those who
shared their experiences.

Picture Credits

Sandy Dawson; p. 18, 24, 36, 46, 69, 74
Mike Haskey, Columbus Ledger-Enquirer; p. 58
Don Coker, Columbus Ledger-Enquirer; painting on dust cover art
Paul Pierce; p. 1, 2, 3, 5, 9, 15, 25, 29, 37, 41, 47, 51, 61, 63, 65, 71
Tom McDougall, Communicorp; p. 21, 55, 59, 75
E. Alan McGee; p.14, 40, 50, 86

The Springer Ghost Book

A Theatre Haunting in the Deep South

by Paul Pierce

EERILY,
Red R.